Disturbance

Marianne Kavanagh

Disturbance

HODDER &
STOUGHTON

First published in Great Britain in 2019 by
Hodder & Stoughton
An Hachette UK company

1

A CIP catalogue record for this title is
available from the British Library

Hardback ISBN 978 1 473 63937 9
eBook ISBN 978 1 473 63939 3

Typeset in Plantin by Palimpsest Book Production Limited,
Falkirk, Stirlingshire

Printed and bound by CPI Group (UK) Ltd, Croydon, CR0 4YY

Hodder & Stoughton policy is to use papers that are natural,
renewable and recyclable products and made from wood grown
in sustainable forests. The logging and manufacturing processes
are expected to conform to the environmental regulations
of the country of origin.

Hodder & Stoughton Ltd
Carmelite House
50 Victoria Embankment
London EC4Y 0DZ

www.hodder.co.uk

For Matt

The moment of crisis arrived with no fanfare, no warning, on an ordinary working day at the end of November. It was very cold. Even at ten in the morning, the slate roof of the extension outside her office was still sparkling with frost, a shimmer of silver in the clear light.

She could hear the fear in his voice. 'You'll have to come and get me. I can't move.'

At work, Mike had leaned down to retrieve a file from the bottom drawer of his desk and a kind of electric shock, like a cattle prod in his lower back, had made him cry out.

After she'd ended the call, Sara sat quite still, letting the implications sink in. She'd promised to leave straight away – to go to his office, collect him, and take him to see the GP – but she was frozen to the chair. She must have known, even then, that picking up the car keys and walking out of her safe and predictable job was going to change everything. If she'd stayed put, working three days a week in the wills and probate department, she would have had more objectivity. She might have been able to cope.

Eventually, Sara dragged herself to her feet and went to make her excuses. When she told Jane, the office manager, that she had to go because there had been an accident, Jane put on her sympathetic face, thinking that Sara was talking about a car crash. But then Sara explained about Mike's back, and having to take him to the doctor, and Jane raised her eyebrows and said, 'Couldn't he get a taxi?' Sara, silenced by the stupidity of the suggestion, just stared. After an awkward pause, Jane swallowed and dropped her eyes to her keyboard, which Sara took to mean that she'd won the argument and had permission to leave.

It was a frustrating, thirty-minute drive through slow traffic. Sara's car – a black second-hand Polo with a reluctant gear stick – shook with elderly nerves each time it stopped at traffic lights.

When she got to the office, Mike was lying on his back on the floor, surrounded by his employees. They stood at a respectful distance, no one daring to acknowledge her arrival, hushed and downcast like mourners round a grave. Mike was very still. She could see from the greyness of his skin that this was much worse than the grumbling pain of the past few months.

He opened his eyes. 'You took your time.'

Four of them helped him to the car. It was clear that every movement hurt, but he didn't say a word, the muscles in his jaw rigid.

As she started the engine, she said, 'Maybe we should . . .?'

He said, 'Don't start. For God's sake, don't start.'

Fear fluttered in her stomach.

In the weeks that followed, Mike worked from home, lying in a state of desperate immobility on one of the big white sofas in the formal living room. Coffee stains appeared on the velvet cushions and office detritus on the silk rug from Marrakech. Crazed by pain, he rumbled with suppressed rage, bellowing out orders, hurling out blame. Sara scurried about like an overworked waitress, trying to cater for his every need but becoming so muddled and forgetful because of all the shouting that she ended up delivering entirely the wrong things – a charger when he wanted his reading glasses, extra strong mints when he needed his painkillers – so that Mike boiled over with frustration and roared, 'Are you doing this on purpose?'

Her mistakes multiplied. Every time, without fail, she rushed out to fetch his prescription from the chemist at exactly the moment he needed her most. Once, she came back to find him apoplectic because a motorcycle courier had shouted through the letter box that he couldn't leave the documents without a signature and Mike had been in too much pain to hobble to the door.

'You knew he was coming.'

Sara trembled. 'I had no idea.'

'They sent you an email.'

'If they did, I didn't see it.'

His outburst was savage. 'For God's sake, Sara! Fucking concentrate on what you're doing!'

The house quivered with tension. She flinched each time he yelled. She cried when he threw a whisky glass that narrowly missed her head. She was bawled out so often for misunderstanding what he needed that she ended up doubting her ability to make a cup of tea.

The worst of it was trying to get Mike to eat. Normally a man of large appetites, he lost interest in food completely. This worried her. As she kept telling him, he shouldn't be taking painkillers on an empty stomach. One cold winter morning, she spent hours making the kind of chilli-laced soup he would normally have devoured with gusto and carried it through to the living room on a tray, the white bowl nestling on a jaunty red-checked napkin.

Mike looked up from the sofa. 'What's that?'

'Lunch.'

'Take it away.'

She stood there holding it, uncertain what to do. 'Mike—'

'I don't want it.'

'But shouldn't you—'

His flailing arm, dismissing her, caught the edge of the tray. It flipped up, tipping the contents of the bowl on to Sara's front. The soup was hot. She cried out.

He said, 'Just go away and leave me alone.'

By Christmas, the atmosphere was so sharp and jagged you could have cut yourself. Edward shut himself in his room, protected by headphones that blocked out everything but electronica.

James, her elder son, was disgusted. 'Is this what it's going to be like from now on?'

She said, 'He's worried about the business. He doesn't know if they can manage without him.'

James gave her a look that was almost pitying. At eighteen, he forgave his father nothing. 'That doesn't mean he can take it out on us.'

It took its toll in the end. You can only be in crisis mode for so long. When Mike, for the third time that week, woke her at three in the morning demanding painkillers, Sara found herself weeping in the bathroom with the shower full on so that he couldn't hear.

Of course she knew that none of this was Mike's fault.

But it wasn't her fault either, which Mike didn't seem to understand.

★

Early in the New Year, just after the boys had gone back to school, the doorbell rang. For a moment, Sara was tempted to ignore it. Mike was now able to climb the stairs, swearing at the walls, and was upstairs in his study. The moment of calm was precious.

She opened the door to a young woman about the same age as James, with large brown eyes and clear skin, pink from the cold. Everything about her seemed on the brink of unravelling – dark shiny hair falling from a haphazard bun, stray threads trailing from a hem. When she spoke, the warmth of her breath puffed the air into steam. 'Hello. My name's Katie. I live just round the corner, and I wondered if . . .'

Sara frowned, trying not to look too welcoming.

'. . . if you'd like someone to walk your dog.'

For a moment Sara was confused. How did she know about the dog? Then she realised that Bundle's demented barking in the back garden – so much a part of her everyday life that she didn't even notice it any more – was so loud that it could be heard by anyone passing the front gate.

Katie hesitated. 'It might not be a good time.'

There was a vivid sweetness about her, a sheen of health and vitality.

Sara stood back and opened the door wider. 'You'd better come in.'

As Katie passed, her voluminous cloth coat – old and baggy, made for a much larger woman – wafted out cold air.

Sara had forgotten that the house could seem intimidating. She saw Katie's expression of awe as she glanced up at the huge modern chandelier, a cartwheel of crystal that caught the edges of the January light. The hall was double height anyway, with stone stairs and a black iron balustrade curving up to the gallery above, but the brilliance of the decoration – white walls everywhere – expanded the space still further, turning the Georgian rectory into a palace of ice.

Sara led Katie through the house, all the way to the great glass room at the back. Building the extension had been an indulgence, because no one could pretend that the original layout had been cramped, but the result was worth the expense. Exterior and interior were perfectly united. The working part of the kitchen was right at one end, with ingenious cupboards that hid everything from view. You could sit at the long wooden table overlooking the garden completely shielded from the hum of fridge and dishwasher.

In the early morning, Sara would watch the greyness lift from the yew trees and it felt as if she were outside, on the lawn. At night, she could look up and see the stars.

'Coffee?'

Katie said, breathless with astonishment, 'This is so beautiful.'

Sara allowed herself a smile. 'I know. I love living here.'

At that moment, Bundle, who had been ferreting about in some distant part of the garden, hurtled towards the house. Sara pulled open the sliding doors and he raced inside, claws clacking on the flagstones.

'How old is he?' Katie was hard to hear, caught up in a muddle of woman and dog that seemed to delight them both.

'Two.'

'They're a lot of work, aren't they, springer spaniels? Full of energy.'

Bundle, weaving in and out of Katie's legs, was a blur of black and white. Sara said, 'He's Edward's dog, really. But no one pays him much attention these days.'

6

Katie looked up. Her eyes held an eagerness to please that was so intense it was almost blinding. 'It's the same with all my clients. They just don't have the time.'

It didn't take much to get Katie to talk. Unlike most people, she didn't bridle at direct questions. As she took off her coat and scarf and Bundle settled at her feet, behaving like the good dog he'd never been, the words spilled out in a rush. Katie had a dear little face, with a kind of startled look, like a kitten. For a moment, the tightness in the house loosened. It felt like a small reprieve from the darkness of recent weeks.

Sara said, 'So how many clients do you have?'

'Three so far. But I've only just started. So that's quite good, isn't it?'

Katie said that her dog walking business was a way of supplementing her student loans, really – she was in her first year of a degree in tourism and hospitality management, and had hoped to cut costs by living at home, but her parents had sold up and moved to Spain. The move had been very sudden – one minute her father had been offered early retirement, the next they'd packed up and left. She'd been really worried about finding somewhere to live within a bus ride of the campus, but she'd met Pete in the pub, and he said that if she wasn't fussy about staying in town and didn't mind going a bit further out into the country, she could live rent-free in the tiny house he'd just bought in the village, tucked into the cul-de-sac at the end of Sara's garden.

Sara looked out of the great glass doors at the back. The trees were far too tall to see anything of the cramped modern estate beyond the fence.

Katie said that Pete didn't want any money from her – the house was in such a bad state. No one had lived there for years because it was wedged into a damp corner and the windows were too small to let in any light. As soon as he got planning permission from the council, he was going to knock it all down and start again. So it was all a bit grim. Black mould had flowered all over the ceilings and the boiler was on its last legs. The bathroom was a kind of lean-to, added on as an afterthought, and slugs clung to the shower screen as if they'd got confused and thought they were still outside in the garden. But Katie said at least it was a roof over her head, and it was fine until she could afford something better.

When she paused to draw breath, Sara said, 'So how long have you lived round here?'

'Since the summer.'

'Do you like it?'

Katie hesitated. 'It's a bit different. I'm used to having cafés and restaurants and shops and a cinema. I mean, I'm sure I'll get used to it. People like peace and quiet, don't they?'

Katie said it wasn't that easy meeting people in the village, because everyone went off early in the morning and didn't come back until after dark, and so many of the houses were hidden behind walls or shrubs or hedges, so you never saw anyone to say hello. She said it was sad because most of her friends apart from Anna and Baz had moved away, or gone to universities in other parts of the country, and she didn't really feel she'd got to know anyone on her course yet. Her dog walking clients were out at work all day – she had keys to all the houses – so if she was studying at home rather than going in to lectures she could spend a whole day not talking to anyone at all.

Sara saw a shadow behind Katie's eyes, as if the loneliness frightened her. 'I know what you mean. We've been here fourteen years and I still don't feel I've got to know anyone.'

Bundle, sprawled at Katie's feet, gave out a long shuddering sigh.

'Even the village shop's empty,' said Katie, 'during the day.'

'I don't think I've ever been in it.'

Katie was surprised. 'Not even for a pint of milk?'

Sara explained that she was normally out at work herself but had taken unpaid leave for a few months because Mike had hurt his back and needed her to be around to help him. Katie looked sympathetic, but Sara cut her off – any mention of back pain seemed to compel people to come out with pet theories about chiropractic or surgery or acupuncture, as if Sara hadn't heard of any of them or was too stupid to have done any research. She told Katie that the solicitor's office where she worked had been very understanding and were happy for her to take as much time as she needed.

What she didn't say was that no one had been in touch since she'd left. Sometimes it felt as if she'd dived down to the bottom of a pool and the waters had closed over her head, causing her to disappear without trace.

Katie looked impressed. 'It must be really interesting being a lawyer. Hearing people's secrets.'

Sara shook her head. 'Most of the time, I'm just filling in forms.'

But she could tell, from the shining admiration in her eyes, that Katie didn't really believe her.

Sara could have put Katie out of her misery and told her she'd got the job, but there was something so appealing about Katie's openness and honesty – something so unusual about talking to someone who hung on her every word – that she was reluctant to bring the conversation to a close. 'So how are your parents settling in to life in a new country?'

'They love it, I think.'

'You haven't been out to visit?'

Katie lowered her eyes. 'It's a bit difficult. They've got a spare bedroom, but Dad snores really badly, so Mum needs it to get some peace.'

'That's a shame.'

Katie looked unhappy. 'Mum says I'd be welcome any time. I could sleep on the sofa. But they couldn't put me up for more than a day or two because the flat just isn't big enough. I can see what they mean. We'd all get on top of each other.'

Sara said, 'Which part of Spain is it?'

For the first time since they'd met, Katie seemed lost for words. Sara waited, curious.

Katie said, in a muffled voice, 'I really miss them.'

'Of course you do.'

Katie hung her head.

With a little more prompting – a gentle nudge here and there – the whole story came tumbling out. Katie had just started going out with someone called Danny when the move to Spain was first mooted. Her parents didn't approve. Caught up in the bliss of a new relationship, Katie had ignored them. A rift had opened up. When Katie was offered the small dilapidated house, just weeks before her parents packed up and left, and Danny had moved in, her parents were appalled. The damage seemed irreparable.

'Why didn't they approve?'

'They said he was too old for me.'

'How old?'

'Twenty-four.'

Sara made sure she didn't smile. 'Are you still together?'

Katie shook her head.

'What happened?'

'I don't know.' Katie's expression was bleak.

Sara stayed very still, her eyes on Katie's face.

When Katie spoke again, her voice was shaking. 'I thought it was forever. But then he left me. After he'd gone, everything fell apart. I couldn't get up. I couldn't leave the house. Anna came and dragged me out of bed and took me to the doctor, and he said I was depressed and put me on anti-depressants.'

Bundle, sensing a change in mood, raised his head.

Katie bent down and stroked his silky ears, her cheeks bright red as if someone had slapped her. 'I've said too much, haven't I? You won't want me to walk Bundle now.'

Sara was astonished. 'But I do. Of course I do.'

Katie opened her eyes wide. 'Really?'

'I can see the way you are with him. I'd love you to walk him every day. Twice a day if possible. I should have said so earlier.'

Katie moved to the edge of her chair, eager to make amends. 'I promise I'm reliable.'

'I'm sure you are.'

'I'm getting therapy now. To make sure I don't get depressed again.'

Sara said, 'We all have times when things get too much.'

Katie's mouth trembled. 'You're such a kind person. I'm so glad I've met you.'

Sara smiled.

★

'A dog walker?' James was surprised out of his usual laconic indifference.

'Just for a while. It's one less thing to worry about.'

Bundle was extremely irritating. Inside, he barked to go out. Outside, he barked to come in. She'd bought him for Edward for his twelfth birthday, thinking a dog might provide reassurance and help with his social interaction. But her research was flawed. It turned out that springer spaniels are full of energy and easily bored, which was exactly the wrong sort of dog for a boy who hated surprises.

James leaned back against the wall. Tall and angular, completely different from his father, he looked older than eighteen. In only a few months, he would have finished school altogether. 'You should have asked me.'

Sara shook her head. 'You're much too busy.'

She felt his eyes following her as she cleared the table. The house was unusually quiet. Edward was in his room. Mike was in his study. James said, 'So when does she start?'

'Next Monday.'

Sara didn't tell him all the details – the dilapidated house, the absent parents, the depression.

He said, 'I wouldn't have thought the dog was the problem.'

She looked up. 'What do you mean?'

'You know what I mean.'

Sara's voice was firm. 'In a few months, everything will be back to normal.'

James bent down and picked up his bag, heavy with books. 'I'll be away the whole of the summer. As soon as exams are over.'

'I know.'

'And if I get the grades, I'll be gone for good.'

She said, 'James, you mustn't worry about me. Everything's going to be fine.'

James adjusted the weight of the bag on his shoulder, but still made no move to go. 'He's getting worse.'

'James—'

'You can say what you like. He's getting worse.'

They held each other's eyes.

She took a deep breath. 'He's your father. I don't want you to fall out with him.'

James gave her a look of incredulity. 'It's a bit late for that.'

The following morning Mike was even more irritable than usual. By the time the boys had left for school he had already created a level of noise in the house that was singing inside Sara's head. She felt as if she were standing on an island in the middle of rush hour traffic, or on a runway beneath the belly of a low-flying plane. On her way through the hall, as Mike was dragging himself round the living room haranguing someone on the other end of the phone about deadlines and delivery, she opened the heavy front door on to the gravelled drive just to remind herself that a world existed outside the hell of his temper. The sky was a frozen grey. Sara closed her eyes, trying to blank out sound, concentrating on nothing but breathing in, breathing out, breathing in, breathing out.

A voice said, 'It's all kicking off today.'

In front of her was the postman, wearing his personal all-weather uniform of olive bucket hat, knee-length khaki shorts and brown hiking boots. He was a familiar sight round the village. Sometimes you came across his metal trolley of letters and packages jammed into a hedge, as if it had got tired of waiting and wandered off by itself.

Sara jerked out of her reverie. 'I'm sorry, what did you say?'

The postman nodded towards the house. 'I said, it's all kicking off today.'

Now that her moment of calm had been shattered, she could hear it all over again – the booming percussion of Mike's voice punctuated by the distant cacophony of Bundle's manic barking.

She tried to smile. 'Just one of those mornings.'

The postman scratched his cheek. He had quite a weathered complexion, being out all hours in the wind and the rain. 'Sounds upset.'

What could she say? She didn't want to be disloyal. 'Not really. Not more than usual.'

He looked disbelieving. 'I could hear it all round the cul-de-sac.'

Sara was silenced.

'If I were you, I'd do something about it.' He hoisted his mail bag higher on to his shoulder. 'I couldn't listen to that all day.'

She watched as he trudged across the gravel, muscles bunched in his calves.

Mike expressed no interest in meeting Katie. When Sara first told him about employing a dog walker, he gave her his usual flat stare, as if he thought she was mad but it wasn't worth having an argument.

Sara guessed he was worried about the cost. Since he'd been forced to take time off work, he'd become obsessed with household expenditure. She had her arguments prepared – they didn't have a cleaner any more, she'd been using the cheap supermarket near the bypass. But Mike didn't raise the subject, so neither did she.

Their first meeting wasn't a great success. Katie had just arrived as Mike was making his way across the hall. He gave her a terse nod and disappeared into the living room.

Sara said, 'He's not a morning person.'

Katie gazed after him with an anxious expression.

Later that week, Katie was putting on her coat in the cavernous hall when a roar of frustration spilled over the black balustrade from the floor above. Katie glanced at Sara, a question in her eyes.

Sara said, 'He hates losing things.'

There was a thud, and then a crash, as if something had been thrown against a wall.

Sara said, 'The stupid thing is, whatever he's looking for is usually right in front of his nose. He just can't see it.'

'That's just like my dad,' said Katie. 'He had us all looking for his glasses once, and it turned out he'd had them in his hand the whole time.'

But mostly the house was silent when Katie brought Bundle home in the afternoons. Mike was always working – propped up on the sofa, or closeted upstairs in his study, staring at several screens – and the boys were making their way home from school. So it became a habit, if they were both free, for Katie to sit in the kitchen having a cup of tea while Sara started preparing the evening meal.

It was Sara's favourite time of day in winter, the half hour before turning on the lamps and drawing the curtains. There was a softness to the dying light, a blurring of edges that encouraged intimacy and confession.

They talked about general subjects at first – how Mike had his own business and was a bit of a workaholic, how James was hoping to study maths at university, how Katie's friend Anna used to be a teaching assistant until the job had been axed, so she now worked in the charity shop and gave Katie first refusal on anything that might be useful.

But as the weeks passed, and conversation moved to more personal matters, Sara found herself shutting the door to the hall to discourage eavesdropping. Bundle was mercifully quiet. Exhausted by racing up and down Ogden Hill or skidding through the icy ruts of Smith's Field, he flopped on to the floor and slept.

Katie said her therapist was called Maxine. She saw patients in the converted garage attached to her house – which was always cold because the heating was turned down so low – and wore bright red lipstick and black knee-length boots that shone under the fluorescent light. She used to be a nanny – which you could tell, because she didn't like being interrupted and believed in setting boundaries – but had recently switched careers. They'd met in the charity shop. Maxine had been searching through the winter coats, lifting each one out on its hanger to search for flaws. Katie had admired her thoroughness.

'Do you like her?'

Katie said she'd only had one session so far, and they'd talked about the importance of self-esteem. Maxine said you couldn't let other people walk all over you, and you had to believe you deserved the best. This meant radical personal transformation and cutting yourself off from negative influences, including people who tried to control you and tell you what to do.

'She says I have to give myself permission to grab hold of what I want, and that it's time to put myself first and be the centre of my own life.'

Sara nodded.

'But she says she can't do it for me. Her job is to nudge me in the right direction, but it's my responsibility to make it happen. I have to give one hundred and ten per cent commitment to personal growth.'

Maxine had explained that she was going to give Katie a series of homework tasks. Some of the assignments might feel quite difficult because Katie would be pushed out of her comfort zone, but change was challenging and there was no gain without pain.

'Have you talked about Danny?'

Katie shook her head. 'Not yet.'

'It will be good when you can. So that you can sort out your feelings a bit more.'

Katie didn't respond straight away. After a while she said that her friends Anna and Baz were so angry with Danny for the way he'd treated her that they'd banned all mention of his name. They thought she'd get better more quickly if she pushed him out of her mind. But it was really hard to do that, because she still didn't really understand why he'd left. It kept going round and round in her head but none of it made sense.

Sara kept her eyes on the task at hand, chopping onions and skinning tomatoes.

Katie stared into space, momentarily silent.

A few days later, Sara came home from shopping to find Katie and Mike sitting together at the kitchen table. This was a shock. Mike looked as if he'd been there for hours, shirtsleeves rolled up, elbows on the table. Sara was so used to Mike's domineering presence – neck and shoulders like a rugby player, a voice that seemed to boom through a loudhailer – that it took her a while to realise that he was drunk. He'd filled a glass for Katie too, but she hadn't touched it. Sara wondered how long she'd been sitting there, bombarded by words.

Mike leaned forwards, wagging his finger in Katie's face. 'It's what I'm always telling James. You can't sit around waiting for life to give you a break. Make your own luck. Create your own opportunities. So many people want it all on a plate. But it doesn't work like that. You've got to get off your backside and do something.' Mike reached for the whisky bottle. 'I started a cleaning business when I was fourteen. Nothing complicated. But I'd earned enough for a deposit on a flat by the time I was twenty. And do you know why?'

Katie stared back, glassy-eyed.

'I worked out what people wanted, that's why. Thorough, reliable and cheaper than the competition. Not rocket science. Just common sense.'

Sara tried to attract Katie's attention, to communicate somehow that she could leave whenever she wanted to.

Mike poured himself a generous measure. 'There's so much crap talked about enterprise and business these days. But anyone can do it. Anyone can start their own business. You just need focus. Determination. Be willing to get your hands dirty.'

Sara said, 'Katie has started her own business. At the same time as studying for a degree. She's a dog walker.'

Mike took a mouthful of whisky. 'You can't afford to hang about. When you're young, you think you'll go on forever.

But one day you realise it's crept up on you. Old age. Your best years are behind you.'

Sara said, 'I should get on with supper. The boys will be hungry.'

'That's why you can't fuck around. You've got to seize the moment. Decide what you're going to do and do it. Don't waste your life waiting for the right time because there never is a right time. You've just got to get on with it.'

'Mike, maybe Katie—'

'Life happens while you're making other plans. Who said that? It's true. It all goes so fast. I'm going to be fifty in June. God, that's depressing. Beginning of the end.'

Sara said, 'Maybe—'

'You see it all on TV. Dementia and cruises and retirement living. I might as well shoot myself now.'

'Mike, we shouldn't hold Katie up.'

Mike fixed Katie with a heavy-lidded stare. 'So how old are you?'

'Eighteen.'

Mike said, 'You remind me of someone.'

Katie looked panicked.

Mike swivelled round. His eyes were bloodshot and unfocused. 'Don't you think so, Sara? Who does she remind you of?'

'I don't know.'

'Yes, you do. You know exactly who she reminds me of.'

'One of James's friends maybe.'

He mimicked her, making his voice sound unpleasantly high and whiny. 'One of James's friends.'

'It's late, Mike. We mustn't keep her. It's time for Katie to go home.'

There was a small silence. Then Mike threw back his head and laughed. The sound reverberated round the room.

Sara caught up with Katie by the front door. 'Don't take any notice of him.'

'Why was he laughing?'

'I've got no idea. It's what happens when you drink too much.'

Katie nodded but still hesitated.

Sara made her voice calm. 'Don't give it another thought. He was rambling. He'll have forgotten all about it in the morning.'

After Katie had gone, and Sara had rushed round in a whirlwind of activity because everything had been so delayed, they had supper. Mike lapsed into a kind of brooding silence and concentrated on shovelling mashed potato and chicken stew into his mouth. Once, when Sara looked up, she saw James staring at his father with an air of puzzled distaste, as if the family meal had been interrupted by a random stranger who'd wandered in off the street and hadn't yet been asked to leave.

Later that evening, Sara came back into the great glass extension to find Mike sitting at the table in the dark. She felt a small tug of alarm. He had his back to her, a hulk of shadow facing the black void of the garden.

She said, 'Can I put the lights on?'

When he didn't reply, she turned on the lamp by the shelves, a gentle illumination that no one could object to. She tried not to look at him too closely, but she could see that he had slumped forwards and that his hands were still nursing a glass of whisky.

'Do you want a cup of tea?'

Still he said nothing. At the sink, she filled the kettle. The black night pressed down on the glass above, making her feel small and insignificant.

When she couldn't waste any more time wiping clean surfaces and rearranging mugs in the dishwasher, she made the tea and brought it back to the table.

He said, as if they'd been in the middle of a conversation, 'She's pretty, isn't she?'

Her heart sank.

'Trusting. Innocent.'

Sara was unwilling to sit down, but there didn't seem to be any other option. She lowered herself on to the edge of the chair, ready to move quickly if the mood turned ugly.

'Works hard, too. Turns up twice a day, regular as clockwork. Takes the bloody dog out.' His voice was harsh, like iron scraping on stone. 'Reliable, honest, loyal.'

She raised her eyes to his face.

'I give it six months.'

She kept her voice light and casual, as if they were discussing something inconsequential. 'I hope she stays longer than that.'

He gave her a hard stare, as if she were being deliberately stupid. 'You'll tell her to go.'

'Of course I won't.'

'You will. Because that's what you do. You'll pick an argument and say it's her fault.'

It was such a reversal of reality that she was silenced.

Mike looked at her with cold contempt. 'You'll fall out with her. Because you fall out with everyone in the end. No one's ever good enough, are they, Sara? No one ever quite meets your exacting standards.'

For a moment, her head was full of bitter retorts. It was tempting to put the blame where it really belonged.

But looking at the flushed, drunken face of her belligerent husband, she thought it was probably better not to reply.

It was several weeks before Katie told her about Danny.

Katie had been describing her third session of therapy in the cold converted garage attached to Maxine's house. 'She says my fixation with Danny is because I'm clinging to the idea of true love. She says I don't need *Sleeping Beauty* and *Cinderella*, because they're just fairy tales for children, and I have to commit to a completely different way of thinking.'

According to Maxine, the modern trend was about picking up different people for companionship or sex as and when you needed them, a way of life she called random conscious coupling. She said that long-term monogamy was dying a death, a thing of the past, which was perfectly obvious if you looked around you because everybody kept getting divorced.

Katie said, 'It's all about attitude. Being open to change. You have to keep challenging yourself and asking if your needs are being met. If something's not right and you're not satisfied, there's nothing wrong with ditching it and moving on.'

Maxine talked a lot about sex, particularly theories about trust and abandonment, and had an extensive knowledge of fetishes and kinks. Given that the traditional approach had been so disappointing, she thought that Katie would benefit from widening her horizons and experimenting with different kinds of relationship, and suggested she sign up to a number of dating sites catering for a more adventurous market.

Sara said, 'How do you feel about that?'

Katie said there wasn't much point in paying for therapy if you didn't follow the advice you were given, but the idea still made her nervous. 'I'm not sure I'm ready for it.'

'I can understand that,' said Sara. 'It's not long since you and Danny broke up.'

Katie bit her lip.

'There's no rush. Maybe you need a bit more time.'

When Katie looked up, her eyes were full of tears.

It turned out that everyone knew Danny. He'd grown up in the area and was a long-term regular of the Goat, the cramped Tudor pub on the town's main high street that smelled of fried onion rings, beer-soaked carpet and damp. His nan lived in one of the terraced houses by the railway line, next to the recreation ground – the ones with thick black mortar round the bricks as if they'd been drawn with marker pen. But he was a lot older than all her friends, and he'd been away for a few years, so she hadn't met him until they all went to a house party at the beginning of the summer.

She'd noticed him straight away, leaning against the wall in the kitchen, arms folded, head down. Someone shouted her name and he looked up and gave her an intense, assessing glance. He was very thin. His skin was white, like a musician who never sees daylight. He always wore a long black coat that swung around him as he walked.

She had no idea that he liked her. And then one Saturday night as they all trailed back laughing and shouting through the town past the chicken and kebab shops, he waited until all the others had gone round the corner and pinned her against the brick wall outside Sainsbury's Local.

They'd been together six months. The whole time, she couldn't believe how lucky she was. She'd wake in the early morning and look at him in the pale yellow light, lying in the bed next to her, and wonder what she'd done to deserve him. Some weekends they never got up at all. Outside it could be raining or snowing, and it just didn't matter – they'd be curled up in the warm like mice in a nest. If he got hungry, he'd kick her out of bed, and she'd run downstairs and make tea and toast. When she got back her feet were like ice, but she'd burrow back under the covers, and he was like a furnace, pushing out heat, even though he was nothing but bones.

He smelled of burnt caramel. She could recognise him instantly, even in the middle of a crowd.

Danny always knew what he wanted. He could have picked anyone. But he picked her.

Sara, listening, kept very still. This was a story she knew well. All those years ago, Mike had done exactly the same thing – ignored the crowd and focused just on her, as if the simple fact of her presence had been so dazzling, so bright, that he couldn't even see the people around her.

For Katie, the end was brutal. One Friday night in the Goat, when the pub was packed with after-work drinkers, Danny said it was over. There had been no preamble, no warning. It was such a shock, she started crying. He pushed back his chair, jogging the table so that beer slopped over the edge of his pint glass, and his voice was angry as if she'd accused him of something he hadn't done. 'I never said I loved you.'

When she got back, she realised the house had been cleared

of everything that belonged to him. He'd packed up before he'd even got to the pub, before he'd even told her it was finished.

A few days later, the spare key arrived through the letter box, like an afterthought.

Katie's voice was thick with tears.

Later, because she had been concentrating so hard, Sara almost felt that she'd been there in the Goat herself the night that Danny said he was leaving. She could smell the old carpet, the frying oil, the sugary yeast of the beer. She could see Danny in front of her, loud with self-justification.

At the end of the afternoon, when Katie finally put on her coat and scarf and they stood in the great hall, the shadows wide on the white walls, Sara said, 'Can I give you a key? Then you can let yourself in whenever you like, whether I'm here or not.'

Katie's eyes were solemn. 'I'll keep it very safe.'

'I know you will.'

Over the next few days, Katie continued to tell Sara about Danny. The stories tumbled out like gas exploding from a bottle. Every so often, she'd stop and look up, hot with humiliation, apologising for the constant stream of words.

Sara said, 'You need to talk.'

'But I'm wasting your time.'

Sara shook her head.

Everything about Danny was perfect – his light blue eyes, his long fingers. He had a way of creating space that belonged only to them, leaning in close to tell her secrets that no one else could hear. She never had to share him with other people – sometimes on Saturdays they went into town to one of the cafés that served all-day breakfasts because Danny was fond of a fry-up, but he always chose the one behind the car park so they didn't have to talk to anyone they knew. Danny usually ordered everything on the menu, including baked beans and fried bread – but not the mushrooms, because he said they were slimy – and decorated everything with tomato ketchup. He always left the white round the fried egg, though, because he said it turned his stomach.

He laughed at her for getting into debt so that she could study for a degree. That's just playing someone else's game. Use your brains. Work it out for yourself.

Sex had been urgent, immediate, as if they were running out of time. They didn't always make it upstairs – slid from the sofa to the floor in front of the small electric fire that smelled of burning plastic. They did it in the woods once, on the way back from the pub. The grass was wet and the air was rank and rotten. The next morning she had a rash all the way up her legs from her ankles to her groin.

In the beginning, she'd worried all the time that he might leave. But then his toothbrush appeared in the plastic cup on the toilet cistern, and his private stash of beer in the fridge, and he hung up all his work clothes on a black iron rail in the spare bedroom, his shoes in shiny pairs underneath.

He said to everyone in the Goat that he was her lodger. 'I'm renting a room at Katie's.'

Except that he never paid her a penny. And the room was just for his shirts.

He was in sales, Katie said, working on commission. He didn't have to sell the windows, just get people to agree to someone coming round to give them a free quotation. He often got invited in for a chat, especially by the elderly ladies living alone. He could turn on the charm. They wanted to fatten him up – cake, biscuits, lots of sugar in his tea. He used to say, 'They love me. Can't get enough of me.'

One afternoon, they went to see his nan. She'd smoked for so many years that the skin on her face had dried out like the apple you've forgotten at the bottom of the bowl. Every so often, she'd turn away from the telly and squint at Katie through the yellow fog and fire questions straight out, like a policeman – how old are you, where did you go to school, what job do you do.

Later, Katie said to Danny, 'I don't think she likes me.'

Danny said, 'She doesn't.'

One bright February morning, Sara took her courage in both hands and went to the village shop, just ten minutes' walk from her front gates. It didn't look very inviting – a fixed white portacabin on scuffed grass next to the children's swings. Inside was no better – slippery lino, a sparse stock of packets and tins, and a humming chiller cabinet that smelled of cheese. There was no one there except for a small woman with round glasses standing behind the counter who said, giving Sara her change, that it was lovely to see the crocuses peeping through but there was going to be trouble if the forecast was right and they were in for a fall of snow.

Outside again, turning up her collar against the icy wind, Sara couldn't help feeling disappointed. She had wanted a more significant encounter.

A few days later, hoping for a better outcome, Sara went

back and spent a dispiriting few minutes hunting through the biscuits for anything she might want to buy. The shop was, once again, deserted. Even the small woman with the glasses seemed distracted and unwilling to talk.

On the way out, Sara found her path blocked by a woman with tight grey curls and a waterproof jacket. She had an air of authority. 'I see Katie's working for you.'

Sara stared. She had been expecting an inoffensive remark about the weather, so this rather aggressive observation threw her completely.

'Your dog walker, Katie Franklin. She walks our dog, too. Mary Miller saw her with a springer spaniel in Smith's Field and put two and two together.' Her expression was amused. 'You look shocked.'

Sara found her voice. 'Not really.'

'You can't keep anything secret round here. You knew that, didn't you?'

'I—'

'We all love Katie. Just a bit scatterbrained sometimes. She once took Dexter to Meadow Rise and Lulu back to Bay Tree House. But then she probably has better things to think about.'

The conversation, with its assumption of shared interest, felt like an affront.

Later, when Sara reported the exchange back to Katie – remembering to leave out the comment about being scatterbrained – Katie unravelled the whole thing. She identified the woman as Rachel Reeve, a maths teacher at the local state secondary who lived with her rather stooped and miserable husband and two teenage sons in Bay Tree House. Rachel's dog Dexter, a wiry and intelligent animal with traces of Jack Russell, was known to be very fierce.

'She seemed quite abrupt,' said Sara.

Katie said that Rachel believed in plain speaking, but that was probably because she was used to keeping crowds of children under control. 'I thought your boys might know each other.'

Sara thought it might sound unfriendly if she said that James hated the village and spent as little time there as possible, so just shook her head and said that they all went to different schools.

Lulu turned out to be the red setter belonging to Grace Knight, a beautician who lived in one of the modern detached houses in Meadow Rise at the edge of the village. Grace knew everybody. She even had clients in London. She often called you 'babe' or 'sugar' because she wasn't good at remembering names, which seemed surprising for someone who spent a lot of time up close and personal doing eyebrow threading and bikini waxes, but you could always rely on her for the latest gossip, although it was never usually earth-shattering – more on the lines of where someone was going on holiday or what they were thinking of buying their mum for Christmas.

'She has her own YouTube channel,' said Katie, eyes big with awe, 'with tutorials about skincare and beauty products and how celebrities do their make-up. She's got thousands of followers.'

Sara could hardly keep up. 'I thought you didn't know anyone in the village.'

'It's because of the dogs. You know what it's like. People with dogs always talk to each other.'

Sara tried to think back to the rare occasions when she'd taken Bundle out, but she could remember only rain and mud and overwhelming irritation because he never came when she called.

Mary Miller, who'd seen Katie walking Bundle in Smith's Field, owned Daisy, a large honey-coloured Labrador, and lived in a small cottage right on the main road. According to Mary, everyone had been curious about Sara and her family for years, because the Old Rectory was by far the biggest house in the village and no one could quite see over the hedges.

Katie said she could hardly get past the church these days without people stopping her to ask questions. It had cheered her up a lot. She felt she was starting to make friends in the village.

'Questions about us?'

Katie nodded.

Sara wasn't sure whether to be flattered or appalled. 'What do they want to know?'

'Everything. What you do as a job, where you shop, what colour the curtains are.'

For a moment, Sara felt frightened. 'What do you say?'

Katie looked serious. 'I tell them I've only been walking Bundle since the New Year and I don't know very much about you.'

Sara was still anxious. 'You wouldn't ever pass on any personal information, would you?'

Katie was shocked. 'Of course not.'

'I wouldn't like to think people were talking about us.'

'It's only gossip. Having a chat and passing the time of day. It doesn't mean anything.'

Later, when Sara thought this over, she came to the rather nervous conclusion that getting to know her neighbours might mean a level of intrusion she wasn't really used to. It was a strange idea. She had never thought of the village as a community. It was just an address, a place to live. No one could pretend it was pretty – not much more than a string of houses clinging to the main road, surrounded by flat agricultural land under a wide grey sky. Most of the time people drove through it on their way to somewhere more interesting. You only found the Old Rectory if you took a turning just past the garage with its dark and oily interior, and drove up a long spindly lane with overgrown hedges frothy with blackthorn. After a while, if you kept on driving, you found yourself passing an estate that used to belong to the council – brown pebbledash houses ranged round a scrubby square of grass with a climbing frame, rusty swings and the fixed portacabin containing the village shop. Further up the lane was a squat thirteenth-century stone church with a square tower and a stained-glass window of St George and the dragon, glowing scarlet and purple, which most people didn't know about because there was only a Sunday service every other week and the wooden door was usually locked. Beyond the church, past a row of cottages and set well back from the road in a couple of acres of garden, was the Old Rectory with its smooth façade of honey-coloured stone.

It was the isolation that had attracted her. She liked the feeling that you could live your life without the constant interaction that so many people demanded. It felt like a sanctuary.

'You're sure?' Mike had stood in the hall, gazing up at the gallery above, clearly wanting it all so badly that he could hardly breathe. A house like this summed up everything he'd ever worked for – not just wealth but the trappings of wealth, the conspicuous exhibition of success.

The estate agent had taken himself off to a distant part of the house – the scullery, perhaps, or the small whitewashed room just inside the back door with hooks for waxed jackets and wooden shelves for wellington boots. He had recognised their need to be alone. He had already seen the commission from an imminent, indisputable sale.

'Yes,' she said. 'I'm sure.'

In time, the ability to shut herself away saved her sanity. They didn't get the diagnosis until Edward was five. Perhaps they should have done something about it earlier, before his behaviour became quite so marked, but her instinct had been to hide him away and protect him. There were so many things that upset him – loud noises, strong smells, sudden movement. If something pushed him over the edge and he started screaming, there was nothing she could do.

She saw the judgement on people's faces. They thought she was a bad mother who couldn't control her child.

At home, behind the high hedges, they were safe. They were lucky to have so much space. When they first moved in, Mike had persuaded her to employ a gardener. But old Mr Priest kept trimming and pruning and creating neat lines and angles, even though Sara explained again and again that she wanted something less ordered and suburban. Mike had said, in those early days when they still laughed together, that he thought the garden revealed her secret self. He said it showed the fire and passion she preferred to keep hidden.

In the end it was a relief when Mr Priest said it was all getting too much and he'd decided to retire. Sara no longer had to explain her antipathy to blowsy flowers and regimented annuals.

Edward dug in the dark earth next to her, transferring

worms and snails to a wooden trug. Sometimes he'd lie on his stomach, staring through the blades of grass as if his concentration could magnify ants into armies.

At the start, she hid what was happening. The excuse she gave herself was that Mike was working long hours and under a lot of stress. In any case, she didn't want to shatter his illusions. Every evening, coming home for the boys' bedtime, he was so relentlessly positive, so determined to see only the best in his family, that it seemed cruel to disabuse him.

Edward, just out of babyhood, was deaf to his surroundings. Sitting motionless in front of the TV, he stared at the screen as if absorbing every particle of pixelation.

Mike was uneasy. 'Is he all right?'

She made light of it, lying through her teeth. 'He's just tired.'

He deferred to her judgement. He thought she knew what she was doing. So she kept up the pretence that everything was fine and eventually, when this was impossible, that she was coping. The lie exhausted her. She enfolded herself like a live nerve in layers so thick that no feeling was left exposed.

When the boys were small, she and Mike hardly saw each other. As the business grew, he was away for weeks at a time – conferences, sales trips, visits to clients. He wished he could spend more time with them – of course he did. But when you run your own company, every minute is devoted to its survival. Even at weekends, he was upstairs in his study working.

Luckily for Mike, she craved solitude. All day she longed for freedom from small sticky hands, from the physicality of feeding, washing, holding, restraining. At night, in the cool darkness, she had responsibility for no one but herself. She lay still, listening to his steady breathing, her skin wired like an alarm because one more touch would have made her scream.

When Edward was nearly two, they decided to get an au pair. It was Mike's idea – he thought it might help if there was someone around to share the load. Sara was worried about having a stranger living in the house, but the agency sent Hilda from the Danish Faroe Islands, and Sara liked her immediately. She was small and fine-boned with shoulder-length blonde hair and an air of calm capability. Hilda said she lived in Tórshavn in a red house with a green roof, and had five siblings. In her musical English, the words dancing to a different rhythm, she said that being part of a large family meant that you always had company and someone to talk to, but there was usually a queue for the bathroom and her little sisters stole her clothes. Sara listened entranced to her descriptions of black cliffs, puffins and kittiwakes, feasts of fermented cod, angelica and sorrel.

She said to Mike, 'Can we go there? Can we go to the Faroe Islands?'

But Mike said he didn't have time for holidays.

By the time Hilda arrived, Edward's sensitivity was already very marked – he hated mess of any kind and shrank back with fear if anyone came near him. But Hilda smiled, and said very little, and gradually Edward tolerated less and less distance between them until they were almost sitting side by side on the same sofa. She was very easy to have around. Even Mike liked her. Sometimes Sara would get back from work and Mike would be catching up with paperwork at the kitchen table while Hilda padded round in her dressing gown, blonde hair a mess, obviously relaxed and at home.

When Hilda left, Sara realised she couldn't manage on her own any more. By now Mike was so often travelling for work that he was hardly ever home. By chance she met Amanda at the GP's surgery. It could have gone badly wrong. Even before Sara had sat down on one of the blue plastic chairs, Edward had launched himself full-length on to the floor by Amanda's feet and started untying her shoelaces. But Amanda just glanced down and turned back to her dog-eared magazine as if the whole thing was completely unimportant. When her name was called, she stood up and gently shuffled beyond Edward's grasp.

Sara said, 'I'm so sorry.'

She smiled. 'Little scientist, that's what he is. Trying to find out how things work.'

Amanda was a local childminder. To begin with, Sara left him with her just a few hours a week, precious time that she filled with all the tasks she couldn't manage with Edward in tow. But once he was settled, and Amanda had agreed to take and collect both boys from school, there seemed no reason not to go back to a job she enjoyed and was good at. She chose a local firm that dealt with family law, and was assigned to the wills and probate division.

It wasn't so much work as a chance to breathe.

Amanda turned out to be one of the few people that Edward ever really liked. All the time she looked after him – until a place came up for him at a specialist school nearby with a bus that delivered him almost door to door – she was his champion and defender, determined to see his behaviour as logical rather than strange. She said that Sara mustn't worry about his delayed speech because Einstein didn't say a word until he was six, and that was only because the soup was too cold. Until that moment, he hadn't had cause to complain.

She said, 'It makes sense if you think about it. If there isn't a problem, don't make a fuss.'

After a while, Sara realised this was true.

The black cloud of Mike's fury made the house dark.

His obsession with saving money had intensified. He told Sara they couldn't rely on the kind of income he'd been able to bring in before, and that they'd have to economise in order to reduce overall spending. To Sara, this made no sense. She knew from happier days when Mike had been less secretive that the house was paid off, there were a number of investment accounts and insurance policies, and that Mike had a fully paid-up pension. She couldn't believe that they were in that much financial difficulty.

'He's worried about the business,' she said to James. 'He's had to take a lot of time off.'

The worst of it was that the austerity drive turned into a kind of petty madness that did nothing much to rein in expenditure but greatly increased the general atmosphere of bad temper. Mike switched off all the lights, plunging the house into gloom. He turned down the heating so low that James, studying in his room, had to hunch over his desk in coat and gloves. He scrutinised supermarket bills and vetoed expenditure on anything but own brands so that Edward, faced with unfamiliar packaging, kept going into meltdown.

'I haven't noticed him cutting back on alcohol,' said James, blowing on his hands.

'Don't begrudge him the odd drink.'

'The odd drink? Have you seen the number of bottles in the recycling bin?'

'James, he's going through a really difficult time.'

James looked at her with irritation. 'I've noticed.'

When she could, Sara escaped to the garden. It had always been her refuge in times of stress – a place she loved that rewarded her care and attention. It was the hard physical work she enjoyed most, digging the beds, picking out the stones and old tree roots, freeing up the clay clods into friable, rich-smelling soil. She liked the feeling that she was creating the best possible conditions for the plants to grow. In the February frosts, there wasn't much she could do, but she cut back the lavatera and ceanothus and tidied up the hedges. The air was sharp and clean. Sara turned her face to the sky and willed herself to be positive. Mike had to get better. There must be an end in sight.

One evening, as they were finishing supper, James asked if he could take the car.

Mike looked up with his usual impassive stare. 'Which car?'

'I'm not insured to drive yours.'

'Your mother's car?'

'Yes.'

Mike considered this. 'Why?'

'I want to see a friend.'

'Which friend?'

'You don't know him.'

'I don't know him?'

'No.'

Across the table, Edward echoed, 'No.'

Sara put a warning hand on Edward's arm.

Mike picked up his wine glass and drained it.

Sara said, 'I think your father's wondering whether it's a good idea to go out on a school night.'

James looked at his father with feigned interest, as if keen to understand his views.

There was a taut silence.

Edward started making a sort of anxious humming sound, like someone standing on the edge of the topmost diving board wondering if the whole thing might be a mistake.

Sara took a deep breath. 'Maybe tonight's not a good idea.'

James was still staring at his father.

Sara said, 'Maybe tomorrow would be better.'

Mike reached for the wine bottle.

James stood up and left the room. As Mike filled his glass, Sara heard James walking across the hall, then a kind of scuffle as if he was putting on his shoes. The front door slammed. Moments later, they heard the engine of the Polo and then the crunch of gravel as the car pulled out of the drive.

Edward had stopped humming, but his eyes were on Sara's face, waiting to see how worried he should be.

Mike's words were slurred by wine, 'He's lying.'

Sara said, 'You don't know that.'

Mike laughed.

Sara stood up and started gathering the dirty plates together.

Mike picked up his glass. 'You know what I think? I think he's gone to meet the lovely Katie.'

'If he wanted to meet Katie, he could walk round to her house.'

Mike leaned forward. 'What if they did it here? Under your roof? What would you say to that?'

A knife from the pile of cutlery on the top plate fell on to the table.

Her voice sounded much too loud. 'That's enough.'

Mike looked up, a slow grin spreading across his face.

Thanks to Katie's descriptions, the faceless inhabitants of the village were beginning to become people with names, jobs and families. Katie said that Mary Miller, who had been one of her very first dog walking clients, was the one who'd asked the most questions about Sara, but it was probably just habit because she'd only recently retired as a receptionist in the local health clinic.

'She wanted to know all about Mike's back,' said Katie. 'She said the pain can be excruciating. She remembered a patient at the surgery who was in such agony he wanted to throw himself off a cliff.'

Mary and her Labrador Daisy were both plump, arthritic and permanently out of breath so spent most of their time in Mary's hot little kitchen crammed with dog paraphernalia – Labrador fridge magnets, a 'Puppies of the World' wall calendar and a tapestry cushion of a black Highland terrier in a tartan beret. There was nothing Mary liked more than a long afternoon of gossip over tea and biscuits.

It turned out that she'd somehow got hold of completely the wrong impression about Sara because she'd once seen her waving her arms about and shouting at Mike in the front seat of the BMW, which made her think that Sara had a bad temper. Katie said that Sara was quiet and kind and never even raised her voice, so what had looked like a row was probably just Sara singing along to the radio. Mary also thought that Sara was unfriendly and kept herself to herself, but Katie explained how busy she was, working and looking after the boys.

Sara said, 'People don't understand what it's like to be shy.'

Katie paused, as if this was a new thought.

'You have everything you want to say in your head, but you don't know how to start, so people think you're cold and reserved. Or you blurt it all out at the wrong time, and everyone thinks you're rude.'

'I've never thought you were rude,' said Katie, her eyes anxious.

'But that's because we've got to know each other.' Sara smiled. 'You know what I'm really like.'

Katie said that Grace Knight had also been very keen to find out more about Sara, but this might have been for business reasons as she was always keen to introduce new clients to her beauty salon on the high street, a little slice of a shop two doors down from the Goat. Everyone loved Grace because she had the knack of making even a small treatment, like a facial or a manicure, feel like a complete makeover. As Katie said, you walked in feeling plain and ordinary, and walked out feeling like someone in a magazine. Naturally enough, both Grace and her red setter Lulu were beautifully groomed. Lulu was so used to being admired that she would stand quite still – staring into the middle distance, the wind ruffling her coat – like a top model posing for a photograph.

'We were talking about Mike,' said Katie, 'and Grace said aromatherapy might help to relax him.'

Sara shook her head. 'He won't consider it. I know he won't. He won't even do the exercises the physio's recommended.'

'What if you bought him a session as a present?'

'There's no point. He won't try anything new. I've spent hours trying to persuade him, but he says it's a waste of time.'

Katie's other main client was Rachel Reeve – the amused maths teacher – but she also occasionally took out Sally Cook's Labradoodle if Sally was down in Cornwall looking after her mother.

'The Cooks live in the thatched cottage overlooking Smith's Field,' said Katie.

Sara nodded, struggling to keep up. Even now, with all Katie's patient explanations, she was easily confused by all the different names.

Katie said it was quite exciting, really, getting to know everyone. According to Mary Miller, the village was a very sociable place to live. Sometimes the gossip seemed a bit relentless, but it was only because it was a small community and people wanted to help out where they could. When Lauren Shipman's husband was laid off and Lauren lost her job at the shoe warehouse, there was a rota of people cooking meals for the children until they got back on their feet, and everyone was always calling in on Sheila Clark, who was ninety-four and pretty much housebound, to check if she needed any shopping done.

Sara looked awkward. 'I would never have known any of this if it hadn't been for you.'

'You were out at work all the time.'

Sara shook her head. 'I should have made more of an effort.'

It felt to Sara as if Katie had woken her from a kind of hopeless inertia, a beige and anodyne life that she'd come to accept because she didn't know that anything else existed. For the first time in months, she looked up and took notice of the world around her. The free newspaper that came through the letter box on Thursdays had always gone straight into the recycling because Sara had dismissed it as nothing but advertising – mobile hairdressers, tree surgeons, minicabs. But now she found herself searching through for local events and snippets of news. She wanted to find out more about her neighbours. She wanted to make up for lost time.

Katie said, 'You could always invite them over.'

Sara looked up, surprised.

'They're dying to see the house. It wouldn't have to be much. You could ask them round for coffee one day.'

There was a small, awkward silence.

Sara said, 'I can't.'

'I could help. I could buy the biscuits and everything.'

Sara shook her head.

Katie said, 'I know you like being private, but—'

'It's not me.' Sara felt the embarrassment tying her up in knots. 'It's Mike.'

'He doesn't like people coming round?'

'No.'

Katie was still confused. 'Ever?'

'Not really. Particularly people he doesn't know.'

Katie thought about this. 'But he's all right with friends?'

Sara didn't want to answer this directly. 'He'd just rather the house was quiet. He doesn't like noise if he's working at home.'

They looked at each other, both acutely aware of the

enormous echoing space around them, the high ceilings, the fact that conversation in the huge glass extension could only be heard by the birds.

Katie said, 'You wouldn't think sound carried much in a house like this.'

'He's very sensitive,' said Sara. 'Very easily distracted.'

Katie's eyes opened wide with alarm. 'What about me? Do I disturb him?'

'No,' said Sara quickly, 'not at all. You make things better. You take Bundle out and stop him barking all the time. Mike loves having you around.'

Katie opened her mouth to speak and shut it again.

'He used to be more sociable,' said Sara, anxious to make Mike sound more reasonable, 'years ago. When I first met him, he loved going to parties. He used to stay up all night. But he's in too much pain these days. He doesn't really feel like seeing anyone.'

They contemplated this with some sadness.

'If you want to find out a bit more,' said Katie, 'about who people are and what they do, you could always go round and see Mary. She knows all the stories. She doesn't get out much, but she picks up every tiny scrap of gossip. Half an hour with her and you'd know everything about everyone.'

Sara was immediately enthusiastic. 'I could take her some flowers.'

'Cake would be better. Or chocolate biscuits. To go with the tea.'

Sara felt a quiver of excitement. Katie was opening up opportunities she'd never even thought of. 'If I make a few visits round the village, people will stop thinking I'm unfriendly. They'll see I'm making an effort.'

'Book yourself in for a facial at the salon,' said Katie, 'and Grace will love you forever.'

They smiled at each other.

'And maybe when Mike goes back to the office,' said Katie, 'when everything's back to normal, maybe we can arrange something then.'

Sara nodded.

'Shall I say that? If anyone asks?'

'Do you think they will?'

'They might,' said Katie, looking uncomfortable.

It was clear that Katie had been under pressure for some time to get Sara to issue an invitation.

'I think it's better not to mention it.' Sara tried to sound neutral. 'It could be months yet before Mike's fit again, and I don't want people to get all excited.'

There was another awkward silence.

'Maybe in the summer,' said Sara, 'when the weather's better.'

It was important to keep things positive. The last thing she wanted was for Katie to report back to the rest of the village that Mike was a bad-tempered bully who refused to let his wife have a few neighbours round for coffee.

A few days later, Sara knocked on the door of Mary Miller's cottage, only a pavement's width from the traffic hurtling along the main road, and was immediately welcomed in.

'Katie said you might call.'

'I'm not disturbing you?' Sara tried not to show how horrified she was by the clutter and stuffiness inside.

'Not at all, dear. It's lovely to meet you after all this time.'

In the hot little kitchen at the back, there was hardly any room to sit down.

'So how's your poor husband?' said Mary. 'I hear he's in terrible pain.'

Sara said he was finding the enforced inactivity very hard. 'He just wants to get back to work full time.'

'Of course he does. What man wouldn't?'

'But he's definitely improving. I can see little changes for the better day by day.'

Mary leaned across the table and patted Sara's hand. 'He's very lucky to have you, dear.'

It turned out that Mary had a soft spot for Mike. She'd once been struggling back from the portacabin with two heavy bags and he'd insisted on taking them from her and walking her all the way to her front door.

Sara was surprised. She'd never heard this story.

Mary said, 'You mustn't worry if he's not quite himself at the moment. I saw so many people with back problems at the surgery and you know it's like Jekyll and Hyde – man to beast in a matter of seconds. They get frightened, you see. They think it's never going to end. And men are never good at talking about their feelings, are they? Just keep their heads down and struggle on.'

Daisy the Labrador, stretched out by the stove, opened her mouth in a huge yawn.

Over a packet of Tunnock's caramel wafers, Mary filled her in on the latest village gossip. Jane Cannon's husband wanted a divorce – it had been on the cards for years, but he'd waited until their youngest had left for university – and Jane was frightened they'd have to split their assets and sell the house, which would break her heart because she loved it with a passion and never wanted to leave. Sally Cook's son-in-law Omar, who was a web designer, had gone in for a routine check-up and come out with testicular cancer, and Sarinda Nunn's husband had high blood pressure and suspected gout. Rachel's younger son Arthur had a girlfriend his mother knew nothing about, whose sister had got pregnant while still at school and swore blind it wasn't the biology teacher even though everyone knew he had form.

Daisy wheezed and coughed, a honey-coloured balloon.

'So much happening,' said Sara, bewildered by this avalanche of information. 'I had no idea.'

'That's the thing,' said Mary. 'It all looks happy on the surface. But you never really know what's going on behind closed doors. There's a rumour that Malcolm Friar's been renting porn again. Either that or someone's hacked his account.'

'I always thought it was quite a peaceful village.'

Mary nodded in a knowing kind of way. 'Sometimes I look at the headlines and I wonder why they never pay us a visit. You could fill a whole paper with what people get up to round here.'

After two cups of tea, Sara said she ought to be getting back in case Mike needed her, but she'd love to pop in again one day if Mary had the time.

'You're always welcome.' Mary smiled. 'And remember what I said. Don't worry if he's a bit crotchety. Once his back's better, your lovely husband will be back to his old self.'

Sara was suddenly anxious. 'Did Katie say something?'

'About what?'

'About Mike?'

Mary said, 'The only thing that Katie's said is that privacy is very important to you, and I know exactly what you mean. No one wants their secrets plastered all over the neighbourhood for everyone to hear.'

When Sara got back to the house, the light was fading. Mike met her in the hall. 'Where were you?'

'Why?'

He glowered at her.

She said, in a bright voice, 'Katie will be here in a minute.'

He turned his back and disappeared into the living room. She found herself standing alone in the great empty space.

Over the next few weeks, her interest piqued by Mary's revelations, Sara began to work out how local gossip worked. The fastest-moving stories were those that incited collective outrage, especially if the perpetrator was rude or unkind. If the guilty party was an outsider – or at least someone that no one in the village knew very well – rumours whipped round like a sharp wind, causing shivers of shocked disbelief.

The whole village stood behind anyone who had been wronged. Judgement was swift, and there were no second chances.

One Thursday afternoon, Katie was taking Dexter, Rachel Reeve's dog, for a walk round Smith's Field when she caught sight of a short middle-aged man with a large bulldog some way off on the corner near the holly bush. He was wearing an olive-green waxed jacket, knee-length wellingtons and a flat cap, and his shoulders were hunched against the cold. Katie was just wondering who he was, and whether she ought to wave, when the bulldog started to run, bowling towards them with such speed that the distance between them disappeared in seconds. Hurtling into view, he took a flying leap at Katie, steadied himself on his hind legs, and began rhythmically thrusting his willy into her thigh.

Katie, trapped in the icy ruts of mud, looked round in desperation. A few feet away, Dexter was barking at top volume, but the bulldog's owner didn't seem to have noticed. He strode ahead, apparently unperturbed, while the fevered humping went on behind him.

Without warning, the bulldog, a large and muscular animal, adjusted his grip, grabbing Katie so hard that his claws dug into her skin. Katie yelled out in shock. In response, Dexter – who had traces of Jack Russell – threw himself at the bulldog's back leg and bit him.

Katie gasped. She had visions of Dexter being eaten alive.

But the bulldog, with a whelp of pain, let go of Katie's thigh, dropped down on to all fours, and retreated several steps. Breathing heavily, his great tusky teeth pushing up the folds of his jowls, he glared from Dexter to Katie and then – to Katie's great relief – shot off after his owner like a cannonball.

As Katie told Sara later, she was touched by everyone's concern. Rachel Reeve said she was a bit worried that Dexter had gone on the attack, but very glad that Katie wasn't hurt. Grace Knight said she thought it was diabolical the way some owners behaved and she hoped Katie wasn't too upset.

The story shot through the village. All Katie's clients were outraged. No one could identify the man in the green waxed jacket, and it was universally decided that he must have been a visitor from outside the area.

The following day, Sara bumped into Sally Cook in the portacabin. By this time, she had learned quite a lot about Katie's dog walking clients and was about to say hello, with a degree of confidence that this was the woman with the Cornish mother and the Labradoodle, when Sally launched into a long and complicated story about how she'd been thinking about what had happened to Katie at the exact same moment that her husband started watching one of those dog training programmes on TV. Apparently, according to the voiceover, experts believed that humping was sometimes a display of dominance, but mostly it was just play. It rarely had anything to do with sex.

Unusually, the shop was quite full. A small knot of people had gathered by the counter and Sarinda Nunn was resolutely ignoring those wanting to pay, her whole focus on the discussion in front of her.

Mary Miller drew herself up to her full height. 'I don't care whether it's got anything to do with sex or not. As far as I'm concerned, it's disgusting and that man should be ashamed of himself.'

There were murmurings of approval.

Sara realised, with a shock of excitement, that she was so much a part of the small circle of indignation that it was somehow taken for granted that she agreed with everything her neighbours were saying.

★

Despite being sure it wouldn't do any good because Mike would never listen, Sara decided to find out more about aromatherapy.

Grace's salon was on the town's cobbled high street, tucked into the historic stretch of half-timbered buildings that had been carefully – and incongruously – preserved in the latest round of regeneration. Behind the wattle and daub façade were upmarket estate agents, small boutiques and expensive coffee shops, with the dark and insalubrious Goat leaning out at a drunken angle. Beyond this tantalising glimpse into the past, the cheaper end of the high street was all plate glass and brightly coloured fascias, tailing off into a small muddle of pound shops and vacant premises. Right at the end, next to the keycutter and locksmith's, was the charity shop where Katie's friend Anna worked, its window full of second-hand cookbooks and black high-heeled shoes.

In the salon, the air was thick with a kind of damp warmth smelling of hot wax and essential oils. Grace herself was a work of art – so buffed and polished that everything about her shone like glass.

'Men are funny about aromatherapy.' She gave Sara a knowing look from under her thick black eyelashes. 'They think it's all about scented candles and bath bombs. You might want to call it sports massage instead.'

'Would it be a good idea for someone with a bad back?'

Grace drew back. 'I'm a trained masseuse.'

'I didn't mean you'd do anything that wasn't safe,' said Sara, realising she had somehow got it wrong and caused offence. 'I meant, would it make him feel better?'

Grace seemed mollified. 'He'd still have a bad back, but

he might feel more relaxed. And that's got to help with the pain, hasn't it?'

But as Sara reported back to Katie later, Mike was unimpressed. He said if he wanted to try out a new treatment, he wouldn't ask a fucking beautician.

It was a mistake to repeat it word for word. Katie's eyes widened with surprise.

Sara said quickly, 'It doesn't mean anything. He only swears to let off steam.'

Katie looked doubtful.

'You won't tell Grace, will you? She's been so kind.'

Katie said that of course she wouldn't pass anything on. The last thing she wanted was for Grace to be hurt. It was just really sad that Mike wouldn't at least give aromatherapy a chance, because everyone said Grace was brilliant at massage. 'You wouldn't think it from looking at her, with the eyelashes and extensions and everything, but she's really strong. It must be all the Pilates.'

When Sara next saw Grace for a manicure – she had begun to call into the salon on a weekly basis – she made up an excuse about Mike not being able to come in because he was completely snowed under with work. Grace read between the lines and said Sara wasn't to worry – a lot of men were a bit scared of massages and it took them a while to come round. Her boyfriend Ryan, who worked at the BMW garage just beyond the bypass, was spending his day off keeping Grace company at the salon, bronzed biceps bulging from the sleeves of his white T-shirt. He said he'd been just the same to be honest until he'd had two hours of shiatsu at a local health club. He'd never realised the tension in his neck and shoulders until it wasn't there.

Afterwards, Sara thought about the way Ryan was so loyal and backed Grace up in everything she said. His eyes followed her round the salon, his face tender with pride as she plumped up the pink cushions on the wicker sofa and straightened the bottles of nail polish on the glass shelves. Seeing the way he looked at her, Sara felt a small flash of loss.

'I wish Mike would listen to me,' she said to Katie later. 'But he's so stubborn.'

Katie nodded. 'Anything's got to be better than being in pain all the time.'

'It's so hard not being able to help.' Sara didn't want to be critical, but it was a relief to tell the truth. 'But he doesn't want me to interfere. He keeps telling me to stay out of it.'

Her only function, it seemed, was to absorb his rage and act as some kind of emotional punch-bag.

But she didn't say this to Katie. It would have been too humiliating.

It had been a busy few weeks. When they finally found the time to catch up, Katie brought Sara up to date with her latest sessions of therapy.

'So how's it going?'

'Really well,' said Katie.

She spoke with such conviction that Sara knew something was wrong.

Katie said that she'd been following Maxine's orders and going out with men from various specialist dating sites. This hadn't been altogether successful. Her increasingly strange encounters had included a tussle on a sofa with a large sweaty supply teacher who thought she was into bondage, and a surreal conversation with an insurance broker who was desperate for her to strap on a dildo. One of her dates had licked her ear and asked if she was into threesomes. Even the silly stuff was creepy, like the time a thin-faced web designer in a tight flowery shirt leaned forward over his triple-cheese pizza and said was she interested in squirty cream because he had a lot of it at home.

Sara listened, trying not to look too appalled.

Katie reached for a biscuit. 'So I asked Maxine if I could go out with people who were a bit more conventional.'

'What did she say?'

'She said, did I mean wine bars with men in shabby suits drinking prosecco and talking about dental work and divorce? And I said, yes. So that's what we're going to do from now on.'

'That doesn't sound very exciting,' said Sara.

Katie looked miserable.

'Are you sure this is working for you?'

Katie bit her lip. 'Maxine says that change is uncomfortable. I don't think I should give up now.'

Sara was doubtful about this but stayed quiet.

Katie said it hadn't all been doom and gloom. A few weeks before, one of her dates hadn't turned up, so she'd been sitting all by herself in the wine bar, trying to look busy by scrolling through the messages on her phone. Al was sitting on the same long wooden bench, but further along, and she realised he must have been stood up, too, because he looked really nervous and worried, chewing his thumbnail and sighing. He was slight and young-looking, with dark skin and brown eyes.

After a while they smiled at each other in a shy kind of way, and Katie said, 'I don't think he's coming, is he?', and he said, 'It looks that way', and they started chatting about general things like forgetting arrangements and the traffic on the bypass. He was a bit vague about what he did as a job, which was something to do with digital media, but he wanted to know all about the dog walking, and it turned out his mother had a Labrador like Daisy, and his favourite breed was a bichon frise.

They ended up sliding along the bench until they were side by side, and when the waitress came back they ordered the vegetarian special and a bottle of wine, and got on so well that they met up the following week.

Once, as they walked along the high street, Al reached out for her hand and Katie's heart sang.

After a few more dates, she invited him back to the house for Sunday lunch, which wasn't a particularly good idea because she had to rush around tidying up and wiping slug marks off the shower door. Also, because he was vegan, she tried to make hummus, but the chickpeas were like bullets and wouldn't mash. So she ended up boiling some pasta and opening a jar of ready-made tomato sauce, which looked as if she hadn't made any effort at all.

Al arrived on time with a bunch of white carnations, and they watched a film on TV, and ate the pasta, and drank two bottles of beer. Then they both fell silent, because it seemed the moment had come. Al leaned forward and put his cheek next to hers. She tried to hug him, but somehow their bodies didn't fit together, as if their bones were in all the wrong places, and she kept being aware of things that didn't matter, like the roughness of his sleeve and the fact that he smelled of something faintly antiseptic, like mouthwash.

He drew back.

She said, 'What's wrong?'

He swallowed. 'I'm sorry.'

He left soon afterwards. Katie sat there in the damp living room, mulling it all over as it got later and later and colder and colder, and decided in the end that he just didn't fancy her.

'Oh, Katie,' said Sara. 'That's so sad.'

'I really liked him. He was so gentle and kind.' Katie hung her head. 'Maybe we should have just stayed friends.'

Sara hesitated. 'You know, sex isn't everything.'

Katie looked up.

Sara said, 'I've got a friend who hasn't had sex with her husband for years. They got out of the habit after their youngest was born, and they haven't done it since. It's just not part of their relationship.'

Katie stared. 'Really?'

'It doesn't bother her any more. She doesn't even think about it.'

'What about her husband?'

Sara said, 'He had affairs, I think, over the years.'

'Why did they stay together?'

'A compromise. For the children's sake.'

Katie shook her head. 'I couldn't live like that. Can you imagine? It must be so lonely.'

Sara looked out of the big glass doors to the shadows of the trees beyond.

The following Saturday, holding a large pack of toilet rolls, Sara made her way down the treacherous steps of the portacabin to find herself once again face to face with Rachel Reeve.

Rachel said, 'So what do you think about the therapist?'

Sara, who wished she'd been carrying something less strongly associated with bodily functions, stared back.

'Maxine. Katie's therapist.'

Sara felt a stab of dismay. 'You know about her?'

'Only because I asked. Apparently, she's not even qualified. She's halfway through an online course. It explains why she's offering cut-price sessions.'

Sara had never asked Katie how much she was paying Maxine. 'Should she be charging at all?'

'Well, exactly. It doesn't seem very professional.'

Sara shifted the mega pack in her arms. 'I'm not sure Katie needs therapy anyway.'

'Her GP suggested it. But there was a nine-month wait for counselling. Services are so stretched. She'd probably be waiting until next year for a course of CBT.'

Sara hesitated.

'Cognitive Behavioural Therapy. Changing patterns of thinking so that your mind works in more positive ways.'

'You sound as if you know quite a lot about it.'

Rachel pulled a face. 'Not really. Only the basics. Mental health is quite an issue in schools these days.'

Sara found herself clutching the toilet rolls more tightly.

'I hear your son wants to study maths.'

'If he gets the grades.'

Rachel fixed her with a direct gaze. 'And will he?'

Flustered, Sara said, 'I hope so. Although he seems to be spending more time planning his summer holiday at the moment.'

'Ah yes. Travelling round Europe.'

Sara was astonished. 'How did you know?'

'It's what they all do. Interrailing and music festivals. Arthur did it last year. I wanted to staple a condom to his forehead.'

Sara recoiled.

'Incidentally, did you know that she was a homeopath?'

'Who?'

'Sarinda who owns the shop.' Rachel nodded towards the portacabin. 'She's a registered homeopath. You know, arsenic for depression. That kind of thing. Of course it's sometimes a bit full on. You go in for a packet of tea bags and she's talking about inherited tendencies. But I thought it might be useful for your husband.'

Sara's voice was cold. 'He wouldn't consider something like that. He's not into anything alternative.'

Rachel smiled. 'Neither am I. I just thought I'd mention it.'

Unsettled by the encounter, Sara wandered home in something of a daze. It was only as the Old Rectory came into view that she wondered how Rachel knew about James wanting to study maths.

It might not have been Katie.

It could have been anyone.

Sara crunched over the frozen grass, deep in thought.

Late one afternoon, Katie opened the front door just as Sara rushed into the hall in a panic of distress. As they stood there staring at each other, Mike's disembodied voice yelled out, 'Why are you so fucking useless?'

Katie looked shocked. Sara worked hard to get her breathing under control, trying not to show how frightened she was.

'How am I supposed to work? How am I supposed to do my job when you're so fucking unreliable?'

The air trembled with emotion.

'His laptop.' Sara's voice was shaking. 'He's shouting at his laptop.'

It wasn't convincing.

There was a thud, and then the musical crash of breaking glass.

Mike shouted, 'Sara! Sara, get in here!'

Katie put her finger to her lips. Then she called out in a clear carrying voice, 'It's me, Mr Parsons. It's Katie. Can I help?'

After a while, sounding infinitely weary, Mike said, 'No, it's nothing. Forget it.'

Katie touched Sara's elbow and the two of them crept across the hall, out of Mike's line of sight. When they reached the kitchen, Sara shut the door and leaned back against it, momentarily shutting her eyes with relief as if they'd only just managed to escape some terrible danger. Before Katie could speak, she said, 'It's a bad day, that's all. A bad day.'

Katie stared back, her expression full of concern.

'I forgot to pass on a message from his PA. It wasn't really important, but it just set him off. He hates inefficiency. He can't bear wasting time.'

Katie said, 'But shouting like that . . .'

Sara took a deep breath. 'It's not him. It's the pain. He keeps trying to manage without the pills.'

'Why? Why would he do that?'

'He doesn't like being dependent on them. It makes him feel weak.'

'But he needs them.'

Sara nodded. 'If he doesn't take them, he's in agony.'

'Can't someone talk to him?'

Sara didn't want to sound defeatist. But she had to be realistic. 'He won't listen to anyone. And especially not to me.'

They stood there, unable to move.

Sara said, 'I don't want you to worry.'

Even to her ears it sounded pathetic.

As time went on, Katie began to admit that Danny had his faults.

She told Sara about a Saturday morning some weeks after he'd come to live with her. They were lying in a mess of crumpled sheets when Danny leaned over to the floor and rummaged around in the pile of clothes by his side. He lay back on the pillows and tossed something on to her stomach. It was an old-fashioned watch with a finely worked bracelet and a small white face.

Katie felt a rush of pleasure. As she explained to Sara, it was the first present he'd ever given her. It wasn't exactly what she would have chosen herself, because it looked like the kind of thing you'd see in a glass cupboard in a junk shop, but she was excited and happy all the same, turning her wrist this way and that to admire it.

Afterwards, she thought her body must have known before her head, because she suddenly felt very tired. When she glanced up, hoping for reassurance, he looked away. So she fiddled with the catch and the two sides of the filigree bracelet fell apart, the watch slithering to the duvet in a small gold heap. Neither of them said anything. She reached for her big baggy T-shirt, got out of bed, and went downstairs to make a cup of tea.

When she got back to the bedroom, the watch had gone.

Sometimes over the next few months, Danny would be in the pub, and slide his hand into his back pocket and pull out a wad of tens and twenties, and she'd wonder if he'd flogged something else he'd nicked from one of the old ladies who invited him in for biscuits and cake and cups of tea. But she didn't say anything, because she didn't want to risk making him angry.

When she'd finished telling this story, Katie looked up, her eyes full of guilt. 'That was wrong, wasn't it?'

Sara chose her words with care. 'You forgive people all sorts of things when you love them. You make excuses for them.'

'But I should have been braver. I should have asked more questions.'

Sara thought about Danny. She thought about his bony fingers, his blue eyes, the long black coat swinging out as he walked. She thought about the dark sweet smell of caramel. 'I don't think it would have made any difference.'

'What do you mean?'

'I think you're right. He would have got angry. And it wouldn't have stopped him. He would have carried on doing it anyway.'

Katie said, in a small voice, 'I don't think he was a bad person.'

'Of course not.' Sara put her hand on Katie's arm, a touch of warmth and reassurance.

Katie looked up. 'Thank you.'

'For what?'

'For helping me sort it out in my head. Maxine says I have to draw a line under it. If I even mention his name, she gets impatient and says I'm dwelling on the past instead of thinking of the future.' Katie took a deep breath. 'I'll never forget him. But it doesn't hurt so much any more. Not now I've been able to talk about it.'

Later, lying next to Mike in a bed so wide that there was never any danger of them rolling into each other, Sara stared into the dark and thought about Danny. She tried to imagine his voice, wondering how that wheedling tone would sound. She thought about the collusion, the way he'd get you to agree to anything because he'd carved out a place that only you fitted into, so exactly tailored to your measurements that it would have been stupid to turn your back and walk away.

She remembered the first time she'd met Mike.

It was a Sunday afternoon. She quite often went to art exhibitions on Sundays when she lived in north London because they were usually free and surrounded you with lots of people without obliging you talk to any of them. Leaning forward to examine a tear in a canvas – it looked intentional, as if the surface had been attacked with a knife – she had felt someone's eyes resting on her face. She turned her back and moved on to the next painting. When she got to the end of the room, she glanced behind her, and a large man with bulky shoulders and a thick neck was gazing at her with an expression of puzzlement. His face had a kind of unfinished look because his hair was a pale reddish gold and his eyelashes were so fair they were almost non-existent. This was quite arresting. You couldn't help searching his features for what was missing. So they stood there, staring at each other across the gallery. When he started striding towards her, she looked away, because she didn't want to appear to be inviting contact.

'Have we met before?'

Not the most original of opening lines, obviously, but it sounded like a genuine question. She shook her head.

'Are you sure?' He smiled, the edges of his eyes becoming a fanfare of lines that turned his ill-defined face into something altogether more interesting.

'Quite sure.' She knew he was older. She could see that. He was thirty, it turned out. She was twenty-two.

'Do you like them?' He nodded his head towards the paintings.

She didn't want to encourage him, so tried to appear non-committal.

'The blue one at the end,' he said. 'The one with the yellow stripe. My friend Charlie did it.'

She looked round the room in a vague kind of way and then gave him one of those tight, would-you-excuse-me type of pursed-lip smiles and moved away.

Of course, that didn't stop him. He wouldn't let one small brush-off stand in his way. Somehow they ended up together in front of a different painting a few minutes later, and this time he told her about Charlie's scholarship to the Courtauld, and how amazing it was because no one else in Charlie's family could even hold a pencil let alone draw, and it wasn't as if Bletchley, where they'd both lived as teenagers, was a

town with a reputation for fine art. By the time they reached
the exit, Mike had formally introduced himself and asked if
he could buy her a cup of coffee. Such was the force of his
personality that she couldn't think of a good enough reason
why not.

London still didn't feel like home. It must have been because
of the cloying attentions of her over-protective mother that
she'd ended up in a city where she knew no one at all, renting
a room in a shared house, eating mainly pasta and washing
out her underwear every night in the bathroom sink. But the
job was promising. She had managed to get a junior position
as a legal assistant, and was working her way up the career
ladder quite nicely. The only drawback was her earnest and
acne-covered boss who would gaze at her with hungry longing,
his skin glowing bright red.

She wasn't happy or unhappy. Her life was neutral. She
watched how other people behaved and copied them. She
fitted in well enough.

Then Mike appeared.

She didn't know why he wanted her so badly. She gave
him very little to go on. Perhaps that was the point.

Sometimes she wondered if it was all a case of mistaken
identity. Early on, Mike had decided that her rather cool
exterior hid an exciting personality and clung to this misunderstanding even when reality was trying to prove something
different. He'd look at her with fondness, his mouth curving
into a smile, and say, 'I know what you're thinking', even
when she didn't have an opinion one way or the other. He
pre-empted her more facile remarks with clever views he was
sure she held. He believed her silence spoke volumes.

Mike was very loud, so disagreement would have been

hard – she would have had to shout with considerable force to make herself heard. But it was also true that she quite enjoyed being given a new personality, because her own bored her to tears. It felt as if someone had slipped a very expensive coat on to her shoulders and she was looking in the mirror, twisting this way and that, admiring her reflection and thinking how much it suited her.

Mike even gave her a sense of humour. She'd say something she genuinely believed, like 'Cyclists should be fined for going through red lights,' and he'd throw back his head and roar with laughter, as if was the funniest thing he'd ever heard. She enjoyed that. It made her feel witty and intelligent.

Of course, she should have known better. Of course, she shouldn't have pretended to be someone she wasn't. But in her defence, she was very young. Mike had to take the blame. He can't have been blind to the fact that young people tend to look up to those who are slightly older. Wealth and experience are bewitching to those who have neither, and even then Mike was raking it in. He loved making money. He was a born entrepreneur.

Mike asked her to marry him on their third date. She pulled a face to show she thought he was mad, and he laughed. He said he'd known the first moment he met her, and that she should congratulate him on his patience so far. It became a kind of joke, or perhaps a kind of bullying. On a visit to Sheffield to see Charlie, who seemed as confused and uncomfortable as she was, he introduced her as 'the future Mrs Parsons'. Driving back, he told her he'd already picked out the house they were going to live in, and boasted he'd bought an antique ring with emeralds and diamonds, ready for when she caved in and agreed.

Was this romantic or manipulative? At what point does persuasion become coercion?

Mike kept telling her that she was in charge and that his whole life was in her hands. But it didn't feel like that. She felt like a small child being pulled along by invisible string.

In the end, as is always the way, a random event changed everything. Four months after they first met, Mike turned up at her place of work in the middle of the afternoon. She was astonished and angry to be called down to reception because a Mr Parsons was waiting to see her. She didn't approve of his overbearing style of courtship interrupting her working day – it felt crass and unprofessional. In the lift on the way down, she almost resolved to teach him a lesson and tell him it was over.

In the polished neutrality of the atrium, Mike was sitting on one of the black faux-leather banquettes, his head bowed. When he looked up, his expression was so bleak she felt a rush of fear. His beloved father had just died in hospital. He didn't know where else to go. She sat down next to him and took his hand, and he turned his head into her shoulder and sobbed.

It was this moment that changed her life forever.

By the end of February, as long as he took his strong prescription painkillers – which Sara couldn't always rely on – Mike was beginning to keep his temper under control. Sara allowed herself to feel optimistic. There was no reason why life shouldn't return to normal. Mike always kept his back very straight, as if he had a broom handle glued to his spine, and there was a new wariness about him as if his confidence had been dented. But he was starting to drive again, lowering himself into the BMW with great care, and went into the office two or three times a week.

Sometimes, when there was no one in the house, Sara lay on her back on the cold stone floor and listened to the silence.

One morning she suggested it was time for her to go back to work.

He looked up from his laptop. 'Not yet.'

'But you're so much better.'

'It's unpredictable.'

Sara nodded, as if this was worth considering. 'As long as you don't push yourself too far, you're fine.'

Mike looked at her as if she were stupid. 'You have no idea, do you?'

Sara opened her mouth to speak but thought better of it.

He said, returning to the screen, 'What's important is the business. Everything I've built up over the years. We have to focus on that or we'll lose it.' He jabbed at a couple of keys. 'It makes more financial sense for you to be on standby.'

'On standby?'

'To help out if I need you.'

She cleared her throat. 'A sort of assistant? Carer, chauffeur, PA?'

He raised his eyes to her face.

She said, 'It doesn't have to be me. Someone else could do that.'

'Help me out of bed, get me dressed, drive me to work?'

'You're past all that now.'

Mike took a deep breath. 'That's my point. We don't know.

I've got a lot of things at a critical stage, and you might have to step in and give me a hand.'

She said, 'I have to tell them something at work. I have to say when I might be able to go back.'

'Tell them you'll ring them in six weeks.'

'They need me.'

He looked tired. 'It's a part-time job helping a bunch of solicitors. Anyone can do it.'

The shock felt like ice.

He said, 'It's not going to be forever. But right now I've got nineteen people depending on me for their jobs and we need to work together.'

'I don't think you're listening to me.'

He exploded, suddenly and with fury. 'For God's sake, Sara! Can't you think of someone else for once?'

It would have been funny if it hadn't been so tragic. Words crowded into her head, jostling for position. 'Have you calculated the impact of my projected loss of earnings?'

'What?'

'We'll be less well off without my salary.'

He gave her his usual flat stare. 'Hardly.'

She shut herself in the downstairs toilet and cried for an hour.

Later, she rang Jane, the office manager, and apologised for what had become a prolonged period of absence. Jane said she wasn't to worry, and these things happened. In fact, they'd recently taken on a new member of staff who could probably take over Sara's role without too much trouble, so she shouldn't feel under any pressure. If at any point in the future she felt she wanted to come back, they'd probably be able to find something for her at roughly the same sort of

level, but there was no hurry, and Sara should take all the
time she needed.

When the call was over, Sara sat in the kitchen looking out
at the grey garden. Her hands shook. There was a ringing in
her ears, and she felt as if she was choking, as if she couldn't
breathe.

When they went to bed that night, Sara said, 'I've told the
office I'm not coming back.'

Mike turned, his back rigid, to switch off the bedside lamp.
'Good.'

James had always been able to goad his father into violent
outbursts of temper. But now, after weeks of practice, he had
perfected his technique. Sara watched, powerless to intervene.
They were like two rutting stags locking antlers.

As she explained to Katie one afternoon, it was just an
unfortunate set of circumstances. In the old days, before the
problems with his back, Mike had been away so often that
no one in the family had seen him very much. She herself
had become so used to his absence that if they came face to
face on the stairs unexpectedly, she found herself nodding
to him politely, as if they were fellow residents in a block of
flats.

Mike had hardly ever been home in time for supper.
Sara usually left his plate by the microwave covered in
clingfilm.

But now everything had changed. Because of Mike's

enforced move to working from home, father and son had been thrown into each other's company, and there was a simmering tension just under the surface the whole time.

Sara said, 'I keep asking James to be a bit kinder, but he can't resist.'

Mealtimes were full of potential clashes. Sometimes the aggression in the air was so thick that she couldn't swallow. She found herself leaving most of the food on her plate.

'It'll be easier once James has gone to uni,' said Katie.

Sara tried to smile. 'He can't wait to leave. He'd go tomorrow if he could.'

Hostilities between James and Mike soon reached a peak.

A week or so after the discussion about Sara going back to work, Mike's treasured personal possessions began to go missing. The first report he filed with the police was about his antique Rolex watch, which he used to wear all the time – so much so that his wrist looked strange and bare without it. He'd maintained it meticulously over the years, replacing worn parts and getting it cleaned frequently, so it was in perfect working order. There was high drama when he couldn't find it. The whole house was ransacked, wardrobes emptied, sofa cushions hurled across the room. Sara only stopped him turning every single drawer in the kitchen upside-down by pointing out that if the watch was, indeed, hidden among old corkscrews and biodegradable rubbish bags, pitching it on to the hard stone floor would probably jam its tiny cogs and crack its handsome face forever.

James said, 'You're going senile.'

Mike looked up, his eyes full of thunder.

Sara said, 'I don't think that's fair, James. Your father's always very careful with his watch.'

James shrugged. 'Not quite careful enough.'

Mike made a sudden movement towards his son that dissipated into a kind of ineffectual shove against the table.

Sara said, 'He only ever takes it off at night.'

Mike glared at her. 'You must have put it somewhere.'

She stared back, astonished.

James said, 'That's got to be the solution. It's Mum's fault.'

Sara said, 'James—'

Mike shouted, 'It was by the side of the bed!'

Sara struggled to stay calm and rational. 'Would it help if we went back over your movements yesterday and see if anything jogs your memory?'

Mike knocked over a chair and left the room.

Shortly after this, Mike lost his laptop – the light, slim, incredibly expensive laptop he carried with him everywhere. Again, Sara tried to help him run through in his mind when he'd last had it, whether he'd taken it to his most recent meeting, if there was any possibility he could have left it in the BMW or in the office. Mike yelled at her to stop treating him like an idiot.

James said, 'He's losing it. Alzheimer's. Dementia.'

'Don't, James. It doesn't help.'

He raised his eyes to her face. 'What doesn't help is the way he's trying to blame it on you.'

'But you can see it from his point of view. The laptop's his life. It's got everything on it.'

James patiently explained that it wasn't a long-term problem. Everything on the laptop had been backed up two or three times over in different locations and protected by so many anti-hacking and anti-theft encryption programs that there could be no breach of security. 'It's just an inconvenience.'

Mike was certain the laptop had been stolen. Again, he made a formal notification to the police.

Not long afterwards, Mike lost the keys to the BMW. The air went blue. Edward retreated to his room and didn't come out for hours. When Sara suggested they should sit down and retrace his steps, Mike smashed the large water jug she'd bought in France on their first holiday after James was born, shattering the glass across the flagstones.

She cleared up with enormous care, anxious that the dog she disliked so much would end up with a needle-like splinter in his paw.

But for days afterwards, cooking a meal or clearing the table, Sara would catch sight of something glinting on the floor. When she went over and knelt down, there it would be, hidden in plain sight – another sharp little shard.

A few days later, as rain threw itself against the great glass doors of the extension and the sky turned from a bluish mauve to gunmetal grey, Sara said, 'Grace is taking a lot of trouble with her appearance these days.'

'Is she?' Katie put down her cup of tea.

'You know – spray tan, hair extensions.'

'But she always does, doesn't she?'

Sara nodded, as if Katie was absolutely right.

'She's a walking advert, if you think about it,' said Katie. 'People look at her, and she's so beautiful they start thinking about having a manicure or a facial. So she has to look perfect all the time.'

'Yes,' said Sara. 'I expect that's what it is.'

Katie was puzzled. 'Do you think there's something else?'

With some reluctance, Sara said she'd been wondering if it was anything to do with Ryan.

'Ryan?'

Sara shook her head and said it was nothing.

Katie persisted.

Sara said it had been a split second, that's all, and who knows what was really going on, but she'd been driving down the high street past Sainsbury's Local and the Goat, and had stopped at the traffic lights, and glanced over to a white van unloading boxes outside the delicatessen, and she thought she saw Ryan, Grace's boyfriend, down at the end of the alleyway by the bins, his whole body wrapped round someone who definitely wasn't Grace.

Katie's mouth dropped open. She said that just wasn't possible – not Ryan, he adored Grace, worshipped the ground she walked on. Sara immediately agreed, and said she must have got it wrong, although Ryan's honed physique was pretty unmistakeable even from a distance. Katie asked what they'd been doing, and Sara made the kind of face that said, use your imagination. After that, they sat in miserable silence. Katie asked Sara what they should do, and Sara said she thought they shouldn't do anything, and Katie nodded and said Sara was right, and with a bit of luck it would all blow over, and Grace would be none the wiser.

Not long after this conversation, Sara bumped into Mary Miller by the post box and asked after Daisy's arthritis. Mary was touched and invited her in for tea so that she could see for herself. The kitchen at the back of her small cottage smelled of hot pie. Daisy was lolling by the stove like a stranded seal.

Sara was struck all over again by intense claustrophobia. It seemed impossible that anyone could live in such a confined space.

Mary squeezed past, holding a tray perilously laden with crockery and biscuits. 'And how's Edward doing?'

'Let me take that. You sit down.'

'Getting on well at school?'

But Sara was too focused on preventing a crash of china to reply.

Once they were settled at the tiny round table, Mary said she often saw James waiting at the bus stop in the morning and thought he was turning into a very fine young man. 'Any girl would be lucky to have him.'

'I think he's too busy with his exams at the moment,' said Sara.

'I wondered about Katie.' Mary settled herself more comfortably on the wooden chair. 'Pretty little thing.'

'She is, isn't she?' Sara smiled. 'But they're just friends, I think.'

Mary filled her in on Sally Cook's volunteering with the homeless, Sheila Clark's great-nephew's new wife, who came from Bulgaria and was either a psychiatrist or a paediatrician, and how Lauren Shipman's husband had finally got a job at the food-to-go factory, working mainly with wraps and sushi.

Mary glanced behind her as if worried about unseen eavesdroppers, although the only other pair of ears belonged to the dog on the tapestry cushion. 'And of course, you've heard about Ryan?'

Sara shook her head.

Mary said it was very sad, and Grace was devastated, but Ryan had been caught out doing what he shouldn't.

'What happened?'

Mary said that he'd been seen in broad daylight having it off with a strange young woman, Sara's original story now embellished to include extra details about her height and the colour of her hair.

'Who told you?'

Mary shook her head, looking solemn. 'My lips are sealed.'

When Grace confronted him, Ryan had insisted he was innocent, that he'd never even looked at another woman, and Grace was the only one for him. But Grace was having none of it. She had suspected for a long time that Ryan was having affairs on the side. She kicked him out that same night, throwing his sports bag, Lycra shorts and protein shakes into the road outside their house.

Later that day, Sara told Katie what Mary had said, and Katie dropped her eyes and said in a small voice that things like that always got out in the end.

Mary had planted an uncomfortable thought in her mind. Was there a flicker of interest between James and Katie? It was irrational, of course, but Sara didn't like the idea of two such special people in her life being paired up by village gossip. She felt it was somehow disrespectful. No one should be making up stories about James.

There was also something unpleasant about the idea of James being dragged into Katie's personal therapy. As soon as Sara started remembering Katie's descriptions of her recent sexual encounters, she started feeling light-headed and had to sit down. Had Mary been dropping hints? James kept everything so secret. He never talked about his friends or brought them home. Was there something going on?

Sara remembered Mike's horrible suggestion that James might be sneaking off to see Katie late at night. At the time she'd dismissed it as yet another example of Mike's prurient sense of humour, but now she wondered if she were somehow missing the obvious. James kept himself so distant and aloof that it was hard to know what he was feeling about anything. Even the goading of his father seemed to be some kind of game, testing Mike's temper to the point of explosion.

Of course, she respected her son's privacy. She didn't want to pry. But she had to protect him. The last thing you want is to be tied down too early. If you make a mistake when you're young, you can end up saddled with the wrong person for life.

One evening, she asked Katie to stay to supper, claiming she'd cooked far too much and it would never get eaten otherwise. Katie was initially apprehensive but agreed once she found out that Mike wouldn't be there – she was still very nervous in his company and flinched whenever he swore. To begin with Edward was terrified to look up and find Katie sitting opposite him at the long wooden table. But Katie, with great tact, didn't force any kind of interaction. She seemed to understand that Edward just needed to be left alone.

Sara found herself remembering Hilda, their Faroese au pair.

During the meal, Sara watched James closely. Katie prattled away as usual, talking about her friends Anna and Baz, and Friday evening at the Goat, and the modules she'd chosen for the summer term, and James looked at her with the kind of cool indifference that would have made most people dry up and grind to a halt.

By the time Katie left – walking the long way round by the road even though there was only a fence between them – Sara was quite certain that Mary had got carried away, and had seen romantic possibilities where none existed.

It was a huge relief.

The next time Katie stayed to supper, James said very little and went upstairs to his room the minute the meal was over. He seemed to find Katie boring. Sara felt ashamed that she'd ever listened to Mary's insinuations.

Later, James said, 'Why do you like her so much?'

'Who?'

'Your dog walker.'

She smiled – all that worry, and James couldn't even work out why she and Katie were friends. 'I just do.'

He looked at her as if he didn't believe her.

She said, 'What made you ask?'

'You never like anyone. What's different with her?'

It was such a cruel observation. Sara felt suddenly childlike, as if she wanted to cry. For a moment, she was desperate to explain how much it took for her to trust people, to feel happy in their company. She wanted to say that there was nothing wrong with being discriminating, especially when it came to female friendships.

But later she was glad she'd said nothing. James hadn't meant to wound her. It was just a misunderstanding.

★

In March, as the buds on the honeysuckle and climbing roses burst into life, there were ominous signs that Mike's recovery was stalling. The lines on his face deepened as if someone had scored his skin with a Stanley knife.

Sara said, 'Are you remembering to take your pills?'

He shouted at her to stay out of it and leave him alone. The fury in his voice made her heart plummet with fear.

Shortly afterwards, he took himself off to see a private specialist, and there was talk of steroid injections and surgery.

'So what will you do?'

'I don't know.'

He seemed smaller somehow, diminished by pain. She stared at him, wondering at the disappearance of her bombastic, domineering husband.

As the days passed and Mike withdrew into silent intro-spection, it felt as if his grip on them all had loosened. The house was strangely quiet. He didn't shout at Sara for her lapses of memory or throw recalcitrant objects at the walls. He stopped yelling at Bundle. Even mealtimes were calm, with Mike ignoring – or perhaps not even hearing – James's attempts to nudge him into explosions of temper. Looking at him sitting there, hunched over like an old man, Sara wondered if Mike was finally considering some kind of surgical proce-dure. He'd always dismissed it before – every operation carries risks, and he'd been told that there were no guarantees and that radical interventions sometimes made the pain even worse. If he was seriously thinking of going into hospital, he must be in agony.

She wanted to ask if she could help him decide, but always managed to stop herself in time. He would only tell her not to interfere.

With his father so preoccupied, James didn't bother asking for permission to use the car. If Sara didn't need it, he drove off on Friday and Saturday nights, often coming back so late that the whole house was asleep by the time he came in. Sara rejoiced in his independence but wished he told her more about where he was going and what he was doing. It felt sometimes as if James had found a magic key and could let himself out while she was still imprisoned until further notice.

Liberated from his father's moods, Edward seemed braver and more resilient. Some of his artistic projects – miniature constructions made from thin cardboard, each piece meticulously cut and folded – left his bedroom and took up residence around the house. One of them grew bit by bit over several days at the end of the long wooden table in the kitchen, so neat and detailed that it looked like an architect's model of some kind of ancient catacomb.

She said, 'Is it a house?'

Edward shook his head.

'A palace?'

Edward frowned.

She didn't understand but admired his creativity.

Sadly, the brief respite from Mike's temper was short-lived. One night, Bundle, excited by something he couldn't quite see, nosed Edward's tiny masterpiece off the table. By the time Edward came down in the morning – the first to arrive in the great glass extension – the intricate structure had been flattened and squashed, chewed into a mess of damp pulp.

Edward's agonised wailing sent Bundle to the opposite corner of the room where he crouched in terror, whining and scrabbling at the floor.

Mike, who had got up early and was working on his laptop in the living room, limped through to the kitchen, disturbed by all the commotion. He was scathing. 'Of course the dog's going to get it if you leave it out like that.'

Sara was near to tears herself. 'I didn't think.'

'Obviously,' said Mike.

She couldn't stop herself. 'You could have moved it! You knew as well as I did how precious it was!'

Mike looked at her with contempt. 'That's right. Blame everyone but yourself.'

'Why is it always my fault?'

He shouted, 'Because the dog is your responsibility!'

'Why? Why is he my responsibility?'

Edward had his arms over his head, trying to block out the noise.

Mike's fury ripped through the air, a jagged dislocation of sound. 'Once, just once, can you keep the fucking noise down so that I can do some work?'

When Sara looked up, Katie was standing in the doorway, her face pinched with shock. The row had been so loud that no one had noticed she'd let herself in.

James appeared beside her, tall and white, naked except for a pair of shorts. His dark hair was sticking up at angles. 'What's going on?'

'I'm going upstairs.' Mike pushed past him, knocking him sideways against Katie.

On the far side of the kitchen, making little keening sounds, Edward was squatting on his heels in a tight protective huddle.

'Mum?' James was still dazed with sleep. 'What's happened?'

Katie lifted the lead from the hook on the wall and made encouraging patting sounds on the pocket of her coat to get

Bundle's attention. The dog struggled to his feet, his rear end buckled under in a kind of squat as if someone had kicked him, and crept after her to the front door.

Later, Sara thanked her for taking Bundle out so quickly.

Katie's eyes were sympathetic. 'I thought Edward needed some space.'

'He did. He can't really cope with arguments.'

'Is he all right now?'

Sara took a deep breath. 'I think so. I got him off to school in the end.'

'Sara,' Katie spoke in a rush, 'are you OK?'

'I'm fine.'

'Are you sure?'

Sara nodded with such finality that Katie couldn't ask any more questions.

Over the next few days, in ways she didn't quite understand, Sara felt as if a grey curtain had fallen over her life. The tension in the house was still there, but she could no longer work up the energy to feel that it mattered. Something inside her had finally been used up and couldn't be replaced. This led to a strange detachment that wasn't altogether welcome, as it wiped out the brisk efficiency of her usual routine. Sometimes she would find herself standing halfway up the stairs, or in the blue-and-white guest room overlooking the garden, wondering where she was going and what she was doing. Lists were half-written. Appointments were forgotten. Her brain felt disconnected, unmoored, floating free in her skull. It was as if all the tiny electrical sparks had stopped firing across its synapses.

When Mike yelled at her because she'd forgotten to pick up a prescription from the chemist, or collect his dry cleaning, or buy him more whisky, she stared at him blankly, wondering at the redness of his face.

He said, 'Are you ill?'

'Tired.'

He glared at her. 'Go to bed.'

But she didn't want to lie down and stare at the walls.

To Katie, Sara pretended that it was an old problem she'd had before, hinting at low iron levels and anaemia, and Katie insisted she sat down and had a cup of tea while she herself took over chopping up onions and garlic and peeling potatoes as the light faded from the sky. She began to stay for supper more and more often, becoming such a normal part of the evening routine that it seemed strange when she went back to the hovel instead. Edward was no longer worried by her presence. Overall, he was probably much more disturbed by the dog.

Late one evening, when Mike and the boys had disappeared to distant parts of the house, and they were clearing the table in companionable silence, Katie said, 'He never stops, does he?'

'Who?'

'Mike. He's always up there, working away.'

Sara nodded. 'It's his life.'

'You'd think he'd want to take a break and do something relaxing.'

She couldn't hold it back any more. 'Maybe he is.'

Katie looked confused.

Sara's voice was edged with misery. 'All I know is that he doesn't want me to see what he's doing. If I knock on the door, he yells at me to go away.'

Katie opened her mouth to speak but seemed uncertain what to say.

Sara said, 'It's always been like this. Ever since the boys were small. It's his escape. It's more real to him than we are.'

'Work?'

Sara couldn't quite bear to put it into words.

The two of them stared at each other, communicating difficult possibilities.

Katie said, 'A lot of people are addicted to gaming.'

Sara's eyes filled with tears.

'Sit down.' Katie put a hand on her arm. 'I can finish clearing up.'

'It just makes me feel so useless. So tired. That he'd rather do that than . . .' Sara couldn't finish. She stared down at the table, defeated.

There was a small silence.

'Does it run in the family?'

Sara looked up, confused. 'What?'

'The tiredness thing.' Katie picked up Mike's empty wine glass.

'I don't think so.'

Katie said, 'Do you think you should go and see your GP?'

'No.' Sara pulled a face.

'Just for a check-up. To make sure you're all right.'

But she'd spent weeks ferrying Mike to clinics and hospitals. She'd had enough of doctors.

That night, because of Katie's random comment, Sara found herself thinking about her family for the first time in months. It made her uncomfortable. She remembered her mother's hunched shoulders, her shrinking timidity, her belief that her main function in life was to keep her only daughter safely bubble-wrapped from all possible dangers. Lying there in the dark, Sara tried to shut off the memories and think of something more soothing, but she no longer seemed to have the ability to stop things happening. She floated along like a dead leaf on water, a dried husk carried by the current.

Her father had walked out when she was very small. She could hardly remember him. Her mother said, 'He couldn't face up to his responsibilities,' which made Sara feel as if she'd been something unpleasant, like a debt or a duty.

The final separation had been brutal. By that stage, her mother hardly left the house, a shadow of a woman, listless and defeated. She had tried very hard to stop Sara leaving home, but Sara had ignored her. The minute she finished school, she went to London and spent an eye-opening summer working as a chambermaid in a dirty four-storey hotel in Bloomsbury, wiping shower tiles, polishing mirrors, and wondering at the various manifestations of bodily fluids around and inside sheets, sanitary towels and long, stringy condoms.

At the wedding, her mother had been overwhelmed, twisting a white handkerchief round and round in her hands.

Mike had said, 'She's very emotional, isn't she?'

Sara had allowed herself a tight little smile.

The pictures kept coming. She remembered the narrow suburban street of terraced houses where she'd grown up, the small concrete gardens at the front just big enough for the plastic bins. Two doors down was a girl about her age, with straight red hair and freckles. They used to soak pink rose petals in water and pretend it was perfume. What was her name? Lisa. They played together all the time. Lisa stood in the sunlight, raising her arm to shield her eyes. 'I knew I'd like you because you've got a nice face.'

You treasure compliments. You store them up and keep them safe.

Sara lay still, listening to the grumble of Mike's breathing.

She thought about Katie. She remembered the time she'd said, 'You're so wise, Sara,' and hearing it had made her dizzy with pleasure, as if she'd been spun round in a giant teacup or drunk a shot of neat gin. Close female friendships are so important. Of course, Katie hadn't quite got it right. She was too young to understand. It wasn't about wisdom at all. It was knowing how to listen. This was something Sara had worked out years before. Keep eye contact, even if your thoughts are racing ahead. Keep eye contact, but say nothing.

She hadn't always remembered to follow her own rules. In the wills and probate department, faced with those who were lazy or whose work was slipshod, she had sometimes said what she really thought. She had realised her mistake immediately, from the shocked look on their faces, even though everyone knows it's hard to maintain civil communication when people let you down. Your temper can get the better of you. You start shouting, and then the words take over and flood out of their own accord, becoming evil and hard and mean.

Mike knew this.

Sara stared into the darkness, the bulk of her husband in the bed beside her.

One Sunday morning at the beginning of April, Mike looked up from his laptop and said he wanted a party for his fiftieth birthday at the end of June.

Sara stared with astonishment.

'Don't start,' said Mike. 'There's no need to go on and on and try to make me change my mind. It's not worth arguing about.'

'You're not well enough.'

'I said, don't start.'

She persisted. 'What about James's exams?'

'What about them?'

'He needs peace and quiet to study.'

'I checked. They'll be over by then.'

'But what if—'

'Sara, for God's sake. It's just a party. A bit of a celebration.'

It wasn't fair. He was asking too much. 'I thought you didn't want to celebrate. You said you hated getting old. You didn't want to be fifty.'

There was a small silence. The air quivered.

Mike's voice was cold. 'You never want me to enjoy myself, do you? Anything that gives me pleasure, you kill it stone dead.'

This didn't deserve a response.

He said, 'It's a way of thanking everyone.'

'For what?'

'For all their support over the past few months.'

Sara frowned. 'So it's a work party.'

Mike looked at her with irritation. 'A birthday party.'

'How many people?'

'Does it matter?'

Sara caught her breath. 'Of course it matters.'

'Fifty, maybe. A hundred. I don't know. I'll make a list.'

Inside, in her head, a little voice was screaming.

He said, 'It's three months away. All you've got to do is order some wine.'

She looked him directly in the eye. 'Please tell me you're joking.'

He wouldn't back down. 'Nothing formal. Just a nice summer party. Friends, family, people from work, eating strawberries and drinking champagne. They can all admire the garden.'

'Family?'

'You. The boys.'

The relief was so severe, she couldn't speak.

There was an unpleasant glint in his eyes. 'Did you think I was going to ask Ursula?'

She said, trying to sound offhand, 'I have no idea.'

Mike laughed.

The next day, Sara spilled out the whole story – softening it by saying that Mike didn't really understand how much work was involved, even for something so apparently informal.

Katie was surprised. 'I thought he didn't like having people over.'

Sara said he was making an exception because it was all about public relations and corporate entertainment.

Katie said, 'Not just friends, then?'

This was all getting a bit complicated, so Sara said that it didn't really matter who was coming to the party – she was just dreading the whole thing. Mike said he wanted it to be simple and low-key, but she knew he didn't really mean it. He was expecting a grand occasion, something showy and spectacular, which meant hours of planning and preparation, and she was just so exhausted these days. She could hardly get round the supermarket without feeling drained and befuddled.

Katie leaned forwards. 'You mustn't worry. I'll help.'

'Don't you have exams?'

'Coursework. And I finish in May.'

Sara said, in a rush, 'Only if you let me pay you.'

'But I didn't—'

'By the hour. A proper rate. I insist.'

Katie, pink with a mixture of embarrassment and gratitude, eventually agreed.

When Sara told Mike, he was furious. 'You're making a fuss. It's a few drinks, that's all, not a bloody wedding reception.'

Sara said she'd been thinking about what kind of food to serve at the party, and was wondering whether to stick with a few of his top favourites, like lamb souvlaki followed by chocolate brownies and home-made ice cream.

He shot her a weary look, as if he knew he'd been outmanoeuvred.

A few days later, he emailed her a long list of names. As Sara explained to Katie one afternoon as they sat at the long wooden table having a cup of tea, it was a real mixture of work colleagues, business associates, and people he'd known since childhood. Mike had always been good at keeping hold of contacts who might be useful. He was busy networking before anyone had even heard of it.

She said, sounding flat, 'He wants to be the centre of attention the whole time.'

Katie nodded. 'I can see that. He's that kind of person.'

Sara took a deep breath. 'But he's just so – I don't know, uncritical. He needs an audience he can perform to, but it doesn't matter who it is. Anyone will do.'

Katie looked confused.

Sara said, 'I choose my friends with care. I have to be sure I can trust them, and that they won't let me down. Otherwise, what's the point? You're just going to end up disappointed.'

Katie nodded, in complete agreement. 'So will they be coming?'

'Who?'

'Your friends?'

Sara took a moment to respond. 'It's Mike's party. Not mine.'

'But he wouldn't mind, would he? If you invited a few people?' Katie smiled. 'I'd love to meet your friends. All this time I've known you, and I've never met a single one.'

Sara glanced up at the clock and said she hadn't realised how late it was, and Katie – who was sensitive to small changes in atmosphere – took this as her cue to leave.

Easter came and went. James hardly left his room, conscientiously working his way through his revision timetable.

Mike broke his iPhone by throwing it across the kitchen, narrowly missing the great glass doors.

Katie's unorthodox therapy continued.

'Maxine said you don't get anywhere without ambition, and successful people never settle for second best.'

Sara nodded.

Katie's expression was quite fierce. 'She said it's natural to feel angry that some people are born into lives of wealth and privilege while other people scrabble around in the dirt begging for scraps. It's no good pretending that money isn't important. To get what you need, you have to barge your way to the front of the queue, even if it means trampling over everyone else to get there first. The important thing is being clear and focused about what you want, because you're worth it, and you deserve it, and you can't let other people take it from under your nose.'

'And what did you say to that?'

Katie's shoulders sagged. 'I said I didn't really like elbowing other people out of the way, and she said that was because I didn't have any goals. She said that if I really knew what I wanted, I wouldn't think twice, because success is all about being ruthless.'

'Single-minded,' said Sara.

Katie looked woebegone. 'She said there are winners and losers, and no one wants to be a loser.'

'I suppose she's right in a way.'

Katie screwed up her face.

Sara said, 'You're not sure?'

'I said it all sounded a bit competitive. She didn't like that very much. She gave me one of her angry looks and said I wasn't trying hard enough.'

Sara thought this sounded like a totally toxic relationship. But she didn't want to hurt Katie's feelings by saying so. 'If you're not getting on with Maxine, you could always try a different therapist.'

Katie opened her eyes wide. 'I couldn't do that. She'd be furious. She demands total commitment from all her clients.'

Later, Sara thought that she should have tried harder to make Katie see sense. But she wasn't thinking as clearly as usual. Most days, she felt she was operating in a kind of fog. Even simple decisions were difficult. Sometimes she tried to think rationally, to work out why she no longer felt in control. But she seemed to have lost her powers of analysis. She felt completely useless, like an empty takeaway carton in a gutter, or a piece of tissue paper on the floor.

Because of this, the prospect of Mike's fiftieth birthday party at the end of June – crowds of people invading her house and garden – made her feel dizzy and afraid. All she'd done so far was send out the invitations. The rest of it – the cleaning, the catering, the organisation – loomed in the distance, becoming ever more impossible to arrange.

She kept this hidden from Katie. She was ashamed of her incapacity. Fortunately, Katie was less aware of undercurrents than usual – she had a series of essay deadlines and kept rushing home to the hovel to work.

More importantly, Sara made sure that none of her anxieties were visible to James. Stress had to be kept to a minimum while he was concentrating on his exams. When study leave started in the middle of May, he would no longer be going into school and it was vital that the house stayed calm and quiet.

To her intense relief, Mike – despite his continuing back pain – was beginning to ease himself back into his usual routine. He seemed to have decided to manage his condition through a combination of painkillers, alcohol and willpower. Work absorbed him, and she could tell from overheard phone calls that he was pushing hard for new contracts. This sudden surge of activity meant that she didn't always know where he was going to be, which led to unpleasant surprises, like finding him in the living room or the kitchen when she thought he was at the office, or hearing his car sweeping into the drive when she'd assumed she was going to have the house to herself. But he was generally around much less, and hardly ever at home in time for the evening meal, which meant that she and the boys could eat in peace.

James, focused on revision, was monosyllabic. Sometimes,

sitting opposite him at the table, Sara felt close to tears. It felt as if he'd already left, as if his head was way beyond his mother and his younger brother. She wanted his success with all her heart. At the same time, brilliant results meant she would lose him to a new and independent life.

One morning, car keys in hand, Sara opened the front door to find herself facing the postman. He was, as usual, dressed in khaki shorts and brown hiking boots, his bucket hat crammed on to his head.

'Shall I take them?' she said, nodding towards the letters in his hand.

He looked down with surprise, as if he hadn't expected to find himself clutching a pile of envelopes.

There was an awkward silence.

'What did you do, then?'

Sara stared. 'What?'

'I wondered if you'd had him put down.'

Sara struggled to understand.

'The dog.' The postman shifted the heavy bag on his shoulder. 'Only I can't hear a thing these days. Nothing but birdsong.'

'Oh,' said Sara, realisation dawning. 'No, he's fine. He's out at the moment. In Smith's Field, probably. Or up Ogden Hill. We've got a dog walker.'

'A dog walker?'

'Yes.'

'Ah,' said the postman. 'That would explain it.'

They stood in the May sunshine.

Sara held out her hand. 'Shall I take the letters?'

'I used to feel really sorry for him, barking away. You could hear him all round the cul-de-sac.'

Sara willed him to leave but couldn't think how to make it happen.

'I thought he might have mental health problems. You know, sudden rages. Unpredictable. Aggressive.'

Sara said, 'I really ought to be going.'

'I'm glad you didn't.'

'Didn't what?'

'Have him put down.'

The grey fog thick in her brain, Sara couldn't think what to say.

'I mean, you wouldn't want to do it, would you? But you can see why it happens, because they're dangerous when they're out of control. You read about it all the time. Turn on their own family sometimes.' The postman looked down at the bundle of letters, secured by an elastic band, and then – as if struck by a novel idea – held it out to her.

Watching him crunch away across the gravel towards the tall wrought-iron gates, Sara slowly exhaled.

For a moment, she felt light-headed, as if she might fall.

At the beginning of June, Mike announced that he was going to a weekend conference in Germany.

Sara decided against asking questions.

He glared at her. 'Nothing to say? No little digs? No barbed remarks?'

'I hope you have a lovely time.'

He looked away, disgusted.

It was bliss. In his absence, they all relaxed. On Saturday, James took a couple of hours off revising for his final exams, and the three of them watched a film on TV. Edward even took off his earphones and hung around in the kitchen while Sara cooked spaghetti.

Bundle, as if sensing a change in atmosphere, seemed much less agitated.

Mike was due back on Monday evening. That afternoon, when Katie was hanging up Bundle's lead on the hook in the kitchen, Sara said, 'It feels like a holiday.'

'Because he's not here?'

Sara looked guilty. 'I shouldn't have said that.'

Katie shook her head. 'You deserve a break. I don't know how you've managed to keep going. Everything would fall apart without you.'

Sara said, with sudden earnestness, 'I wish you'd known us before all this happened. He's a good man, you know. Very driven. Very ambitious. But only because he wants the best for his family. He loves his sons. He'd do anything for them.'

Katie's eyes were full of sympathy.

'I just wish the pain would go away.' Sara knew she sounded desperate. 'He won't even talk about it any more. He won't discuss treatments, or what the consultant says, or whether he's still thinking about surgery.'

'I'm so sorry.'

'He doesn't want me to see what's going on. But I know how stressed he is. It can't be right, can it? Swallowing hand-fuls of pills. Getting drunk every night.' Sara dropped her voice to a whisper. 'I'm really worried, Katie. I don't think he can carry on like this.'

Katie had left by the time Mike came home. The taxi from

93

the airport crunched over the gravel soon after Edward came back from school. James was upstairs studying. When Sara came into the hall, drawn by the noise of Mike's arrival, she found Edward rooted to the spot, transfixed by his father's sudden reappearance.

Mike looked as if it was only force of will that was keeping him upright. His skin was grey. He seemed to have new lines cut into his face. As he turned to take off his coat, he stepped backwards and stumbled over a pair of shoes that had been left near the front door. He cried out, a kind of guttural roar that flattened the air like a sledgehammer.

Edward flinched.

Mike shouted, 'What the fuck are these doing here?'

Sara rushed over to pick them up.

'How stupid can you get? What are you trying to do – kill me in my own home?'

Crouched on the floor, Sara looked up. 'Mike—'

His eyes were like bullets. 'Don't start.'

Edward, wide-eyed with fear, was swaying like a sapling in a high wind.

'Please, Mike.' Sara was finding it hard to breathe. 'Please leave it now. Come and have a cup of tea. Edward didn't mean any harm. It was just a mistake.'

Mike looked at her with fury. 'I wasn't blaming Edward.'

In the middle of the tirade that followed, as his swearing bounced off the white walls and the air was blasted with abuse, Sara froze. Out of the corner of her eye, she saw James at the top of the stairs, his hand on the black iron balustrade. She took a step forward, trying to stop him. But it was too late. There was a kind of rushing in her ears, a blurring of sound and pressure.

'That's enough!'

His voice echoed through the space.

Mike, mid-bellow, looked up.

The silence fell like a sheet of ice.

All three of them were now staring up at James. His fists were clenched. Sara felt sick. In one blinding moment, she knew for certain that there was going to be physical violence – that everything over the past few months had been leading up to this moment, that it was inevitable that her son and her husband were going to lay into each other, to fight for dominance, to batter each other into submission.

She could see blood.

Mike broke the spell. 'I need a drink.'

As he crashed off towards the kitchen, Sara realised she'd been holding her breath for so long that she felt faint.

James came down the stairs in record time. They gathered as near as they dared to Edward, talking in low voices until he stopped shaking.

After a while, she looked up and met James's eyes.

He said, 'You can't let him get away with it.'

She nodded.

But he hadn't finished. 'I mean it. I'm not going to be around forever. Once I've gone, you and Edward will be on your own.'

'I don't want you to worry.'

'So you keep saying.' James was still staring at her, willing her to focus. 'It can't go on like this. You have to do something. He's got to be stopped before it's too late.'

★

'So did he crawl home in the early hours and throw up in the flower bed?'

Sara, startled out of her thoughts, nearly fell into the cans of baked beans. Rachel, sunglasses balanced on her grey curls, had stuck her head round the carousel of birthday cards.

'Arthur's hangover lasted two days. He tried to pretend it was a migraine.'

Sara said, 'I don't—'

'But I expect James is more sensible, being a mathematician. It's perfectly possible to celebrate the end of exams without giving yourself liver damage.'

Sara wished she was anywhere but the village shop.

Rachel smiled. 'I hear there's a big party tomorrow.'

'I'm sorry?'

'Mike's fiftieth. Lamb on skewers, vegetarian lasagne and home-made ice cream.'

Sara could only stare.

'I think it's very kind of you to give Katie the extra work. Poor girl. She has no support from her parents at all.' Rachel had skirted the end of the aisle and was now standing next to Sara, contemplating the packets of soup. 'I do wonder if it's safe for her to live in that horrible house. She says there's fungus growing out of the skirting boards. Something to do with the heat and the damp. I know she wants to keep costs down, but some of the basic accommodation on campus is quite cheap. I said she should find out what's available for next year. Part of the whole university experience is living with other students.'

Sara felt a familiar tension round her temples, as if she was wearing a hat that was way too tight.

'And she needs to get rid of that therapist. She's not even

reliable. Keeps cancelling at the last minute. You can't do that, can you? Not if you're looking after people with mental health issues.' She gave Sara a sideways glance. 'Katie says you're a keen gardener.'

Sara took a deep breath. 'Yes.'

'You've got green fingers, apparently. A riot of colour.'

'In fact,' said Sara, rapidly deciding she didn't need any milk after all, 'I ought to be getting back. There's still a lot to do.'

'And how is Mike?'

For a split second, Sara wanted to be brusque and rude, to put an end to a meaningless conversation that was making her feel cornered and uncomfortable, but she swallowed the impulse and said, 'Up and down.'

Rachel gave her a shrewd look. 'How brave of him to have a party when he's in so much pain.'

What was that supposed to mean? 'It was his idea.'

'I'm sure it was.'

'He wanted,' said Sara, 'to thank everyone at work for being so supportive over the past few months.'

'As well as celebrating his birthday.'

'Yes.'

There was a hint of a smile playing round Rachel's mouth.

Walking home over the dry, scrubby grass under the midday sun, Sara felt a surge of irritation, more than ever convinced that Rachel was treating her as one big joke.

At the Old Rectory, Katie had polished the great glass doors of the extension to a brilliant shine.

'They'd run out,' said Sara, putting down her shopping basket on the table. 'So we'll have to drink it black.'

Katie's normal air of dishevelment had increased. Damp wisps of hair clung to her forehead. 'What about tomorrow?'

'We can get some in the morning.'

Sara glanced up at the lush green loveliness of the garden, the managed chaos of astrantia and hellebore, silene and aquilegia. The weather forecast was good for the next day – hot sunshine and clear skies – and it would be a perfect June evening. She pictured the long trestle tables set up on the lawn, the salads, the strawberries, the jugs of Pimm's.

They had been hard at work the whole day and the house was poised in a state of readiness. Every room had been dusted and cleaned. Even the small white boot room had been swept. In the old scullery, the huge American-style fridge freezer was full of champagne, white wine and beer. In the kitchen, the fridge was packed with food for the party.

Sara had written a long list and was slowly ticking off the tasks one by one.

Weeks later, when the horror was starting to recede, she realised the list had stayed behind the kettle the whole time, the paper curled and spattered by tea, coffee, brandy.

James had already left for the Isle of Wight. When she asked if he was sure he wanted to miss his father's party, he'd given her a long-suffering look.

'You know the answer.'

She said, flustered, 'I just thought I'd check.'

He shook his head as if she'd lost her mind.

She couldn't bear to watch him leave. It felt like the beginning of the end. She focused on Edward, fussing over him until he got upset and started shaking and she realised he wanted to be left in peace.

Bundle, sensing abandonment, howled.

But it was better once James had gone. Emotional anticipation is always much worse than the event itself. Added to this, Mike had left for Birmingham early that morning, and wasn't expected back until midnight – he was visiting new clients and taking them out to dinner – so the atmosphere in the house was light and happy. After lunch, Katie started folding cutlery into white napkins and counting out plates while Sara made the vegetarian lasagne and marinated the lamb. Late in the afternoon, when their energy started to flag, Sara suggested that Katie stay for supper, and they ate pizza on their knees while they watched *The Hobbit: An Unexpected Journey*, which Edward knew so well that he quivered with excitement each time Gandalf spoke. After that, because Katie was due to come back in the morning anyway, Sara asked if she'd like to stay the night.

'Can I have a bath?'

'Of course. Help yourself.'

Katie's face lit up like a child at Christmas, and Sara remembered the cold lean-to in the dilapidated hovel, the slugs on the shower door.

It had been a long day. Katie and Edward were already in bed when Mike rang. He said that dinner with the clients had been cancelled and he was on his way back. He was in a lot of pain. He needed to get home and sleep.

As Sara told the police the next day, she couldn't remember hearing Mike's car, or the slam of the front door. She didn't hear him come to bed. Their lives that day had been so separate. It was as if she and Katie had been on one path, and Mike had been on another, and it was complete chance that they'd all ended up in the same place in the early hours as Friday nudged into Saturday.

On the morning of Mike's fiftieth birthday, Sara woke at six – as she always did – and got up as quietly as possible, paying serious attention to every move so that she didn't disturb him. In the bathroom, she got dressed in the clothes she'd worn the day before, because they were going to end up dirty from cooking anyway, and crept downstairs to let Bundle out into the garden. She stood for a moment looking out at the long sweep of the lawn as the light intensified and the day expanded into heat and wakefulness. Then she reached for her list. There was still a lot to do.

Katie came downstairs at about nine, and they had a cup of tea together before they started preparing the salads.

At around ten o'clock, Sara made Mike a cup of coffee and took it upstairs. He was still as she'd left him, a hump under the bedclothes, turned away towards the wall. The room was already warm, and the light was yellow and creamy. She went to his side of the bed, next to the window, and stood there, looking down at his face.

Two irreconcilable thoughts lurched into her head at the same time: he's dead, he's sleeping.

He was still under the sheet, his head on the pillow, so it seemed logical to think that he might wake up. But another part of her brain could see that he wasn't breathing. He looked different anyway, as if the central part of him – the part that made him a person – had somehow disappeared. She put the coffee on the bedside table and thought, 'He won't be wanting that now,' and stared at it, not sure what to do.

Time became long and stretched out all around her, like old elastic or pulled chewing gum, and she saw that her hands were shaking.

Then came a gap that, thinking back later, could never be filled with memory, however hard she tried, until she was in the kitchen, finding it hard to breathe, and Katie looked at her face and said, 'Oh God, what's happened?' and somehow knew it was something to do with Mike or Edward and ran out of the room, racing for the stairs. Sara slid out a chair from the table and sat down and remembered at that exact moment that it was ten o'clock on a Saturday morning, and Edward was still asleep, and might wake up at any moment and blunder through the doorway and find his father lying there, lifeless, so she ran upstairs too, and she and Katie met on the landing, crashing into each other just outside the bedroom, and Katie said in a high voice, 'I'll ring for an ambulance,' and disappeared so fast that Sara said to nothingness, to empty air, 'There's no point. It's too late.'

Some time later – seconds or minutes, she didn't know – she found herself in Edward's room, sitting on the end of the bed and staring out of the window at the blue sky. She knew she had to wake him, to prepare him for the strangers who were about to arrive – because random, unplanned events were so frightening for him – but she couldn't bring herself to do it. When he woke, it would be the start of a completely different life. It seemed so momentous, so final, that it felt like standing on the edge of a pit, and looking down into darkness, knowing you were about to fall but being unable to stop yourself.

She put her hand on his leg under the white sheet, feeling the hard bone of his shin. It would be impossible for him to understand. He would be confused and upset.

She thought about the warm light in their bedroom.

She leaned forward and gently shook Edward awake.

It was the paramedics who called the police, after they'd examined Mike's body and failed to find a heartbeat. Katie let them in – two police constables in white shirts and black boots, radios crackling – and one of them went upstairs with her while the other, PC Bush, who had short grey hair and very blue eyes, took Sara and Edward into the big white living room. Edward was rocking back and forth on the balls of his feet saying, 'Where's Dad? Dad's dead,' over and over again, and Sara explained that he was on the autism spectrum, and wasn't really able to process what had happened, and PC Bush nodded and said that was fine, he didn't need to ask him any questions. They sat down on one of the sofas, and PC Bush asked her to tell him what she knew, and Sara passed on all the dry, useless details, embarrassed by how little there was to say.

When she talked about being careful not to disturb Mike when she first woke up – because the day before had been long and stressful, and he needed as much sleep as possible – she started crying, and Edward became even more distressed. PC Bush asked if he could call someone to look after them, but Sara couldn't think of anyone except for Katie, and she was already there.

PC Bush asked whether Sara had moved anything from the bedroom, or whether she'd left everything just as she'd found it, and she said she hadn't touched anything at all. He wanted to know if Mike had any health problems, and Sara explained he'd had trouble with his back for months, and gave him the name of their GP, but couldn't remember the name of the private consultant. They talked about Mike running his own company, and how the meeting in Birmingham had been important because he'd been hoping for a new contract the business badly needed.

Eventually PC Bush creaked off in his black leather boots to find his colleague upstairs, and Sara took Edward outside into the garden so that they could watch the sparrows in the birdbath. Bundle stood on the lawn, barking, barking, barking, but in her mind Sara turned the sound down so that it was like watching an old black and white film with the odd crackled flash and spark.

The police stayed for a long time. A police sergeant visited briefly, but didn't ask any questions, and was gone before she could offer him a cup of tea. At one point, PC Bush came out to talk to her again and said they'd bagged up all the medication they'd found. 'Had your husband been drinking, do you know?'

'He drove back from Birmingham. He wouldn't have had anything at all.'

'What about when he got home?'

She tried to picture what had been lying about near the sink when she first got down to the kitchen, but it had all been so automatic, clearing away mugs and plates and bowls and debris from the night before, that she couldn't remember. Had there been an empty whisky glass? She'd already run the dishwasher through and unloaded it all before she'd even taken up the cup of coffee. 'Maybe. I don't know.'

'You didn't hear him come to bed?'

'No.'

'So he might have stayed up late?'

She nodded.

'Watching TV? Working?'

'I think so. I don't know. If he was in his study, he always had the door shut.' Then she said, in a rush, 'But I don't think he would have stayed up last night. He would have been tired. He would have come straight to bed.'

A little later, when she thought PC Bush had gone back

inside to talk to his colleague, she looked up to see both police constables walking along the far boundary of the garden, searching the shrubbery, looking up at the high green hedges.

The police were still there when she rang James. With great care, keeping her voice steady and calm, she said she had some bad news, and he said, 'What's happened?' with a level of anxiety in his voice that made it clear that he knew it was something serious.

Later, he said that his friends took all the decisions about getting him home – finding someone to drive him back from the festival, taking him straight from some tent in a field all the way to their front door. He was home by six. It was when she saw him standing in the hall – her son, her eldest – that she broke down. She hugged him, and he smelt of tobacco and wood smoke and unwashed clothes.

He said, 'Can I see him?'

She went with him upstairs and watched him walk into the room and stand there, looking down at the body of his father.

By the time James arrived home, Katie had already been hard at work for a couple of hours cancelling the party. She had found Sara's master list, neatly subdivided into categories with phone numbers and emails attached, and worked her way through, getting help from shocked friends and colleagues who offered to ring some of the guests themselves – even, in some cases, to go round and break the news in person. The background to the daze of hours was Katie's voice saying, 'Yes, very sudden,' and 'We don't really know, I'm afraid,' and 'Yes, of course we will.'

Sara knew she should be doing more but knew, equally

clearly, that she couldn't do anything at all except sit with Edward while he rocked back and forth on his chair.

At about seven, the undertaker appointed by the police came to take Mike's body. By this time, Edward was in a pretty bad way. He depended on routine – similar things happening at similar times, nothing abrupt or unexpected – and the day of Mike's death had been unpredictable from beginning to end. Sara and Katie stayed with him in the garden while James went to stand in the hall, watching as his father left the house for the last time. The expression on his face when he came outside to join them made her catch her breath, as if she'd been punched in the stomach.

When it was all over, when she couldn't put it off any longer, she went upstairs to Mike's study. There was nothing useful on his laptop and she couldn't get into his phone. But right at the bottom of his desk drawer, under hotel receipts and random letters, she found a business card he must have kept from one of their secret meetings in Hong Kong or Vancouver or Paris – a little square of white card with a work email and two phone numbers.

It must have been some time in the early hours in Sydney when she finally got through.

She said, 'It's Sara.'

There was silence at the other end of the line.

She said, 'I'm so sorry, I've got some bad news.'

Still, there was nothing.

Sara said, 'Mike died this morning.'

At the other end of the line came the sound of a woman crying.

★

Sara could never remember much about the day after Mike's death. To her intense relief, Katie stayed on to help, disappearing only once when she went home to pick up some clean clothes. James, normally so capable, had mentally retreated to a place of isolation that Sara couldn't reach. She hadn't been able to answer any of his questions about Mike's death – why he'd died, when he'd died, how he'd died – and after a while he just sat there, staring into space.

Once, someone rang the doorbell, and Katie leaped to her feet and went out to the hall to deal with it.

Sara turned off her phone. She didn't want to talk to anyone.

The hours passed. James went up to his room. Edward sat on one of the white sofas playing games on his laptop. Bundle padded around the house, nudging cushions and jumping at flies.

Late in the morning, Sara said, suddenly panicked, 'I don't know what to do with all the food. There's so much of it. Enough for eighty people.'

It seemed such a huge and urgent problem.

'We'll think about it tomorrow,' said Katie.

Sara said, 'All the strawberries. All the strawberries you got ready. They'll all go to waste.'

Katie nodded.

They sat looking out at the garden.

It was still hot when Katie took Bundle out for a walk. They were gone a long time. When they got back, Sara hadn't moved from the kitchen table, staring at the sun on the lawn.

Katie hung up the lead on the hook by the door.

Sara said, 'Ursula's coming tomorrow.'

'Who?'

'I ought to check what time she's getting in. Although she said she didn't want me to come and meet her. It's much more stressful getting through immigration if you're worried about delays and people waiting for you.'

'Who's Ursula?'

Sara said, 'Mike's sister. She lives in Australia. I said she could come and stay. I had to, really.'

Bundle, panting because of the heat, stretched himself out by the great glass doors.

'She sounded terrible on the phone.' Sara's voice was very quiet. 'It must have been a horrible shock.'

Katie sat down at the table, her eyes full of sympathy.

'All I could hear was the sound of her crying.'

The air was heavy with sadness.

Sara said, 'It's not going to be easy, having her here. I haven't seen her for years. She's never even met the boys.' She hesitated. 'She doesn't like me very much.'

Katie looked astonished. 'Why?'

Sara didn't answer for a moment. Then she said, 'I don't know. I never really worked it out. I think it's because I married her brother.'

'But that doesn't—'

'It's not rational.' Sara looked up. 'I know that. She isn't a very rational person.'

'But what happened?'

'It's a long story.' Sara stared into the middle distance. 'Do you mind if we don't talk about it now?'

Katie was mortified. 'Of course. I'm sorry, I shouldn't have asked.'

'It's not your fault. It's mine for bringing it up in the first place.'

They often talked like this, each of them apologising to the other, like people arguing over who should go through the door first.

Sara took a deep breath. 'The important thing is that we make her feel welcome. Gather her in and look after her. Now that Mike's gone, we're the only family she has left.'

Despite these brave words, Sara's heart still beat uncomfortably fast the following morning when she answered the front door and found Ursula standing on the stone steps. Time had changed her. She was much thinner than Sara remembered, with long stringy muscles in her arms like a long-distance runner. She wore a sleeveless black dress and a spiky silver necklace that bristled in all directions like an anti-climb security device.

Her face was expressionless. 'So here we are.'

Sara stood back to let her in. Her suitcase was red and shiny, a hard shell on wheels. It rattled along, sounding loud and self-important in the empty hall.

In the kitchen, Ursula took out a packet of cigarettes. Sara slid open the great glass doors, and Bundle raced inside, barking loudly. Ursula stood back as he shot past her and skidded to a halt by the skirting board.

There were silver strands in her hair.

It pained Sara to look at her face and see a family similarity with James.

'Coffee?'

It was so early that the boys were still asleep.

Ursula shook her head and walked out into the garden. Bundle followed her, still barking at top volume. The morning was dewy and calm, with the steady self-confidence of a day that's going to become warmer and more beautiful. Ursula lit her cigarette and stood there smoking, her back to the house, blowing out a cloud of tar and nicotine into the limpid air.

As if summoned by Sara's desperation, Katie appeared beside her in T-shirt and shorts, ruffled and sleepy. She mouthed, 'All right?' and Sara shook her head.

Ursula ground out her cigarette on the lawn and wandered back to the house. She stopped and looked over at Bundle, who was now standing foursquare by the yew tree, barking into the shrubbery.

'There's something wrong with that dog.' Her voice had a slight Australian accent.

Sara said, 'He needs a walk. Katie's going to take him out.'

Katie said, 'I'm sorry about your brother,' but Ursula was busying herself with taking out another cigarette from the packet and didn't appear to have heard.

On their way out, Bundle was so excited he did a kind of sideways jump, like someone sailing off a trampoline, and knocked over Ursula's suitcase.

Once Katie and Bundle had left, the silence was oppressive.

Ursula sat down on one of the garden chairs. Sara felt she had no choice but to join her.

'So what happened?'

Sara started to lay out the little she knew – that it was an unexplained death, so there would have to be a post mortem, and probably an inquest to look into the results – but Ursula cut across her.

'I know all that.' She flicked ash in the general direction of the lawn. 'Just tell me what happened.'

Sara said, 'But that's the point. I don't know what happened.'

Ursula gave her a hard look.

To her intense irritation, Sara found herself stammering as she repeated everything she'd said on the phone the day before. This time, when she said they'd taken away Mike's medication, Ursula said, 'So they think it's an overdose?'

'They don't know. They have to run tests.'

'It might have been his heart. Dad died of a heart attack.'

Sara nodded, lowering her eyes. Perhaps Ursula hadn't remembered that she'd been at the funeral all those years ago. Sara hadn't wanted to be there – she felt it should be a family affair. But Mike had got his way, as he always did, and Ursula had stared at her the whole way through, angry and resentful at the intrusion.

Ursula said, 'So there's going to be a post mortem?'

'Yes.'

'And when does that happen?'

'Today.'

A shadow passed across her face. 'When do we get the result?'

'In about a month.'

Ursula looked at her with fury.

Sara said with apology, as if the whole thing was her fault, 'Because of the toxicology tests.'

'So what about the funeral?'

'We have to wait for the coroner to release the body.'

'When will that be?'

'We don't know. When they're ready.'

Ursula turned away and looked towards the distant trees at the end of the garden.

Her interrogation continued. Sara knew that it was in her power to stop it at any time – she could say that she was tired, or upset, or needed to lie down. But she felt the justice of Ursula's barbed, aggressive questions. She had loved her brother. She needed to find out everything she could.

At one point she asked if Sara thought Mike might have committed suicide.

Sara shook her head. 'No.'

'But he was in terrible pain. You said so yourself.'

'He wouldn't have killed himself.'

Later Ursula said it might have been murder, and Sara looked at her in bewilderment, because the police had ruled out forced entry, so that left only her, Edward or Katie as possible perpetrators. She opened her mouth to explain this, but Ursula had already rushed on to the next question, as if it had just been a stray thought that she'd immediately dismissed.

They must have been sitting in the garden for at least half an hour when Ursula went right back to the beginning and repeated all her original questions – Mike's usual routine, how much he drank, his state of mind, whether he'd ever been careless about his medication, how often he saw his GP – and Sara finally realised, much too late, that Ursula was still in shock, that none of this was normal or rational, and all these incredibly detailed queries were just automatic, because she didn't know what else to do. Sara looked at Ursula's taut, strained face and felt a great surge of compassion.

She said, 'Let me make you something to eat.'

Ursula shook her head.

'Or maybe you want to rest? You must be tired.'

They sat in silence. The day was filling up with heat. Already Sara could feel the sun pricking the surface of her skin.

They both heard Bundle's distant barking. The walk was over. Katie was bringing him home.

Ursula stood up. 'It's all right if I stay?'

'Of course. I'll show you your room.'

'Just tell me where it is. I'll find it.' Ursula managed to sound both crushing and offhand.

'You're in the room just above here.' Sara gestured up to the window overlooking the garden.

In the doorway, before she stepped into the kitchen, Ursula turned round, a flat expression in her eyes.

'Are you pleased he's dead, Sara?'

It was a shock. She felt she should be outraged, but she was too tired to feel anything at all.

Ursula said, 'You enjoyed it, I could tell. When you rang to tell me he'd gone. I could hear the smile in your voice.'

With a sinking heart, Sara realised that this was only the beginning.

The door to Ursula's room stayed shut all morning. After she and Katie had worked their way through a list of phone calls, and Edward was settled with his laptop at the kitchen table, Sara said she was going upstairs to Mike's study to make a start on the paperwork.

'You don't have to do that now,' said Katie.

Sara took a deep breath. 'I have to do something. I can't just sit around waiting.'

But in the study, sitting at Mike's huge black desk, she found herself staring into space.

Ursula would have been in her mid-twenties when they first met in a bar in north London. Sara was completely overawed. Ursula had the kind of spare, straight figure that looked good in clothes – you felt she didn't have to make any effort because the fabric just sat where it should without being yanked and tweaked. Next to her Sara felt colourless. She wasn't the kind of person who turned heads.

Sara could tell within minutes of meeting her that Ursula had no idea what Mike saw in her. Sara sympathised. She didn't either. At that stage in their relationship, he was obsessed. He stared at her face the whole time, trying to work out if she was happy or sad, too hot, too cold, hungry, thirsty, wanting a change of scene. Sara could see Ursula taking this all in, puzzled, trying to work it out. She kept throwing out questions – 'Where did you meet again?' – as if hoping that some vital piece of information might make things clear.

Looking back on it, this all made perfect sense. Mike and Ursula had always been close. When they were young, the family had moved four times in ten years – some kind of money problems kept secret from the children – and in every new place it had been the two of them against the world. The bond tightened when their mother left. There was an angry divorce. Custody was awarded to their father, and their mother disappeared, never to be seen again. Mike was sixteen and Ursula eleven.

And now here she was, staring at her elder brother, waiting for him to notice her. But he only had eyes for Sara.

She remembered one moment from that first meeting with great clarity. Mike went up to the bar to get drinks, and the minute she judged he was out of earshot Ursula whipped round and hissed, 'Do you love him?'

What a question! Sara wanted to say, 'I have no idea. I hardly know him. I only met him a few weeks ago.' But she could tell from looking at Ursula's face that something so logical wouldn't do. So she said, 'It's happening so fast.'

Ursula looked relieved. 'Don't let him rush you. Be sure it's what you want.'

This sounded like kind advice from an older woman looking out for her welfare. But Sara took it for what it was.

They next met about a month later, just after Mike's father had died. Ursula was hardly ever in the UK – in those days, she was a buyer for a high street fashion company, so was always visiting suppliers in different parts of the world – and had just flown in from somewhere exotic like Mumbai. After the cremation – talking to dusty-looking people with uneven teeth and bad haircuts over cups of tea and ham sandwiches – Sara could feel Ursula's hostility. She was outraged that her brother's new girlfriend had gatecrashed an occasion of such profound importance. Sara came up with some excuse as to why she had to leave early. Mike was torn – should he stay or should he go? – but made the right decision and remained with his sister.

He told her afterwards that they'd been up all night drinking. 'She likes you.'

Sara was surprised. 'Is that what she said?'

Mike looked away. He was never much good at lying to

her face. She often wondered if that's why he became so secretive in the end. It was better that things were hidden away so that she didn't even know they were happening.

But at that stage, right at the beginning, Mike wanted to tell her everything. He hardly allowed a thought to enter his head before he wanted to share it with her. It had promise, this relationship – two people who made a rational decision to be together. She hadn't known him long enough to be sure that she understood everything about him. But she was drawn to his energy and integrity. She knew he wouldn't let her down.

Thinking back, she marvelled at how quickly it was decided. They were never able to spend much time at his flat – large and light, the top half of an Edwardian house – but if she ever stayed overnight, she used to wake up long before he did and wander round half-dressed, looking through the bathroom cabinet and his desk drawers and the pockets of his coat, trying to work out who he was, this man lying naked in the next room.

Sex was pleasurable. She enjoyed it most when he forgot to think about her.

She agreed to marry him on impulse. They were having lunch in a café one day, and he asked her yet again, and she said, 'OK,' and he nearly fell off his chair. He grabbed hold of her so hard it felt as if he were crushing the bones in her fingers. If she'd known his reaction was going to be so painful, she would have sat on her hands.

The wedding was small, expensive and very white. There wasn't really anyone to invite from her side apart from her mother, who spent the whole service sniffing into her handkerchief, and a few people from the law firm where she worked, who weren't quite sure what they were doing there. She didn't ask any old friends from school. There wasn't any point. She hardly saw them any more.

Charlie the painter was the best man.

Ursula did her best. She tried to put a brave face on it all. She said, 'You're everything I could have wanted for him, Sara,' which was such an obvious lie it was surprising she was able to spit the words out.

They went on honeymoon to one of those exclusive resorts where the room opens straight out on to white sands leading to a clear blue sea.

Mike said, 'We're going to remember this for the rest of our lives.'

He was right, in a way. She often thought back to the great wide bed with the white voile curtains billowing in the breeze, and wondered where it had all gone wrong.

To Sara's intense relief, Katie had temporarily moved in. It would have been impossible to cope without her.

For one thing, Bundle's behaviour had become increasingly bizarre. As usual, he stood by the great glass doors barking until someone let him out, and then stood in the garden, feet planted in the earth, barking until someone let him in. But he also ran around the house picking up random objects in his soft mouth and depositing them with great care in the downstairs toilet, and growled at the kitchen sink with an air of menace whenever the tap ran to more than a dribble. He even became fussy about his food, picking over his biscuits and whimpering until Katie or a member of the Parsons family came to keep him company and make encouraging noises while he ate.

Because no one was functioning normally, all this strangeness was accepted without comment. Katie even put a footstool next to his dog bowl so that the person on Bundle-calming duty could sit in comfort.

Katie's arrival wasn't without its problems. She made tea, ran errands, and kept visitors at bay. She spent hours sitting with Edward as he cut and folded his tiny constructions, handing him scissors and tweezers like a nurse in an operating theatre, and filled in all the awkward silences at mealtimes when everyone stared down at their plates, their throats too tight to eat. But she was also slapdash and forgetful – cashmere on a boil wash, cardboard in the general rubbish – and spread chaos wherever she went, trailing second-hand clothes and glittery scarves down the stairs and littering all available surfaces with keys, rings, tickets and hair clips. Incense billowed from her room, and strange indefinable marks – mascara? pen? – appeared on towels and cushion covers. Sara tried very hard not to mind. She recognised that her usual military precision wasn't to everyone's taste, and the cold sad days of mourning were lightened by Katie's almost childlike delight in small things – a robin perched on the windowsill, the purples and pinks in a particularly spectacular sunset.

Ursula, on the other hand, seemed to find Katie extremely annoying. She kept asking why Sara needed to employ someone to walk the dog, and more particularly why the dog walker had to live in. Sara couldn't be bothered to explain, so tried to intimate that this was a particularly British tradition that Ursula had somehow forgotten.

Katie said that Ursula sometimes cornered her and fired out direct questions.

Sara was curious. 'Like what?'

'She wanted to know if I had a boyfriend.'

'What did you say?'

Katie looked miserable. 'I said I did but we'd broken up. And she said that was probably just as well under the circumstances.'

Sara was puzzled. 'What circumstances?'

'I don't know,' said Katie. 'I thought you might know what she meant.'

Sara said, feeling for the right words, 'Don't think too much about what she says. She's a bit strange. And she can be quite cruel if she wants to be.'

Katie said in a rush, as if guilty of telling tales, 'I saw her kick Bundle.'

Sara was shocked. 'When?'

'Yesterday. When he jumped up. He was only playing. He didn't know what he'd done wrong.'

Sara said, 'We'd better try to keep him out of her way.'

A look of collusion flashed between them.

Ursula herself answered questions with staccato monosyllables that killed conversation stone dead. Once, Sara asked if she lived alone, and she said, 'Divorced, no children, no pets,' in a voice so cold that Sara didn't dare say another word.

Sometimes Sara caught her looking at Edward with a thoughtful, analytical expression, like a tourist studying an unusual artefact in an out-of-the-way museum.

One evening over supper, James asked Ursula why they'd never met her before.

'I live in Sydney,' she said.

'But you're here now.'

'Special circumstances.' Ursula stopped poking at the pasta and put down her fork. 'Your father's death.'

She didn't sound like an aunt.

'Didn't you ever want to visit?'

Ursula didn't answer for a moment. Then she said, 'Yes, I did.'

'So why didn't you?'

'Ask your mother.'

James glanced at Sara across the table. Sara pulled a face to show that she didn't know what Ursula meant.

Later, when Ursula had gone upstairs, James said, 'Why's she so angry?'

Sara shook her head. 'I'm not sure. I think it's grief.'

He didn't like this. 'She doesn't need to take it out on us.'

Hours followed hours in a kind of sludge. They knew they wouldn't get the post mortem report for three or four weeks, because the pathologist had to wait for the results of the toxicology tests. But knowing this didn't make life any easier. All the unanswered questions hung in the air like exhaust fumes, foul and poisonous.

Ursula said, 'So when can we have the funeral?'

Sara gave a hopeless little shrug.

Ursula looked at her with scorn. 'Have you thought of asking them?'

But the prospect of ringing the coroner's office terrified her. It felt like stirring up trouble. Not knowing seemed preferable to finding out there were serious reasons for the delay.

When she did eventually make the call, shaking with nerves, she was told there was no news.

'If people ask,' said Katie, 'I'll tell them we're still waiting.'

Ursula was clearly unhappy. Once or twice she borrowed Mike's car and went off for the whole day. Sara assumed she was visiting distant relatives or old friends from her childhood. It would have been helpful if she'd told them where she was going and what time she was expected back, if only so that Sara could plan when to put meals on the table, but she didn't offer information and Sara didn't ask. The whole situation was far too precarious to start making any kind of demands on her. Sara hoped she might realise that it made more sense to go back to Sydney until the coroner released Mike's body. But this didn't seem to occur to her. When Sara asked about work and whether they could spare her – she was still in fashion, but vague about the details – she said, 'I'm freelance. My time's my own.'

That seemed to mean, as Sara said to Katie later, that they were stuck with her.

Letters, cards, emails and texts arrived daily. Sara was taken aback by the outpouring of emotion – *honourable and big-hearted, the kindest man I have ever met, my best and oldest friend, the world will be so much poorer without him.* So many people said she was constantly in their thoughts. She appreciated the sentiment but had no idea how it was supposed to help.

One morning, seeing the expression of despair in Sara's eyes when she opened yet another flowery card expressing heartfelt sympathy, Katie asked if she could give her a hand with the replies. Together they worked out a system of standard templates tailored to all the different groups of people – relatives, work colleagues, schoolfriends, business associates – so that all Sara had to do was sign her name at the bottom.

'I'll send them off,' said Katie. 'You don't have to do anything.'

Sara nodded, unable to speak.

'You don't even have to see them if it's too much.' Katie gathered up the latest batch of envelopes. 'You can look at them all when you're feeling stronger.'

So many people, thought Sara. So many people.

'They just want you to know how much he meant to them,' said Katie.

Sara's eyes filled with tears.

The house felt huge. It didn't seem to matter that Ursula and Katie were staying – the rooms echoed with silence. Sara hadn't realised how much space Mike took up. It wasn't just his physical presence – his muscular bulk, his booming voice – but the force of his personality, the way he'd set the atoms of the air spinning. He'd been away so often that she thought she'd be used to his absence. But somehow the knowledge of his imminent return had always kept his outline present. Now that was gone. There was nothing left.

If someone had asked her a few weeks earlier, when Mike's bullying had reduced her to tears on a daily basis, how she would feel if he suddenly disappeared, she would never have said lost or lonely. It would never have crossed her mind. But here she was, wandering about like a child in a maze. Sometimes she'd stare at a blank white wall and think that the past few weeks couldn't have happened, because death and Mike were so obviously incompatible. For a moment she'd be so sure that she'd been hallucinating, and that Mike would any minute come home and shatter the strange, unnatural quiet, that she could almost hear the slam of the front door.

But however long she waited, he didn't reappear.

News of Mike's death spread quickly. Katie said she was

always being stopped by neighbours anxious for updates. Mary Miller used her network of retired NHS employees to spread the word about the importance of medical check-ups for middle-aged men, and much later Sara found out that sudden unexplained death had been the major topic of conversation in Grace's salon for weeks. Gifts appeared daily on the stone steps at the front of the house – flowers, home-made cakes, bottles of sloe gin.

One morning, coming back from the portacabin, Katie said that Sarinda had been talking about the homeopathic remedies that might help with grief. It depended on all sorts of things, like whether you were sighing or sobbing or liked salty food, so Sarinda said it would be best if she could pop in and give her a consultation.

'I can't face seeing anyone,' said Sara.

'I'll tell her,' said Katie. 'She'll understand.'

Sara thought how strange it was that there were people in the village who cared about her at all. Six months ago, she hadn't known any of them.

The bureaucracy following Mike's death almost overwhelmed her. Sara had believed that modern systems worked quite smoothly, and that you no longer made a phone call to a bank only to get a letter the following day addressed to the person who'd died. But she was wrong. Institutions were sympathetic but inefficient. Access to money was a nightmare. A temporary death certificate eventually unlocked some basic accounts, and there was no mortgage to pay, so she was luckier than most. But all the details about savings and investments were hidden away under cryptic file names on Mike's PC, protected by dense security procedures. Even life insurance was complicated, as neither policy paid out on suicide, so nothing could be settled until the coroner's official ruling on cause of death – which could be weeks away if there had to be an inquest.

At night, Sara lay awake worrying about bills and utilities and how to pay for the funeral.

One Friday evening, Sara opened a bottle of red wine. It disappeared so fast that she opened another. So they sat there at the supper table in a somnolent haze, and Ursula started talking about Mike as a child – silly stories about his paper round, and taking bets on the fastest beetle through a toilet roll, and ruining the paintwork on a neighbour's car by cleaning it with shaving foam. As a teenager, he talked his way out of trouble, charmed his way into clubs, and gate-crashed other people's birthday parties. Her descriptions of him as a young man in his twenties – optimistic, irrepressible, good-humoured – didn't match the Mike any of them remembered, and after a while she must have realised that they all looked sad and uncomfortable, because she stopped talking and stared down at the table.

James fiddled with his wine glass. 'I don't remember him laughing very much.'

'He was in a lot of pain, though, wasn't he?' said Katie.

James kept his eyes on Ursula. 'I don't mean recently. I mean ever.'

Ursula raised her head and looked straight at him. 'I'm talking about the way he was before he met your mother.'

That was a bad moment. Under the table, Sara clenched her hands into fists.

A few days later, Sara was outside in the garden half-heartedly deadheading the roses when James came to find her and said he was cancelling his plans for the summer.

'Are you sure?'

He nodded. 'I can't be on a train across Europe with all this going on.'

'I'm sorry.'

'It's not your fault.'

But she still felt guilty. His life was on hold. He had wanted his independence so badly.

She said, 'After the funeral, there will still be time. I'm sure there will. Before you go off to university.'

James said, 'Maybe I won't go.'

'What do you mean?'

'Maybe I'll take a year out.'

She looked at him with concern. 'Of course you must go.'

For a moment, his usual self-possession deserted him. 'I don't see how.'

She said, with great firmness, 'This isn't the time to make decisions. Let's take it one step at a time.'

Finally, in the last week of July, the wait was over. The coroner's office rang to say that the toxicology results were in, and the post mortem report had given the cause of death as drug overdose. The coroner intended to open the inquest later that day – a formality, and the family wasn't required to attend – and the hearing would be in mid-October. In the intervening weeks, the police would be gathering evidence and talking to witnesses to establish by what means death had occurred.

'Whether he killed himself,' said Ursula, when Sara reported this word for word.

Sara fantasised about giving her a violent shove. Just imagining it gave her a surge of adrenalin. Why did Ursula keep going on about suicide? Apart from anything else, it wasn't fair to broadcast speculation as fact, especially if James or Edward might overhear.

Sara breathed in and let the air escape slowly from her lungs. 'The good news is that they're releasing the body. They apologised for the delay.'

Ursula was staring into the middle distance. 'Did they give a reason for it?'

'No.'

'And you didn't think to ask.' Her tone was mocking.

Sara felt ashamed. She'd been so relieved that the first stage of the investigation was over that she'd hardly said anything at all. 'It means we can set a date for the funeral.'

'Great,' said Ursula. 'I can't wait.'

Katie had been at the Old Rectory for a month. One morning, as she was helping Sara unload clean clothes from the washing machine, she said, 'Don't you think I ought to go home now?'

Sara looked up. 'Do you want to?'

Katie seemed uncomfortable. 'I just feel I'm getting in the way.'

'You're never in the way. It's lovely having you here. I don't know how I would have managed without you.'

Katie said, 'But maybe it should just be the family now.'

'Why?' Sara paused. 'I know it'll all be different when the summer's over and term starts again. But there's no reason to go back home until then.'

Katie said, in a gabble of embarrassment, 'I might need to get a job. As well as the dog walking.'

Sara's eyes widened. She couldn't believe this hadn't occurred to her. 'Oh, Katie, I'm so sorry. Are you short of money? I should have offered before. What if I paid you to be a kind of live-in housekeeper?'

Kate looked horrified. 'But I didn't—'

'I mean, you're not, obviously. You're a friend. But I'd much rather pay you than some stranger through an agency.'

'But it doesn't—'

'Backdated. Because of everything you've done. It's only fair. And I really do need your help organising the funeral. There's so much to do. You can't be out job-hunting if you're here with me.'

Katie hesitated.

'It's just a temporary arrangement,' said Sara. 'To get us through the next few weeks. You'd be doing me a huge favour.'

It was lucky that Katie decided to stay on. A few days later, Sara came out of the bathroom one morning to find her sitting on the chair on the landing with a face so puffy from crying that she was almost unrecognisable, like a child's toy that's been left outside in the rain.

Sara was shocked. 'What is it? What's happened?'

Katie could hardly speak. She'd been weeping all night. Anna had rung just before she got into bed to warn her that Danny had turned up, out of the blue, at the Goat.

'Danny?'

Katie nodded. Anna and Baz and a few others had been sitting at their usual table, and they turned round, and there he was at the bar. According to Anna, he looked exactly the same. He was even wearing the long black coat, despite the sultry July weather.

'So what's brought him back?'

Katie said no one had been able to get much information out of him – he'd just been joking around and laughing about how he'd been away all this time, and now he'd come back and they were all stuck in the same place, exactly where he'd left them. He'd had a couple of pints, played a game of pool, and then left.

Katie had badly wanted to know whether he'd asked after her, but hadn't raised it with Anna because she couldn't risk the humiliation if he hadn't.

'Oh, Katie,' said Sara.

'Anna's been saying for months that he wouldn't dare show his face round here again after the way he treated me. But he's back as if nothing ever happened.'

'Maybe he's just visiting. Maybe he won't stay long.'

Katie's eyes filled with tears. 'I never thought I'd have to see him again.'

Shortly afterwards, with extremely unfortunate timing, Maxine cut off all Katie's therapy sessions for the whole of August, as she'd been asked to deliver urgent family counselling – some kind of crisis intervention – to established clients in Edinburgh.

Sara wondered if this was just a euphemism for providing emergency childcare over the long summer break, but she kept her thoughts to herself. It was bad enough that Katie felt abandoned in her hour of need. The last thing she needed was any suggestion that her therapist might be a fraud.

★

The row blew up about ten days before the funeral.

The day was hot and airless. Sara and Katie were sitting in the living room on one of the huge white sofas, doing a final check on all the arrangements – the flowers, the order of service, the reception afterwards. Ursula had taken very little part in the planning and preparation. Sara had asked her, from time to time, what she thought about a particular decision, but she only ever said, 'Whatever you want,' in a cold and listless voice, as if it wasn't worth her attention.

When Ursula came into the room, they both stopped talking and looked up. She settled herself with long-limbed ease on to the sofa opposite and said she'd been wondering what had happened to Mike's watch. She realised she was at the back of the queue, and that someone else in the family might want it, particularly James or Edward as his sons. But she'd love to have something that belonged to him, so she thought she'd ask just in case.

Sara said, 'It got lost, I'm afraid.'

There was no expression on Ursula's face – just her usual blank stare.

'We searched everywhere – cupboards, drawers, underneath cushions. But we couldn't find it.'

'When was this?'

Sara thought back, trying to remember. 'A few months ago.'

Ursula said, 'He must have been upset.'

'He was.'

'He'd worn it every day for years.'

There was a prickling sensation running down Sara's spine.

Ursula said, 'You're such a shit, Sara.'

Next to Sara, Katie gave a little gasp.

'What did you do? Sell it?' Ursula's voice was quite neutral, as if they were discussing the weather.

Sara started talking very fast, telling her about all the things that had gone missing – Mike's watch, his laptop, his car keys. She explained that Mike had reported it all to the police, but that he couldn't be sure they'd been stolen because it was just as likely he'd mislaid them or left them behind at a meeting somewhere. She said it wasn't like him because he was normally so careful about his personal possessions, but she and James thought he might have been distracted because of all the pain he was in. He was so focused on what he had to do to keep the business going that he might have put something down in the wrong place and then forgotten all about it.

The words tumbled out in a great rush, and all the time Ursula just sat there, looking at her.

Then there was silence.

She said, 'Did you ever love him?'

Katie half stood up, but Sara grabbed hold of her arm and pulled her down again.

Ursula said, 'I always supposed it was the money. That's all I could think. But it was such a waste. For both of you. Who knows – you might have been a different person married to someone else. Nicer. Kinder. Maybe Mike let you get away with things too much. Turned a blind eye once too often.'

Sara was finding it hard to breathe.

Ursula said, 'I'm in a difficult position. Mike and I talked a lot, which you probably didn't know – phone, Skype, emails. Usually about Edward. How much it hurt. Wishing it could be different but knowing it never could. You wouldn't discuss it. Everything screwed down tight.'

A shiver ran through Sara's body.

Ursula's tone was cool. 'He told me that he'd made very sure that you and the boys were financially secure. That was important to him, providing for Edward's future. But I'm guessing you don't know how much there is. Maybe you don't have access to all the accounts. And that's why you're so desperate that it was an accidental overdose. I couldn't work it out at first. Then I talked to various people I know in insurance, and they told me that most policies don't pay out on suicide. That helped me to understand. You have to keep saying that it wasn't suicide or you don't get your money.' She paused, her expression quite calm. 'But that puts me in a bit of a quandary. Because accidental overdose doesn't make sense. My brother wasn't stupid. He would never have made a mistake with the pills he was taking. So I'm really confused. And I don't know what to do for the best.'

Sara kept her eyes on Ursula's face.

She said, 'I know you want me to shut up and go away. I do understand that I'm an irritant and I'm making your life difficult. But he was my brother. I loved him. And until I find out what really happened, I'm going to keep on asking questions.'

Sara nodded.

'That's it?' Ursula looked incredulous. 'Nothing to say?'

'I think death is hard to accept.'

Ursula narrowed her eyes. 'What's that supposed to mean?'

'Nothing.'

'Nothing?'

Sara said, 'I think we should get the funeral over with first.'

'What difference will that make?'

Sara spoke slowly and carefully. 'I think we're both still in shock. Over the next few weeks the police are going to be asking questions. But the priority now is to plan the funeral.'

Ursula said, 'Was he depressed, Sara? Was it the only way out?'

Sara felt Katie shift position. It was a tiny movement, almost imperceptible. 'He wasn't depressed.'

'He sounded depressed. Whenever I spoke to him.'

For a moment, Sara held back.

'He sounded,' said Ursula, 'as if the decision he made years ago to stay with you was slowly killing him.'

She had gone too far. She couldn't sit there saying what she liked, twisting the facts, making mean and cruel accusations. Sara took a deep breath. 'You want someone to blame. I understand that. You don't want to think he made a stupid mistake. You don't want to think that he was tired and drunk and in pain and came home and swallowed too many pills, because that makes it seem meaningless, a waste of a life.' Her voice rose. 'But that's what an accident is. Stupid and wasteful and impossible to understand. Don't you think I go over it in my mind every second of every day? Don't you think I go back over every detail and try to work out what happened? I can't believe I didn't wake up when he came to bed. All night I lay there next to him, and while I was sleeping, he was . . .'

Tears strangled her. Sara couldn't say any more.

Katie, next to her, was trembling.

There was a small silence.

'I have to hand it to you,' said Ursula. 'You've still got it. I've never met anyone able to lie so convincingly.'

Katie let out a little cry of shock.

Sara kept very still. It seemed important not to react.

Languid, unhurried, Ursula got to her feet. 'OK – have it your way. Go ahead and plan the funeral. And in the meantime I'll carry on asking questions. See what I can find out.' She paused. 'You never know, the sight of the coffin might prompt a few memories.'

They watched as she crossed the room, her tall spare figure moving with the grace of a catwalk model.

At the door, she turned round. 'And when you find the watch, let me know, will you? I'd like to have it. Something to remember him by.'

Then she was gone.

For a moment, neither could speak.

Katie said, in a whisper, 'She's mad.'

'I'm sorry you had to hear that.'

'But what are you going to do?'

Sara slumped down further into the soft white cushions. 'There's nothing I can do. We'll just have to hold it together until the funeral. And then she'll go home. For a few weeks at least.'

Katie said, 'I just don't understand why she's saying such horrible things.'

Sara felt exhausted. 'I think it's what they call denial. One of the stages of grief. When you just can't accept what's happened.'

It was Mary Miller who first alerted her. Sara went round to thank her for the flowers she'd left on the doorstep – a bunch of old-fashioned sweet peas from her garden in velvety shades of pink and mauve – and they settled down at the table, sad and tearful, and had a cup of tea and talked about what a lovely man Mike had been. Despite the open windows, the little kitchen was as usual stiflingly hot, and Sara was drifting off into her own thoughts when Mary said '. . . which is the one good thing about funerals.' Seeing Sara's puzzled expression, she said, looking flustered, 'I mean, there are always wonderful bouquets and hymns and beautiful words about the dear departed, and I'm sure this one will be no exception. But they don't really make you feel any better, do they? It's seeing family that counts. Such a comfort. You must have missed her so much.'

Sara said, 'Ursula?'

'I mean, people always say they'll get together, don't they? And they really mean it at the time. But it takes something big like a wedding or a funeral to make it happen. Life just gets so busy. Especially these days. I asked her how she'd managed to take so much time off work, but she said she's between projects at the moment, which must be such a relief. It means she can stay as long as she likes.'

Sara realised that she should have been paying more attention. 'You've been talking to Ursula?'

'She came round. Just to say hello.'

This was unwelcome news. 'So you had a nice long chat?'

'Oh yes,' said Mary. 'She brought a lovely banana cake with a cream cheese frosting. We enjoyed that, didn't we, Daisy?'

Daisy, in her basket by the stove, was asleep. Her stiff legs stuck out from the great mound of her body like knitting needles from a ball of wool.

Sara said, 'She and Mike were very close.'

'Oh yes. I could tell.' Mary's voice trembled with emotion. 'She said she still couldn't believe he'd gone. I think that's what happens when you've been so far away. It doesn't seem real. Doesn't really sink in. She wanted to know all about his life here – what it was like to live in the village, and what kind of things he got up to. I told her about the time I was coming back from the shop with two big carrier bags, and how he rushed up and took them from me and insisted on walking me all the way to my front door. And she said, that was so like him. Always looking to help others. And we talked about you and the boys, and how hard he worked all his life to make sure you were well provided for.'

Sara could feel a familiar tightening round her temples. Despite the urgency of the conversation, she found herself wondering if homeopathy was any good for tension headaches.

'And she told me about all his charity work. That was amazing. I had no idea. Thousands of pounds he's raised over the years.'

Sara stared.

Mary gave her a warm and reassuring smile. 'Don't worry. I won't tell a soul. Ursula said he never wanted it to be public knowledge.'

Sara's voice sounded faint. 'He kept quite a few things secret.'

'The mark of a modest man, I think.' Mary beamed at her across the table. 'Not everyone wants to shout about their good deeds.'

When Sara called into the salon for a manicure, Grace said that Ursula had popped in several times for sessions of aromatherapy and massage. 'She was all knotted up with tension. And I said she'd done the very best thing by coming in because you've got to look after yourself at a time like this.'

'Thank God you're here,' Sara said.

'You get a build-up of toxins in the muscle,' said Grace, sniping at her cuticle with what looked like beaked tweezers. 'That's what causes the pain.'

'Did you get much of a chance to chat?'

'Not really.'

Sara said, 'I'm worried about her. I don't think she's really come to terms with what's happened.'

'I know what you mean.' Grace jammed Sara's hand back in the tray of warm water. 'She couldn't believe I hadn't been questioned by the police. She said, that's what you should always do in a case like this. Start with the neighbours. Find out what they know. And I said, well, I live right on the edge of the village, so I wouldn't have seen anything, would I? But she said she didn't mean just on the night itself. She said you have to build up a picture of what was going on before it happened. And I said, like what? And she said, you don't know till you start, because any little detail could be important. That's why the police should be taking their time and weighing up the evidence, not jumping to the first conclusion they think of. And I said to her, but you're not suggesting there was anything funny going on, are you? And she said, I'm not suggesting anything at all. I just think there should have been a proper investigation, that's all, for Sara's sake, to give her peace of mind. Because the last thing she wants is a whole lot of loose ends and everything left up in the air.'

By the time Sara came out of the salon, she was shaking.

She knew, without a shadow of a doubt, that every word of this had already gone round the village.

Worse was to come. Outside Sainsbury's Local, in the modern part of the high street some distance from the salon, she bumped into Rachel. 'Your sister-in-law's very direct.'

Sara forced a smile. 'It's her trademark.'

'I always get told off for asking too many questions, but she could teach me a thing or two. She asked me right out if I thought Mike was depressed.'

For a moment Sara couldn't breathe. 'What did you say?'

'I said I didn't know. I thought it was quite an odd question, if I'm honest.'

'Why?'

Rachel fixed Sara with her usual penetrating stare. 'Because depression is rarely obvious. People are extraordinarily good at hiding it.'

As Sara walked home, she was filled with a strange and disquieting emotion that left her feeling as if her skin was crawling over her bones, squelching and squirming with disgust. It was lucky that there was no one in the house, because she took off all her clothes, piece by piece, as she walked up the stairs, pushed her way into the bathroom, and stood for a very long time under a cold shower.

Sara knew from talking to Mary Miller how common it was. In one of their chats over tea and biscuits, Mary said that her friend Ailsa – who used to be the sexual health nurse at the

GP practice where Mary worked – often said that if she had a pound for every time a patient admitted to playing away she'd be a very rich woman.

Mary said it was so often the little things that caught people out. Obviously, there were the terrible occasions when an unsuspecting partner was diagnosed with chlamydia or gonorrhoea, or discovered genital warts. Sordid secrets often came to light because of sexually transmitted infections. But most of the time the infidelity was betrayed by tiny inconsequential details – a receipt, a misremembered story, texts on a phone.

Mary said you couldn't help wondering if people wanted to be found out. Guilt was hard to bear. It was so tempting to give in to the luxury of confession. Middle-aged men were the worst. They chased after erotic adventures, but then they wanted to be forgiven so that they could slot back into family life as if nothing had happened. Shirts ironed, meals cooked, children upstairs doing their homework – and lovely memories of being a naughty boy to ward off the spectre of old age and decrepitude.

The day before the funeral, Sara gave up on sleep in the early hours. All night she'd been worrying about the way that Ursula was stirring up antagonism against her in the village, and her head was so full of remembered conversations it felt as if she was standing in the portacabin with everyone shouting at top volume.

For a moment, Sara's mind hovered over what had happened in New York, their visit to Ursula in Manhattan just after they married. She felt a plunge of despair. No one knew Ursula the way that Sara did. They saw her as the grieving sister. They didn't know what she was capable of.

Sara turned her head into the pillow.

She had thought of getting rid of the bed. It was too much, lying down on it night after night, thinking of the way he'd drifted from a drugged sleep to death. But at the same time it had seemed somehow cold and callous to let go of her last physical tie with him. She had even thought, in her less rational moments, that a drastic action like that could be wrongly interpreted. Someone might see it as anger, blame, even guilt.

Your mind plays tricks in the weeks after death.

So the bed – the great super kingsize bed – had remained.

Sara lay on her back, trying to calm down and regulate her breathing. But the darkness was suffocating. It felt as if the walls were closing in, making the room small and claustrophobic. After a while, she couldn't stand it any more. It wasn't yet dawn, but she got dressed and went downstairs, careful to make no noise, with the vague intention of taking Bundle out for a walk.

Time should always be put to good use.

Once in the kitchen, she changed her mind. Pulling open the great glass doors on to the garden, she escaped outside into the eerie stillness, breathing in the cool air, feeling the wet grass beneath her feet. The grey light was ghostly, full of shifting shadows. She felt frightened but strangely exhilarated. Bundle, worried by the change in routine, was so subdued that she almost liked him. She sat down on the stone bench underneath the silver birch, and he settled at her feet, quiet and obedient like the dog she'd always wanted.

Katie appeared out of the mist, somebody's old coat over the indeterminate T-shirt she usually slept in. Bundle rose to greet her, tail wagging.

Birdsong echoed in the space around them.

Katie said, 'Couldn't you sleep?'

Dawn is only a beginning. But sometimes it seems to underline your helplessness, the inevitability of a future that frightens you.

Katie said, 'It's all right, Sara. It will all be over soon.'

Sara hadn't been aware that she was shaking until Katie took hold of her hand.

'You've been so brave.' She was leaning forward, trying to give Sara strength from her words. 'It's not for much longer.'

Sara always worked so hard not to give in to weakness. It just made things worse. But Katie's sympathy broke the dam. She buried her face in her hands and started rocking back and forth, making a sort of moaning sound, embarrassing and over the top like something in a bad drama on TV. She almost wished Katie would shake her and make her stop. But Katie just kept saying, 'Oh, Sara, it's OK, it's OK,' which didn't help at all. Bundle, alert to crisis, moved from one to the other, putting his head first on Katie's knee and then on Sara's, and finally, for some reason, this pathetic gesture of solidarity exploded her last heroic attempts to hold it all in. Sara heard herself half shouting, in a voice shaking with emotion, 'No one knows what he did! No one knows!' She could feel the panic rising inside her, that horrible feeling of being out of control. It was getting harder and harder to breathe. For a moment, she felt so sick and faint she thought she was going to black out.

Katie said, 'I don't understand. What don't we know?'

'I can't tell you.'

'Yes, you can. You can tell me anything.'

'It's too late.'

Katie was insistent. 'You have to tell me.'

Sara said, 'You won't believe it. I didn't. I still don't.'

She was bewildered. 'What won't I believe?'

Sara was beyond reason. She couldn't spend another long night staring into the darkness thinking about Mike, the same ugly thoughts going round and round in her head.

So, holding tight to Katie's hand, she told her the whole story.

The week before, on an afternoon when everyone happened to be out – James visiting a friend, Katie with Edward at the shops, and Ursula playing with the heads of gullible villagers – Sara had found herself alone in the empty house with nothing that particularly needed her attention. So she decided to catch up on some basic administration. The road tax on the BMW was due, so she thought she'd look for the MOT. Mike had always been very efficient at keeping track of all the paperwork – normally everything to do with the cars was in his study, in the big grey filing cabinet next to the window. But the MOT was missing. So Sara hunted round the house, in drawers and cupboards, in Mike's briefcase, in the pockets of his suits. She tried to think logically. Maybe Mike had left it in the car – hadn't ever bothered to bring it inside. So she went into the garage and unlocked the BMW, which smelled cold and musty inside because no one, not even Ursula, had used it for a while, and opened the glove compartment.

Right at the back, behind all the petrol receipts, she found a phone. It was just one of those cheap pay-as-you-go ones, so she thought it might belong to James or one of his friends. Maybe Mike had given them a lift somewhere, and found it on the back seat, and put it away for safekeeping. So she picked it up and brought it inside.

She went back up to Mike's study to carry on looking for

the MOT and put the phone in the top drawer of his desk. She thought she'd ask James about it later. But she couldn't get it out of her mind. So after a while, she took it back out of the drawer and looked at it more closely. She tried to turn it on, but it was dead, not surprisingly. So she searched around in the big box of cables and leads and chargers, and found one to fit.

It wasn't hard to get in. Maybe that's what he'd wanted.

'Who?' said Katie.

Sara let go of her hand and rubbed her eyes. They sat in silence for a moment, listening to the clamour of birdsong across the half-light, declaring territory, calling for a mate.

'There were hundreds of texts. Graphic, horrible, explicit texts. I thought, OK, it's phone sex – a middle-aged man having fantasies about women he's never going to meet.' Sara kept her eyes averted. She didn't want to see the shock on Katie's face. 'But then I realised he knew them. He was talking about places they'd been, hotels they'd stayed in. They were making arrangements to meet. Not just bars and cafés. Airports. Train stations.'

Next to her, Katie was very still.

'So I rang them.'

Sara heard Katie's sharp intake of breath.

'I started at the top of the list and worked my way through. I said I'd found this phone in a car park, and I wanted to get it back to the person it belonged to. Just in case it was important. The first one I spoke to was really nice. She said she recognised the number straight away. She hadn't heard from him for a couple of months and wondered if something had happened to him. I wasn't sure what to tell her. I thought the truth might be too much of a shock.'

Katie interrupted, her voice urgent. 'Maybe it wasn't his. Someone could have left it in the car. Someone from work.'

Sara looked up. 'She described him in great detail. So I'd know him if I saw him. So I could give him back his phone.'

Katie was silenced.

'I kept going, working my way through all the numbers. It felt like something I had to do. The same story every time – I'd found a phone and was trying to track down the owner. Most of them didn't want to talk, which didn't surprise me. But I got chatting to a few of them. They talked about him as a friend. Affection in their voices. One of them said she'd known him for years. They met up every few months when he went away on business. Always very generous, she said. Meals out, make-up, jewellery. Even presents for her little boy.'

Katie said, 'Are you sure it was . . .?'

'Prostitutes?' Sara couldn't believe she needed to ask. 'I can show you the texts if you like.'

Katie shook her head, a quick vehement movement.

Sara looked out across the lawn to the sleeping house. 'I'm not stupid. I've always known he had other women. Each time he said he was going away on a conference I guessed what was going on. Working late, running into old friends, the car breaking down – all the old clichés. He was no good at lying. I could always tell.'

'I'm so sorry.' Katie sounded desperate.

Sara felt very tired. It all seemed so pointless suddenly. 'That's not why I'm angry.'

Around them, the garden was waking up, the colour returning.

Sara said, 'I can accept what he did to me. But not what he did to the boys.'

'What do you mean?'

She hated having to spell it out. She took a deep breath. 'I started thinking about the money. How much it must have cost, this secret life. So I went back and looked again. You know how long it's taken me to piece it all together. All the money in different places. But I found it in the end – logins and passwords for two bank accounts I didn't even know existed.' Sara turned and faced her. 'Thousands of pounds, Katie. Over the past five years, he's spent a small fortune. Wiped out two savings accounts altogether. All sorts of regular payments going out every month. Escort agencies, porn sites, hotel rooms, flights. Huge cash withdrawals.' The words were sticking in her throat. 'And you know the worst of it? I can't even ask him how he could do this to us. I can't even sit him down and shout at him. Because he's dead. Because he's gone. Because he's left me behind to sort it all out.'

Katie's eyes were wide with horror.

She said, trembling, 'It's so humiliating. He cared that little. He's spent all the money we'd been saving for the boys' future.'

'Oh, Sara. I'm so sorry.'

'It's as if he took a sledgehammer to our lives and destroyed everything we had. Deliberately smashed it all to pieces.' Sara could hear her voice rising, a wail of emotion. 'So when people stand up at the funeral and say what a great man he was, and how he loved his family and worked hard to make sure that his sons were financially secure, I'll be sitting there knowing that their inheritance has disappeared. That the money I thought was safe has gone. That he threw it all away on sex with random women.'

Faint sunlight shone through the branches of the tree above. She couldn't stop shaking. 'And the irony of it all is that while I'm trying not to break down, while I'm worrying about how we're going to manage, Ursula will be going round telling everyone his death was my fault, because I drove him to drink and depression and suicide. That he was a saint who could do no wrong. That he always put his family first.' Anger was making it hard to speak. 'Tomorrow will be a day of lies. Lies upon lies upon lies. And I've no idea how I'm going to get through it.'

Outside the Old Rectory, the lawn was dry and brown, like industrial carpet.

In the oppressive heat of her room, Sara put on her black dress. It was linen and close-fitting, and within minutes she wanted to rip it off because her whole body felt constricted. She felt shrink-wrapped, like raw meat. But she made herself wear stockings, too, because bare legs seemed disrespectful.

Downstairs in the hall, the others were waiting for her. Katie had made a huge effort – the hem of her cotton dress was perfectly straight and her shiny brown hair was twisted up and bristled with pins. Ursula, because she was always well dressed, looked exactly the same as usual – elegant and slightly remote, as if she wished she were somewhere else.

The chances of Edward submitting to a jacket and black tie had seemed slim, so Sara had bought new white shirts for the boys and hoped this would be enough. As she said to Katie, it was bad enough burying your father without worrying about what you were wearing.

When the hearse rolled into the drive, and she saw the coffin covered in white flowers, Sara felt frightened. She didn't like thinking of Mike in the suffocating darkness.

The five of them got into the car behind.

Sara said to Edward, 'You know where we're going?'

He said, 'To a funeral.'

'Dad's funeral.'

He repeated, 'Dad's funeral.'

Ursula turned and looked out of the window.

Outside the crematorium, mourners swarmed like flies. There were so many people. New arrivals kept surging forward, milling round her in black suits, khaki jackets, faded dresses, tattoos. She recognised a few faces from the office, and some from the village, but most of the rest were unknown. Who were they all? Where had they come from?

A squat man with a snub nose enveloped her in a hug. The unwanted contact made her recoil. He said, 'Thank you for asking me to speak. It's a great honour.'

She wouldn't have recognised him. It was Charlie the painter. He looked like a bad drawing of himself, a loose pencil scribble of grey lines and cross-hatching.

It's age, she thought. I haven't seen him for twenty years.

It was cooler inside the chapel. Sara sat down on the first row, her sons either side of her. Edward was gently rocking in his seat, keeping himself calm. She wondered how many other women had sat like her, staring straight ahead, trying not to look at the coffin. Her head ached. Her throat was tight. She could feel the pressure of bodies building up behind her, the crowd of murmurs and coughs and whispers. With a sudden lurch of alarm, she couldn't remember where Katie was, and was about to swivel round when she felt a hand on her shoulder. Katie was sitting just behind her. As always, she was exactly where she was needed.

By the time the service started, all Sara's attention was on trying to keep control. The panic kept rising. Every time she looked away, the coffin pulled her eyes back. She knew he was angry. She could feel it. It didn't matter that he was dead. This wasn't what he'd planned, and he wouldn't let her forget it. She wanted to shout out that it wasn't her fault, that he was to blame, that he had no right to make her feel this way, and her heart began to beat so fast in her chest that she started to shake. There was a moment when she knew that she had to get up and run away, that she couldn't stay in her seat a moment longer, and she almost pushed herself to her feet. But then everyone stood up anyway to sing a hymn, and the strangeness of the movement she'd imagined with such clarity happening as a matter of course, as part of the service, somehow cut the fantasy dead and brought her back to herself – Sara Parsons, a widow, on the front row of her husband's funeral.

Charlie got up to speak. He stood there for a long time, looking down at a piece of paper that trembled in his hand. The silence was thick and sticky. He raised his eyes. He said this was the hardest thing he'd ever had to do. Mike was his best friend. He'd known him for forty years. For half that time, they'd lived at opposite ends of the country. But it didn't matter because Mike was always around when you needed him. In an emergency, he dropped everything. You could rely on him. If you were in trouble, he'd drive all night through a howling blizzard to make sure you weren't alone.

Sara felt hot and light-headed.

Charlie said that Mike was a family man. A wonderful

father. You couldn't spend two minutes in his company without having to look at photos of his sons on his phone. Mike always said that it was a constant surprise to him that James and Edward were so good-looking. He said they'd somehow managed to bypass his genes.

A ripple of amusement ran round the chapel.

Charlie said Mike had always been proud of his baby sister Ursula, and the way she'd forged ahead in a world of fashion and design that he admired but didn't really understand.

Sara stared down at the black weave of linen in her lap.

Charlie paused. 'And by his side for twenty years was Sara. He knew the minute they met that she was the one for him.'

She could feel the skin of her face burning hot.

'He was so excited. Rang me in the middle of the night and asked me how to get her to agree to a date.' Charlie paused. 'As if I'd know.'

Everyone was laughing.

Charlie talked about how Mike's company had grown from one man and a phone to a full-time staff of twenty with contracts all over the world. Mike was a born entrepreneur, because he was creative, and determined, and had the energy to make it happen. But most of all, because he understood people. He supported them, teased them, made them laugh. He believed in fairness and honesty. He believed in working together, looking after each other, helping each other.

Sara felt sick. Who was this man Charlie was talking about? How could anyone think it was true? The air around her seemed shiny, tiny particles of light dancing and glittering so that nothing was straight any more, the edges of everything she could see – windows, walls, wooden chair backs – shifting into jagged, broken lines. At home, Mike had been a liar and a bully. But no one knew. All they saw was his public face, full of understanding, fairness and honesty. He had fooled them all.

Charlie looked round the chapel. 'This is why so many of us are here today. Some of us have travelled a long way, from New York, from Sydney, from Munich, from Milan. Some of us live nearby, in the village Mike made his home. Some of us knew him all our lives, some for only a few years. But whoever we are, and however we knew him, we had to come today to pay our respects.'

The chapel was silent.

Charlie looked over to the coffin. 'Goodbye, my friend.' His voice broke. 'We're going to miss you.'

Sara pushed her fingernails into the palms of her hands.

Outside, after the service, the crowd of mourners seemed even thicker than before, as if the heat had solidified them into one huge mass.

'Such a gentleman.' Mary Miller was looking up at her, her face wobbling with tears. 'It's so true. We're all going to miss him.'

'I wish I'd known him better.' Sarinda Nunn's little round glasses shone. 'It's been such a privilege to be here today with all his friends, celebrating his life, listening to all the memories.'

The pressure in Sara's head was so strong it felt like a bright light.

Katie said, 'Are you OK?'

She nodded.

By the time they reached the old manor house – much in demand for fashionable weddings – Sara had got herself back under control. The elegance of their surroundings helped. The cream-painted reception room looked out on to a formal rose garden, and long trestle tables had been set up with chilled white wine, smoked salmon sandwiches, and tiny strawberry shortcakes. Someone guided her to one of the chairs at the side of the room and brought her a cup of tea. Sara was stunned by exhaustion. It takes its toll, night after night of sleeplessness.

Katie joined her. She looked tired, too. Despite all the careful pinning, her dark hair was falling down, and her skin looked almost grey. Sara insisted she drank a glass of wine. 'Funerals are hard.'

Katie said in a low voice, 'Can you imagine what people would say if they knew the truth?'

Sara shook her head and looked away.

'It was so hard just sitting there. I kept thinking about the way he shouted and swore at you, the way he treated you when all you were doing was trying to look after him.'

'Katie—'

'That man Charlie going on and on as if he was some kind of saint! I wanted to stand up and tell everyone what he was really like.'

Sara broke away, unable to listen any more. When she looked back, Katie was staring after her, her eyes desperate with the injustice of it all.

The heat intensified and the afternoon took on the heaviness of a dream. People she didn't know kept coming to talk to her, and she watched their mouths opening and shutting, wondering at the amount they had to say. At one point, she asked them all to excuse her, went out into the corridor and locked herself into the cool tiled toilet. Her face in the mirror looked strange, stretched out and shiny as if covered in plastic.

Katie was waiting for her by the French windows. Seeing them both standing together, Ursula detached herself from a group of Mike's employees and sauntered over. 'Congratulations, Sara.'

'For what?'

Ursula waved a graceful arm round the room. 'All this. The planning. The execution.'

Sara stared back, too tired to speak.

Ursula gave her a mocking smile. 'Anyone would think you cared.'

Sara flinched as if Ursula had hit her.

As Ursula left them, Katie grabbed a glass of wine from the table and took a large mouthful, quivering with indignation. 'She can't talk to you like that.'

Sara was trembling. 'She's just angry, that's all.'

'What are you supposed to have done?'

They watched as Ursula turned to talk to Sally Cook, who shot a quick glance in Sara's direction.

Sara said, 'I trapped her brother in an unhappy marriage and drove him to suicide.'

Katie shook her head, bewildered by such a stupid idea.

Sara said, 'She just wants someone to blame. That's what you do when someone dies – lash out at everyone around you, because nothing makes sense.'

Katie reacted with unusual acerbity. 'She should try blaming herself. If she'd been here, she could have helped you look after him.'

Afterwards, Sara thought about how many factors had been at play – the heat, the wine, the waves of emotion. Katie was young and impressionable. Of course she'd understood that everything Sara had told her had been in confidence. But at the same time, her loyalty to her friend was strong. She couldn't stand by and do nothing while Ursula wove a web of lies.

Sara didn't see it happen. Charlie had come to say goodbye, because he had a long drive to wherever it was he lived in the north of England, and she'd been so repulsed by the forcefulness of his fleshy embrace just before he left that she'd wandered outside, leaning in to the pink blush of a rose to calm herself with its scent. She didn't find out until much later that it all started with just a few whispered sentences. Katie gave in to the impulse of a moment. Maybe she thought the gossip would stay within the tight village circle – Mary Miller, Grace Knight, Sally Cook, Sarinda Nunn. But it fluttered off almost immediately, settling briefly on shocked lips before flitting across the room to a different social circle altogether. No one wanted to believe it. It was preposterous. It was incredible. But at the same time it fitted so completely with what they had always known – that Mike was extraordinary, unconventional, a man of extremes.

Gemma, Mike's PA, listened open-mouthed. To her, it made perfect sense. Mike's diary had always been a nightmare because he never told her where he was going or what he was doing. A double life of whoring explained it all.

In the space of half an hour, everyone in the elegant cream reception room knew about the prostitutes. They knew about the squandered savings. They knew about Mike's betrayal of his sons. As the implications of the scandal sunk in, titillation was blunted by dismay. Mike hadn't been such a great family man after all.

Afterwards, Sara was thankful that she'd told James and Edward about the games room. When the story broke, they were downstairs in the basement, out of earshot.

How do you talk to the sister of someone who's frittered away his sons' inheritance? It was too shocking to take in. Mary Miller dropped her eyes. Grace Knight looked upset. Sarinda Nunn pretended to be searching for something in her bag. Ursula was suddenly an embarrassment. You could see the confusion on her face. Only days before, all these women were inviting her into their homes, hanging on her every word. Now it was clear from their body language that they wished she'd go away.

Much later, when they were back home at the Old Rectory and Ursula was upstairs in her room with the door shut, Katie confessed. Sara had wandered right to the end of the garden, wanting a moment of calm under the tall trees, and Katie came to find her. She was distraught, sobbing so hard she could barely speak.

There was no way Sara could be angry with her. Katie had merely reacted to events. Of course it was sad that the story about Mike had got out in public. But funerals are emotional affairs, and people understand that things are said in the heat of the moment. Katie mustn't worry about it. The whispers hadn't even reached James and Edward, downstairs in the basement playing table football. The whole thing would probably die down and be forgotten.

Privately, Sara thought the gossip was already halfway round the county. You couldn't keep something like that secret. It was a lasting blow to Mike's reputation. He was no longer the fearless entrepreneur, the doting father, the loving husband, but a figure of fun, a priapic fool. But there was no point in saying this to Katie. She needed comfort, not condemnation.

Sara's one consolation was that Ursula's mischief-making had been curtailed. Her attempts to brand Sara as the witch who drove Mike to drink and suicide had spectacularly failed.

The morning after the funeral, before anyone else was awake, Ursula and her red suitcase went back to Sydney.

Looking back on the days that followed, all Sara could see was a series of endings. It was as if the funeral had unlocked a door, and everyone made their escape while they could.

First it was Katie. Mortified by having blurted out the secret of Mike's sexual activities, she decided to leave the Old Rectory and move back to her mildewed hovel beyond the back fence. Nothing Sara said could dissuade her.

'I should give you a bit of space.' Katie's kitten-like face was wide-eyed with sincerity.

For a moment, Sara was tempted to sink to her knees and plead with her to change her mind. She couldn't imagine coping – with bureaucracy, with Edward, with life – without her. 'I promise I'm not upset by what happened.'

Katie looked wretched. 'I know.'

'I can't pay you as much if you go.' Sara spoke with unusual sharpness. 'You can't be a live-in housekeeper if you're not here any more.'

But Katie was determined. 'I don't want to get in the way. You need time with James.'

Sadly, this was true – although not, thank goodness, because news of his father's infidelities had reached his ears. Either the villagers were being very careful, or James just wasn't interested, but he didn't seem to have heard anything about the squandered inheritance. What was uppermost in his mind was the immediate future. In the dark days after Mike's death, James had thought about taking a year out in order to help his mother and brother come to terms with their changed circumstances. Sara had been deeply touched but was adamant that he shouldn't put his academic future on hold. It wasn't fair. He had his own life to lead. She said they all had to get used to living without Mike, so they might as well start now.

'What about the inquest?' James looked uneasy.

'You can come back for it if you really want to. But it's just dry and legal stuff. Statements and reports. They won't need you to stand up and say anything because you weren't even here when it happened.'

'Is Ursula going to be there?'

Sara kept her voice casual. 'I don't know. She didn't tell me what her plans were.'

He was still concerned. 'You shouldn't be on your own.'

'I won't be. All sorts of friends will be there.' Sara tried to reassure him. 'I'm not looking forward to it. But I'll be fine. And it'll be good to have the coroner's decision so that we can all move on.'

To her great surprise, James was eventually won over. Not long after the funeral, he found out that he'd got the results he needed and that his university place was confirmed. There was a lightness about him she hadn't seen for months. He said he'd decided to stick to the original plan and start university at the end of September.

Later, driving the ancient Polo to the shops, Sara was overwhelmed with such panic at the thought of James leaving home that she had to pull over to the side of the road, wind down the window, and take in great gulps of air.

It didn't help that Katie had moved out. Sara mourned the old intimacy. Katie still came round twice a day to take Bundle out, but if she didn't get an answer to her knock, she'd use her key and let herself in. Once or twice, Sara missed her altogether, coming downstairs after doing something noisy and absorbing with Edward, like changing the beds or hoovering the landing, to find the house unusually silent and the hook on the wall empty of Bundle's lead.

Right at the very end of August, there were two odd but unrelated incidents.

One morning, Katie said that she'd seen Anna the night before – not in the Goat, which was still too frightening a place to visit because of the possibility of bumping into Danny, but in the wine bar on the high street – and Anna had told her a very strange story. At the charity shop, Anna had been sorting through a backlog of donations and had found a bag filled with items that should have gone off to be valued. From time to time, people would drop off jewellery or antiques that had the potential to raise quite a lot of money, and it was the manager's policy to send them to a retired auctioneer in one of the villages nearby to ask for his opinion about what kind of price the charity should be looking for. Because of some kind of administrative muddle – or perhaps just basic inefficiency – this particular collection of possibly quite valuable donations hadn't been sent away, but had just been shoved to the back of a cupboard.

Sara had started unloading the dishwasher as Katie was talking – it seemed to be turning into a long story and she thought she might as well be getting on with something useful – so had partially switched off when Katie said, '. . . might be Mike's watch.'

The clean mug she'd picked up fell back into the wire basket. 'What?'

'Anna said they've got an antique Rolex.'

Sara couldn't think straight for a moment. 'Why does she think it's Mike's?'

Katie was flustered. 'It might not be.'

'How could it be? How could it end up in Anna's shop?'

They looked at each other, lost and bewildered.

Sara leaned back against the worktop, trying to think it through. 'How did Anna know Mike's watch had gone missing?'

Katie explained that she'd told Anna weeks before about Mike going through a phase of losing things, and her description of the watch must have stuck in Anna's head. 'I'm really sorry. I know it's upsetting, and there was that horrible row with Ursula. And it may not even be the same watch. But I thought I should tell you.'

'I'm glad you did.' Sara rushed to reassure her – she looked so anxious. 'Where's the watch now?'

'Back in the cupboard. Anna promised to keep it safe until you could get there to look at it.'

A few days later, Sara called into the shop. It was a particularly hot day, and the smell of nylon, raffia and old wool had intensified into something overwhelming, like a scream. Anna's colleague, a rather dowdy-looking woman with a T-shirt tucked into elasticated trousers, conducted an ineffectual search before inviting Sara into the stockroom to look for herself. Sara searched all the shelves, rifled through the cupboards and looked behind the cardboard boxes. But it was no use. The bag of potentially valuable items had gone missing, and the retired auctioneer, when applied to, couldn't remember anything about an antique Rolex, or indeed any kind of watch at all.

'It probably wasn't Mike's watch anyway,' said Katie.

Sara nodded. 'It couldn't have been, when you think about it. There's no way that Mike would have given it away to charity.'

The one silver lining – a thought that Sara didn't share with Katie – was that the watch had definitely disappeared, which meant that Ursula couldn't get her hands on it.

The second strange incident was altogether more puzzling.

One afternoon, Bundle was slumped in the corner of the kitchen, tongue lolling, and Sara and Katie were drinking home-made lemonade in long tall glasses filled with ice and fresh mint from the garden. Katie had just brought Bundle back from a long and enervating walk and her hair was flattened by sweat. She said that now she was sitting down, the heat had stuck her thighs together in one big lump and she felt like a fat mermaid. Sara smiled, seeing a fish tail with shining silver scales. Unfortunately, her mind then drifted to the steely brilliance of the Chrysler building in Manhattan, which reminded her of Ursula and New York, and she hastily brought all day-dreaming to an end.

When the doorbell rang, Sara made a face. She'd had enough of well-meaning visitors. Ever since Mike's death, neighbours in the village had taken to popping round with food and drink in case Sara was too distraught to cook. This was very kind, and Sara was grateful that people were thinking of her and going to so much trouble, but the day before Sally Cook had come round with six stuffed vine leaves. Sara had been mystified as to why anyone would think damp, cold rice wrapped in something that looked like spinach would provide any comfort at all.

Katie smiled at Sara's anguished expression and said she'd

go and answer the door, and there was a small pause while she peeled herself off the chair. Sara leaned back and closed her eyes, and didn't really listen to what was going on in the hall, so it was a surprise when she heard a kerfuffle of footsteps, and looked up to see a short, balding man with wire-rimmed glasses standing in the doorway to the kitchen.

'Sara,' said Katie, 'this is Mr Roslyn. He's a private investigator.'

Sara thought for a moment that this must be some kind of joke. As far as she was aware, private investigators existed only in old crime novels and TV detective shows. But Mr Roslyn held out his hand, and then rummaged in his pocket for his card, and said he was sorry for disturbing them but wondered if he could ask a few questions about someone who used to work as their au pair.

Sara said, 'Hilda?' because they'd only ever had one au pair, and he nodded, his expression friendly but serious.

Sara invited him to sit down. Katie said she ought to be going, but Sara said there was no need to rush off. She felt unnerved by the idea of being alone with this rather seedy-looking stranger. So all three of them settled round the kitchen table, and Mr Roslyn unravelled his extraordinary tale.

It turned out that Hilda, the au pair who had lived with them when Edward was small, had a rich aunt in Tórshavn in the Faroe Islands who had recently died. The aunt had left everything to Hilda, but Hilda couldn't be tracked down, so couldn't claim her inheritance.

Sara was confused. 'What about all her brothers and sisters? Someone must know where she is.'

Mr Roslyn shook his head. 'She was an only child. And her parents died some years ago.'

This was something of a shock. Sara felt a wave of great sadness. Why had Hilda lied about her family? For a while, she stopped listening to the conversation and thought back to all the stories Hilda had told her, the pictures she'd painted of feasts and celebrations, crowded rooms full of friends and relations. Sara shivered, despite the heat of the afternoon. She had a horrible feeling that something had gone badly wrong.

Sara realised Mr Roslyn had stopped speaking and was looking at her with an air of inquiry.

She took a deep breath. 'I'm so sorry. I want to help, but I haven't seen Hilda for years.'

Mr Roslyn said he understood that, but all their enquiries so far had led nowhere so he was starting all over again, building a timeline going right back to when she left school. He said any information Sara could give him would be really useful. So she thought hard, screwing up her eyes, and came up with what she thought were the dates Hilda had lived at the Old Rectory.

Mr Roslyn said, 'And did she leave a forwarding address?'

Sara hesitated.

He waited, pen poised over his notebook.

'The thing is,' she said, 'there was a bit of a row before she left.'

He nodded, eyes full of concern, like a doctor hearing about pain.

Sara glanced at Katie. For a moment, she almost wished Katie wasn't there. It was so humiliating. The last thing she wanted to do was dredge it all up again. But then she realised that Katie already knew what kind of person Mike was, and one more story wasn't going to make any difference. 'I found out that Hilda and my husband had been having an affair. While she was living here. So I asked her to leave.'

'Oh, Sara,' said Katie.

Mr Roslyn said, 'So it was quite an abrupt departure.'

Katie took a deep breath. 'Mr Roslyn, there's something you—'

But he cut across her. 'Did she say where she was going?'

'No.'

'And were you ever in contact with her again?'

'No.'

'What about your husband?'

Katie gave a little cry.

Sara felt the tears wet on her cheeks. 'He promised it was over. He said he was sorry and that he'd never see her again.'

Mr Roslyn looked sad. 'Mrs Parsons, I'm so sorry to cause you distress. But could I talk to your husband? In case he remembers anything else that could be useful?'

Sara's voice came out much too loud. 'No.'

He opened his mouth to speak just as Katie half rose from her seat, leaning out across the table.

Sara said, 'You can't talk to my husband. Because he's dead.'

In the days before James was due to leave, there was a flurry of activity, getting together all his student paraphernalia – duvet, pillows, cutlery, plates. Sara was grateful that there was so much to do because she couldn't face the thought of living in the house without him.

At the very last minute, she gave him a crash course in basic cooking and food preparation – how to dice an onion and crush garlic, make an omelette, roast a chicken. She didn't want him to spend a whole term eating nothing but chips. He turned out to be a very willing pupil. One night they even managed a sweet potato curry, the spices freshly crushed in the big stone pestle and mortar, the kitchen hazy with cumin, coriander and turmeric.

The morning before he left, Sara said, 'Anything else you want to learn?'

'Risotto?'

So late in the afternoon, when all the rest of the packing was done, she stood with him at the hob, watching him fry chopped onion, garlic and celery, pour in the dry rice, add the white wine, and then the slow addition of hot stock, bit by bit, the grains becoming soft, the rice becoming creamy and thick. A dreamy activity of watching and waiting: the alchemy of chemical transformation.

Outside, the light faded, the sky becoming dark and grey.

The making of risotto can't be rushed. However tired you are, however much your back aches, you have to stand there until it's finished. It's a labour of love.

'And after you've added the Parmesan,' Sara said, 'you can stir in anything else you like – bacon, mushroom, herbs.'

'Anything?'

Grief was never far away. She couldn't speak.

James looked at her more closely. 'Are you all right?'

Risotto had always been Mike's favourite meal – the one he asked for if he'd been away working.

She said, 'It's just hit me that you're leaving home.'

'I'll be back at Christmas.'

She gave him a watery smile. 'So you will.'

When James finally went, getting a lift with a friend who was starting at another London college, Sara felt bereft. If the house had seemed empty without Mike, it now felt limitless, like a fantasy palace with echoing corridors. In the mornings, once Edward had left for school, and she was alone in the vast white rooms, she didn't know what to do with herself. It made sense, obviously, to go back to work. There was nothing to stop her. But she felt she should wait until the New Year so that she could be around when Edward came home on the afternoon bus. It wasn't the time to think of alternative arrangements. Now that his father had disappeared, Katie had moved out, and his brother had gone, Edward was understandably nervous if he didn't know where she was.

When there were only two of them in the house, he became her shadow. Even if she went outside to put plastic packaging in the recycling bin, he came with her, watching her every move. She managed to persuade him that shutting the toilet door didn't herald imminent abandonment, but it was a close call.

The inquest loomed on the horizon. Each time Sara thought about it she felt sick. She had heard nothing from Ursula – she had no idea whether she was intending to come or not.

One morning at the beginning of October, Sara walked into the hall to pick up the post from the mat just as the lock rattled with the turning key and Katie opened the front door. Sara stared in astonishment. Katie was lit up with joy. She radiated bliss. There was a flush to her cheeks and her breathing was rapid with excitement.

'Katie,' said Sara, 'what's happened?'

But Katie's wide smile said it all.

They sat down and had a cup of tea – ignoring Bundle's plaintive whines from the back garden – and Katie told her everything.

Her descriptions were so vivid that Sara almost felt as if she'd been there herself.

The night before, in the mildewed bedroom of her horrible hovel – which seemed even more damp and comfortless after her weeks of luxury at the Old Rectory – Katie had been propped up against the pillows, rather miserably choosing her options for the spring term, when the doorbell rang. Thinking it was probably Anna, because no one else would come round that late without having rung her first, Katie scrambled out of bed, pulled on a pair of socks, and ran downstairs to open the door.

There, in the porch, was Danny.

He said, 'All right?'

She couldn't breathe.

It was such a shock to see him in person. The real thing. The version of him in her head had been, by comparison, just a copy – faded and washed-out, a supermarket own brand, nothing but a ghost of the original. But the Danny in front of her was perfect – immediately recognisable and so exactly what she had longed for, body and soul, that she could only stare.

He said, 'I'll go if you like.'

'No. Don't.' The words were out before she could stop them.

He looked at her threadbare T-shirt. 'You'll catch your death.'

As if in a dream, she stood back and let him in.

Danny, in her living room, was taller than she remembered, but just as thin, like an exclamation mark.

She pulled at her T-shirt, tugging it down so that it covered more of her thighs. 'Would you like a cup of tea?'

'If you're offering.'

Trembling, Katie went out to the kitchen, and all through the familiar process of boiling water and finding tea bags, her head was firing questions at her that she couldn't answer – not even the simple ones, like 'What's he doing here?'

When she opened the cupboard, there in front of her was his favourite mug, one of the joke ones that spelled out a swear word if you had your hand in the right position. She had never had the heart to throw it away.

In the living room, Danny was sitting on the sofa, still wearing his coat, thin legs in black jeans spread out in a V-shape. 'You're not having one?'

'I won't sleep.' She sat down on a pile of cushions on the floor, not too near, not too far.

The room was silent. Danny drank his tea. At one point, he looked up at the ceiling. But he said nothing about the great black cloud of mould.

'You went away.'

He nodded.

'Where did you go?'

'Oh, you know.'

'But you're back now?'

'Got promoted.' He held the mug so that it swore at her. 'I'm a salesman now.'

She thought of all the little old ladies inviting him in for a chat.

'Got my own car. Ford Mondeo. Alloy wheels.'

The room was dank. The darkness was coming in despite the curtains, seeping inside like fog.

She said, 'Anna told me you were back.'

He looked guarded.

She didn't press it. Maybe this was something he didn't want to talk about.

Danny put the mug on the tray.

Katie had forgotten how much they talked in silences. Their conversations were a series of dots. Perhaps that was the reason she stared at him so often – she was trying to understand what he might be thinking by reading the expressions on his face.

Danny leaned his head back against the sofa. 'So what are you up to?'

'Back at uni.'

'Are you now.' His cosy, camp voice made her heart turn over.

'And working.'

'I know.'

Her heart beat faster. 'Do you?'

'Dog walking.'

Her throat was tight, as if someone was strangling her. 'Who told you that?'

'Anna.'

'When?'

'Just now.'

The thought of Danny asking about her in the Goat made it even harder to breathe than before. 'It doesn't pay that well, dog walking. I should be taking them all out together, really. That's how you make money. But Bundle's a bit manic. And Daisy's so fat she only gets as far as the post box before she has to sit down.'

'You do it every day?'

She nodded.

'How many dogs?'

'Four. Sometimes five.'

'Busy girl.' He smiled, the kind of cracked-face grin that made her think of a clown.

The words fizzled out again.

After a while, Danny shifted in the sofa, spreading his legs more widely. 'My nan asked after you.'

Katie looked up.

'Maybe you could go round some time.'

This was such a strange suggestion that Katie didn't know what to say.

The dots disappeared into a long line of nothing.

Katie stared at the grey wool of her thermal socks, seeing the ribbing of the design and the tiny pinpricks of machining at the toe. She felt a kind of despair. He was sitting there, in her living room, so near she could touch him, so close she could feel his warmth. Everything drew her to him – the way he looked, the way he spoke, the way he kept her at a distance. But the months of weeping were real. She couldn't pretend they hadn't happened. He had hurt her and left her in such a mess that her heart had been mashed into tiny pieces.

'Why are you here?'

He said nothing.

'I mean it, Danny. I haven't seen you for months. What are you doing here?'

Danny's eyes flicked round the room, as if looking for a way out.

'You want something.'

He shook his head.

'So why did you come?'

The air in the room was cold and still.

'I missed you.'

She looked at him, frightened, wary.

He said, in a loud voice, 'I missed you, all right?' He sounded irritated, as if he'd been accused of something he hadn't done. In a sudden movement, he shuffled towards the edge of the sofa, reaching out to touch the very edge of her sleeve. 'I mean it, mate. I don't like it without you.'

Katie started to cry.

Danny dropped down cross-legged in front of her with the careless agility she'd always loved.

She lifted a hand to wipe the tears from her face. 'You missed me?'

He nodded.

'Why didn't you come before?'

They both leaned in closer so that their foreheads were touching, as if they had secrets that no one must hear.

'I did.'

'When?' She couldn't believe her ears.

'Couple of times. I saw you out. Different men.'

'Oh, but that wasn't . . .' Katie, anguished that Danny had seen her with some of her more unfortunate contacts, didn't know how to explain.

'Looked like you were fine. Weren't missing me at all.' His soft voice was back, the wheedling tone that reeled her in.

The misunderstanding was agony. 'But I did miss you. All the time.'

He sounded pleased. 'All the time?'

'All the time.'

He dipped his head and kissed her. His lips were thin, his fingertips cold on her face. She shuffled closer, and he slipped an arm round her and gently tipped her back on to the cushions so that their bodies nuzzled together. It seemed so familiar – the way he smelled, the way he moved, the weight of him.

He said, in a muffled voice, 'You don't know what you do to me.'

It was all so urgent, they didn't even remember to plug in the electric fire.

Afterwards, holding him tightly, she felt safe.

Danny said he could stay, so they went upstairs and got into bed in the muddle of clothes and blankets, pushing the laptop to one side. When she saw him there, lying back against the pillows, she started crying again, because she'd missed him so much. He turned off the light and pulled her head into the hollow of his shoulder, and she started telling him all about the terrible days of misery when she thought she was going under.

He said, 'It's over now.'

She told him about going to see Maxine, and the months of therapy. He wanted to know about the homework tasks. Katie didn't want to tell him at first, especially all the stuff about sexual research through random encounters.

Danny said – she couldn't see his face, because her head was tucked under his chin in the dark – 'You fucked them all?'

She rushed to reassure him. None of them, she said, not

one of them, because they were all disgusting. I didn't fancy any of them. Danny laughed. He said he'd popped back for his nan's birthday a few months ago, and seen her walking along the high street, holding hands with a small dark skinny bloke, a big smile all over her face. Katie changed the subject quickly because she thought he was probably talking about Al who in fact, if she was being honest, was the one person she would have slept with given half the chance.

She told Danny that the therapy had been about much more than meeting random men – it was all about learning to have pride in yourself, and giving yourself permission to enjoy all sorts of selfish pleasures and put yourself first.

'Sounds all right,' said Danny.

Katie explained that Maxine could be a bit fierce sometimes because she said you had to grab what you needed even if it meant taking it away from other people. It was all about pushing yourself to the front of the queue and trampling over everyone else to get there.

'Makes sense to me,' said Danny.

Katie said she wasn't sure. She didn't really want the kind of life that was all about being greedy and making money.

Danny nudged the top of her head. 'You're mad, you are.'

'Do you want to get rich?'

'Fuck off, mate. Of course I do.'

'I'm not sure it makes people happy.'

'Since when?'

Katie didn't want to argue.

All she knew, lying next to him in the dark, was that what made her happy was Danny.

★

Danny's return changed everything. Katie even looked different – there was a dewy intoxication about her, a kind of glowing brilliance that made it almost impossible not to stare. Every morning, Sara sat at the kitchen table and listened, smiling, while Katie – starry-eyed with adoration, brimming over with love – described in detail every conversation she'd had with Danny the night before. He had a way of looking at the world that entranced her. He was funny and clever and thought for himself. She admired his ambition, his drive, his fearlessness.

Sara said, 'So did you find out where he's been living since he went away?'

No, said Katie, that hadn't really come up yet – they'd been too busy talking about his promotion and his mileage allowance and his expenses. She thought he probably felt guilty about leaving so suddenly, because he didn't seem to want to talk about the past nine months, and as far as she was concerned it was all water under the bridge. The important thing was that they were back together again.

Apparently, Katie hadn't told Anna or Baz about the miraculous reunion. She was still a bit worried that they might disapprove, given they were so critical of his previous behaviour. But Katie felt it wasn't fair to be so judgemental.

'It happens all the time, doesn't it?' she said. 'People quite often split up for a while. It's only when you're apart that you realise how much you miss each other.'

Sara nodded in agreement. But privately she was concerned. She had spent too many hours listening to Katie as she spilled out the terrible story of Danny's desertion – the cruel way he'd dumped her in the Goat, irritated by her tears – to feel anything other than a deep sense of foreboding. Romantic reconciliations happened all the time – of course they did. But it seemed from Katie's descriptions that Danny's original exit had been cold and calculating, which made her wonder if an equal amount of planning had gone into his return. What was he up to?

Her best hope was that he just needed somewhere to live – that his latest girlfriend had thrown him out and he thought Katie might put him up for a while. But even this didn't make much sense. Danny hated emotional displays. He must have known he'd be walking straight back into a volatile situation.

She couldn't bear the idea of Katie throwing her life away on someone who didn't deserve her.

She said, 'So what are Danny's plans for the future?'

Katie looked confused. 'I don't know.'

'You don't know?'

'We haven't talked about it.'

Sara nodded. 'But he's moved back in?'

Katie smiled. 'It's so lucky the house has a drive. Only a little one. But at least he can get his car off the road.'

Sara wondered how Katie could possibly think this was important. 'So he's working locally again?'

'Yes. This is his new patch.'

'Selling windows.'

Katie was rosy with pride. 'He's hoping to make salesman of the month.'

That night, alone in her enormous bed, Sara thought about Katie's loyalty and devotion. Katie had forgiven the past. She bore no grudge. The slate had been wiped clean. Sara found this hard to understand. She wasn't even sure if it was something she should pity or admire.

Her mind drifted to the little house just beyond the back

fence. She imagined Danny leaning in to whisper cosy little secrets, his breath hot on Katie's skin. She thought about the bones of his body, his long fingers, his cool lips on her mouth.

She remembered Katie talking about the excitement of making love in the woods, half hidden by the wet grass – so public, so daring, risking discovery as the dog walkers and joggers and drunks wandered past.

How had he made Katie – conservative, conventional Katie – behave with such recklessness?

The following Saturday, Sara bumped into Rachel in the portacabin.

'I saw that boyfriend of hers the other day.' Rachel fixed Sara with her usual direct stare. 'The one in the black coat. It was quite a surprise. He hasn't been around for months.'

'Yes,' said Sara, keeping her voice light and airy, 'they're back together again.'

She felt envious. Because Katie had described him in loving detail so many times, Danny was very vivid in her imagination. But Sara had never actually seen him in the flesh.

Rachel said, 'I don't hear very good things about him.'

Sara was taken aback. 'He's just got a promotion.'

Rachel looked sceptical.

'And a car. A Ford Mondeo. With alloy wheels.'

Too late, seeing the amused expression in Rachel's eyes, Sara realised that Katie's adoration had rubbed off and that she was gushing about silly inconsequential details.

Danny's return had one good outcome. Katie had been receiving numerous texts from Maxine asking her when she'd like to resume their counselling sessions – Maxine had now come back from Scotland and had once again taken up residence in the small modern house with the cold converted garage – and had been dithering about what to do. Then, quite suddenly, she made up her mind. One morning, while walking Bundle over Ogden Hill, the whole of the bypass spread out before her, she rang Maxine and said that she didn't think she needed counselling any more.

Maxine was disapproving, explaining that therapy was like antibiotics, and you should always finish the course. 'Or you'll slide back into your old negative ways and end up depressed again. And I can't guarantee I'll be around to pick up the pieces.'

But Katie, in her new-found state of blissful contentment, was adamant. She said to Sara later, 'I know everything's going to be fine from now on.'

Her optimism chilled Sara to the bone.

One Thursday, James rang to say that Ursula was coming to the inquest.

Sara found herself gripping the phone. 'Really? How do you know?'

'She emailed me. Wanted to check she'd got the date right.'

'I'd better make up the bed.'

'You won't need to. She said she didn't want to put you to any trouble. She's going to stay in a hotel.'

After James's voice had disappeared, Sara sat there for a while, still holding on to the phone, staring into space. She had been trying so hard to make herself feel positive about the inquest. Of course, it would be horrible to hear the details of Mike's death all over again – the witness statements, and all the coroner's interrogations, would bring back every moment of the terrible morning when she discovered him lifeless in their bed. But she had comforted herself that at least this formal inquiry would put an end, once and for all, to rumours and speculation. In addition to this, the coroner's decision on accidental overdose would finally unlock Mike's life insurance policies. There would be no more worrying about money. They'd be financially secure.

But that was the end point. During the journey to get there, she'd have to face Ursula again. This filled her with dread. She'd heard nothing from her for over a month. But she was sure that Ursula's threat to stir things up by asking awkward questions was still very much alive. Ursula hadn't succeeded at the funeral. But maybe Sara wouldn't be so lucky the second time round.

The room was getting dark when Edward came to find her. 'What are you doing?'

'Nothing,' she said.

Luckily, he didn't notice things like tears.

In the weeks before the inquest, increasingly agitated by the prospect of Ursula's return, her memories of Mike grew stronger.

She was frightened by the muddle of her thoughts. There seemed to be no straight paths any more, just roundabouts and T-junctions and the odd bypass hurtling towards a cliff edge. Some days she was quite convinced that Mike was still alive. She knew for certain that she'd be in the kitchen chopping up an onion, and the front door would slam and she'd hear the thud, thud, thud of his footsteps, and there he would be with his habitual scowl, and their evening would proceed exactly as it always did, the picture of marital discord. She knew this. She knew it for a fact. But then Edward would look up from the sofa and say, 'Why did he die?' with that scared look in his eyes, and she'd be drowning again, drowning, drowning.

In clearer moments, she knew he'd gone. The house howled with his absence. He just wasn't there. But he was still inside her head. To begin with, in the early days, it was just the odd comment that pinged into her mind, sometimes so loudly that she jumped. One afternoon she made a chocolate cake for Edward and must have been distracted at the measuring stage because it came out of the oven looking dense and dark with a distinct dip in the middle. As she stared at it in some dismay, Mike's voice said, 'Not up to your usual standard, Sara.' She whipped round, thinking he was standing right behind her. But there was no one there.

As time passed, comments like these became so much more frequent that she felt like a politician being interviewed by a hostile radio host. When she snapped at the cashier in Sainsbury's Local, Mike was in her ear asking if she was going to apologise. She backed the ancient Polo into a lamppost and he wondered what she was trying to achieve.

Not looking good, Sara.

Not quite what you planned, Sara.

Not going so well, Sara.

She suspected that this was some kind of benign aberration quite normal to the process of grieving and that it was nothing to worry about. Perhaps, like Ursula, she couldn't fully accept that Mike was dead and was holding on to a version of reality that kept him alive in her mind. But this didn't make it any easier to bear. The weight of his disapproval was so heavy.

Once, without warning, he swore at her. He had never before used language that was quite so gross, although the contempt in his face – that blank stare from his pale green eyes – had sometimes led her to wonder if that's what he'd been secretly thinking. But one day, as she picked up a mobile phone in his study – the cheap, disposable, pay-as-you-go phone she'd found in the glove compartment of his BMW – his voice rushed into her head, curt and blunt. It was a terrible shock. She was shaking so badly she had to sit down.

After this, she spent a considerable amount of time and effort blocking out Mike's voice. More often than not, she was successful. But there was the odd occasion, particularly if she was tired or under stress, when she lost control and his booming rudeness filled her head for hours.

Worse than coping with Mike's constant attempts to invade her thoughts was having to worry about Ursula. Vivid images and fragments of speech kept rushing into her head. Sometimes in the evenings when Edward was upstairs watching TV, she could sit at the kitchen table looking at the darkness through the great glass doors and lose a whole hour to unwanted memories from the past.

She remembered the morning in Regent's Park quite soon after she and Mike had got together. Mike wasn't with them. It was probably a calculated ploy on his part to stay out of the way so that they'd get to know each other – it must have been his dearest wish for his sister and new girlfriend to become the best of friends.

They were walking along one of the long straight avenues, surrounded by joggers and mums pushing buggies, the sunlight falling through the leaves and dappling the grass below, when Ursula said, 'Do you ever feel guilty?'

It was a strange question. Her dark hair was falling forwards over her face so Sara couldn't see her expression. 'Sometimes. Why?'

Ursula didn't answer.

Sara was still at that stage of their relationship when she wanted Ursula to like her, so she said, 'I know I should spend more time with my mother. That makes me feel guilty. She wants to see me much more than she does.'

Ursula said, 'I was thinking about Carys.'

There was no obvious way to respond to this, so Sara said nothing. They carried on walking, their steps in time with each other.

Ursula said, 'She's not coping very well.'

They walked on.

'It's not surprising, I suppose.' Ursula's voice sounded high and strained. 'After all those years.'

Sara chose her words with care, 'It was Mike's decision.'

'Oh, I know,' said Ursula, 'I know that. It wasn't your fault. He didn't say when you met that he was living with his girl-friend.'

'No, he didn't.'

'He didn't say that they'd been together since they were at school and they'd just bought their first flat.'

Sara remembered the dresses in the wardrobe, the shoes under the bed, Carys's make-up in the bathroom cabinet.

'He was in the wrong,' said Ursula. 'Not you. I know that. But I just wondered if you were OK with it.'

Sara turned slowly and faced Ursula head on. 'Mike never talks about her. I've never met her. So I'm fine.'

Now, at last, Ursula met Sara's eyes. 'You don't feel guilty?'

'For what?'

'For breaking them up.'

'I didn't break them up.'

For a moment, Sara thought Ursula might argue. She seemed to be struggling to hold back words.

Sara said, 'Mike had moved out by the time we met. I never even saw the flat.'

A white lie, but perfectly understandable in the circumstances.

Ursula looked down at the ground.

Sara said, 'I know you're friends. And I'm sorry she's unhappy. But I can't do anything about it.'

Sometimes, in idle moments, Sara was curious as to why Ursula had thought it was a good idea to raise the spectre of the ex-girlfriend with the woman her brother was currently obsessed with. But she didn't worry about it. She knew Ursula was fiercely protective of her brother, and imagined she was equally loyal to her friends. She never thought that Ursula would take it to extremes. Why would she? In those days she thought Mike's sister was a sane and rational person.

According to Mary Miller, Grace had never really got over Ryan. She wouldn't ever talk about him in anything other than scathing tones – she seemed delighted to be rid of him – but sometimes, in unguarded moments, her beautifully made-up face settled into lines of hopeless misery and, beneath the thick black mascara, a lost and lonely look crept into her eyes.

The rumour was that Ryan was equally unhappy. He hadn't come to terms with the break-up either – Mary said his muscle-pumping in the gym was now so excessive that his biceps had ballooned to Popeye proportions – and would still tell anyone who listened that he had never, on his life, even thought of cheating on Grace.

Once you start telling a lie, thought Sara, you have to stick with it or no one will ever trust you again.

Poor Grace. It was one blow after another.

Outside the village shop, Mary said, 'Did you hear about the bracelet?'

Sara shook her head.

'It was her pride and joy. Rose gold with a heart-shaped padlock. Used to belong to her grandmother. And now it's gone. She can't find it anywhere.'

The gate link bracelet had been in the jewellery box by Grace's bed. She didn't remember when she'd last worn it, but she'd definitely seen it at the weekend when she put her diamond studs away. She hadn't been burgled – there was no sign of forced entry – and no one who'd recently been in the house, from the plumber to her best friend Jade, could remember anything untoward.

She searched pockets and drawers and cupboards, looked in totally stupid places like the fridge and the biscuit tin in case she'd had some kind of eccentric moment, and carefully examined every tiny crevice in the car.

'It's a complete mystery,' said Mary. 'Grace's mum thought it might be something to do with Lulu. But Grace said, I know my dog's clever, but she can't unlock a jewellery box as far as I know.'

Someone unkind started a rumour that Ryan might have

taken it, but Grace said that was ridiculous because she'd changed the locks since she'd thrown him out, so he wouldn't have been able to use his key.

Grace rang the police and was given a crime number so that she could claim on her insurance but, as she said, it wasn't about the money. 'I'd give anything to get it back, Sara. Anything. You know what it's like. If someone dies, the things that used to belong to them are so precious. It's all you have left. Something to remember them by.'

Sara thought about Mike's watch and how much Ursula had wanted it.

Finally, the day arrived.

Sara had expected the coroner's court to be much grander. But it was just a small room with high windows, light wood panelling and a gold coat of arms above the bench where the coroner sat. In the morning when they arrived, neither of the public toilets was working, and everyone had to file through a corridor to get to the staff toilets at the back. This didn't inspire confidence. You could see people thinking that a court of law convened to establish the cause of a sudden death should be able to afford the services of a qualified plumber.

Everyone from the village was there, sitting on the benches at the back, except for Grace, who had asked Mary to say she was really sorry but Kayleigh was off with a stomach bug and she had to mind the salon. Sara was pleased to see all her neighbours, and glad to have their support, but wondered if they would have bothered to turn up in force if it hadn't been for the revelations about Mike's sordid sexual adventures. No one had tired of the story yet. Sara could tell, when she walked into the portacabin and everyone looked guilty and stopped talking, that the scandal of Mike and the prostitutes still had a long way to run. It was all so exciting, the idea that someone living in their midst – in the biggest house in the village – had been indulging in the kind of shocking life-style you only ever read about in the tabloids.

She could imagine all the conversations – how no one could bear to think of the grief, anger and humiliation she must be going through. Poor Sara – she must be devastated. Imagine living with someone for twenty years and finding out he had a whole secret existence you knew nothing about!

Sitting on the hard wooden bench, Sara cringed.

Katie was just behind her, on one of the rows reserved for the witnesses. It was comforting to know she was there. They had driven in together, and Katie had promised she would stay by her side all day. She had got up extra early that morning, rushed Dexter and Lulu out for a quick run, and walked Daisy to the post box. She and Sara had decided that Bundle could manage by himself in the garden until they came home.

High up towards the ceiling, on two sides of the courtroom, the windows let in the autumn light. The sky was bright blue. Sara tried to regulate her breathing. It was nearly over. Just this one day to get through.

It wasn't until they were all settled, waiting for the coroner, that Ursula arrived. Sara didn't need to turn round – she could tell from the murmurings behind her who had walked in. She couldn't quite bring herself to look in Ursula's direction, but could see, on the edge of her vision, that Ursula had sat down at the other end of the row, as far away from Sara as possible.

Mike's voice in her head said, *She hates you.*

Sara's heart began to beat faster.

You know why, don't you? He sounded sad and resigned. *You know why she hates you?*

It wasn't my fault, she thought. I had no choice.

She blocked Mike's voice from her head.

When the coroner came in, Sara was worried to see how old and thin he was. His spine was bent, as if he'd spent too many years shouldering heavy responsibilities. Was he up to a long day of questioning and analysis? He looked as if he should be tucked up in a wing chair in front of the fire, a tartan blanket folded over his knees.

The coroner began by explaining how the proceedings worked, glancing up at one point to look directly at Sara over the top of his glasses. Sara nodded to show she was listening, but it was hard to concentrate, because of Ursula sitting so nearby, and the constant fear that Mike would interrupt if she dropped her guard for a moment.

He explained that an inquest was not a trial. They were all there to establish the facts surrounding the death of Michael Parsons, and there could be no language of blame or accusation. He said he also had a separate statutory duty to report on any risks to life or health identified during the inquest so that future deaths could be prevented. In a gentle voice, bowing his head as if showing proper deference, he read out a list of the witnesses he was intending to call, explaining that others had not been required to attend as he was going to redact their statements – in other words, just read out those parts that he felt were important. He would also summarise the post mortem and toxicology reports.

And then, much more quickly than she'd anticipated, Sara, the first witness, was called to give evidence. It was only a few steps to the wooden stand at the side of the court, facing out towards the rest of the room, but it felt like a long slow walk down an endless road. She couldn't stop shaking. So many eyes were staring at her.

The coroner took her through the statement she'd given to the police some weeks before. It was a laborious process. Some sections he read out without comment, but then he'd stop, as if struck by a thought, and ask her to expand. 'Can you explain again, Mrs Parsons . . .?' 'In what way, Mrs Parsons . . .?' There were long pauses while he took notes.

Later, she remembered only fragments of what she'd said. Once, she talked about how much Mike hated being dependent on painkillers, and the coroner looked up and said, 'Can you tell the court a little bit more about this, please?', and she tried to put into words what a physical person he'd always been, and how shocking it had been for him to be reduced to an invalid, and how he kept trying to cut down the dose or manage without his medication altogether in the hope that the pain would somehow disappear if only he tried hard enough to ignore it. On another occasion, she stumbled through the rather sad admission that Mike drank more and more as the weeks passed, but only to dull the pain. He didn't seem to get much pleasure from it. He had a bottle of whisky in his study.

All through her testimony, she was filled with cold dread that she'd say something stupid or illogical. It felt so important to give answers that satisfied the coroner's patient questioning.

During the long pauses while the coroner scribbled away, she glanced up at the high windows and the bright blue October sky.

At one point she worried that the coroner might be slightly deaf, because he asked the same question again and again, rephrasing it slightly each time. Had Mr Parsons ever given any indication that he was thinking of death? Had he ever expressed the intention of wanting to take his own life? She had to fight down the urge to shout out, in a loud clear voice, 'Mike wasn't depressed. He didn't commit suicide. It was an accident.'

But she restrained herself. It seemed better to answer the questions calmly.

Finally, after what felt like hours, he said, 'Thank you, Mrs Parsons. I know this hasn't been easy. You have been very helpful.'

When she sat down, her legs were shaking.

The coroner read out statements from the senior paramedic who had arrived first, examined Mike's body and found no heartbeat, and then from the two police constables and the police sergeant, one after the other – no evidence of foul play, nothing in the room to indicate any kind of disturbance, no blood or obvious wounds on the body, nothing out of the ordinary in the house or grounds.

Sara was flooded with relief when each of the police statements mentioned looking for a note but finding nothing. It made sense that they'd searched so thoroughly. Find a fifty-year-old man dead in his bed, and suicide must be one of your first thoughts.

The police sergeant said that after liaising with the detective inspector, because there had been no indication that any other persons had been involved, it had been declared a non-suspicious death.

The statement from the GP described Mike's chronic back problem, the various treatments discussed, and the drugs he'd been prescribed. It was good to have a summary of the toxicology report read out in public because it confirmed the high levels of painkillers and alcohol in Mike's blood. The post mortem report said that there had been no pathological features to indicate third party involvement. The cause of death was drug overdose.

The atmosphere in the courtroom was dull and tired as if all the air had been used up. The coroner raised his eyes from the paperwork and suggested they all take a break and reconvene at midday for a short session before lunch.

Outside in the waiting area, one of the toilets was now in operation. But the drinks machine was broken. It took all your coins one by one, but when you pressed 'select' they all rushed out again as if you'd won the jackpot.

'How are you bearing up, dear?' said Mary Miller.

'I've brought Ignatia and Aconite,' said Sarinda Nunn, 'in case you need a remedy.'

Sally Cook said she was a bit confused as to why it wasn't all over now that they'd read out the cause of death, but Mary – who'd been to an inquest before, in the course of her professional duties – said it wasn't just about why someone died, but how it happened.

'But we all know how it happened,' said Sally. 'It was an accident. He took too many pills by mistake.'

Beyond the reception desk, right by the entrance, Ursula was staring out into the car park, her back to them all.

Katie went out to one of the nearby cafés and brought

back a tray of tea in plastic cups. Sara was grateful. She was trembling with cold, as if someone had turned off the heating and the windows were wide open to thick snow and blizzard conditions.

Back in the courtroom, the coroner called Gemma, Mike's PA. She was wearing a bright green bouclé jacket and her silver bracelets jangled as she turned the pages of her statement. It turned out she'd been the very last person to speak to Mike apart from Sara. He'd rung her from Birmingham to relay some action points from the meeting, which had gone well, but he said that if the pain in his back got any worse he was going to have to miss his own party the next day. The coroner questioned Gemma for some time. She was tearful at the beginning but gained in confidence as he congratulated her on the clarity of her responses. She said Mike had sounded angry on the phone, and the coroner asked if that was unusual, and she said, no, pain always made him irritable because it got in the way and took his mind off what he was supposed to be doing next. She said he wasn't a good patient because he was so impatient, and then stopped, tied up in knots by her own bad choice of words.

'He didn't always remember to take his pills. But that was sometimes on purpose. He said they made him feel sleepy and he couldn't concentrate. But then if he didn't take them, he'd be in agony.' Gemma paused. 'It was like he couldn't win. Whatever he did, it didn't work.'

The coroner spent a long time writing this down. Then he asked her to go back to the phone call. 'You say he sounded angry.'

'Yes.'

'But that was normal.'

'Yes.'

'You had no indication that his state of mind was in any way different from usual?'

Gemma thought about this. 'No. He was just like he always was.'

The coroner nodded and thanked her for her evidence and for being so clear. 'Is there anything else you'd like to add?'

For one stomach-churning moment, Sara was frightened that Gemma was going to spill out the story about the prostitutes and the porn sites and the thousands of pounds wasted on sordid sexual adventures. It wasn't relevant – of course it wasn't. It had nothing to do with Mike's death. But she couldn't be sure that the coroner would feel the same way. It might open up all sorts of difficult questions about stress and pressure and mental health.

Sara held her breath.

But Gemma, after a short pause, shook her head.

The coroner said it had been a heavy and emotional morning and thanked them all for their attentiveness and co-operation. He said they would break for lunch and reconvene at two o'clock.

Katie took them all to the café she'd found round the corner. She sat Sara at a table by the window, as if she were an invalid or an elderly lady who needed cosseting, and went up to join Mary and Sarinda in the queue for sandwiches.

Well done, Sara.

She jumped.

Mike's voice said, *You can see the way it's going. The coroner doesn't think it was suicide.*

She shook her head, trying to get him to shut up.

So you'll get your money and keep the house and everything will go on as normal.

She shut her eyes tightly.

Ursula won't be happy, though.

'She's never happy,' said Sara, out loud. In a panic, she looked round in case anyone had heard. But the café was noisy with chatter and scraping chairs and orders shouted to the kitchen.

Without warning, the memories flooded back.

About a year after they married, Mike said that he wanted to meet up with contacts in New York. In some ways it was nothing more than a glorified sales trip, but it was also a chance to see Ursula, who was spending six months there on secondment – her company liked offering their buyers temporary placements in their international offices. As Sara had never been to Manhattan except in her imagination, courtesy of improbable rom coms, she jumped at the chance of going with him. They had planned to rent an apartment or stay in a hotel, but Ursula wouldn't hear of it. She said there was a spare room and plenty of space, and that Lee was really looking forward to meeting them.

'Who's Lee?' Sara was hoping that Ursula might have fallen in love and become less spiky.

Mike looked lost. 'I've no idea.'

What Sara hadn't realised until she was on her own for the third day running – Mike at meetings and Ursula and

Lee at work – was that solitary sightseeing was very boring. She made herself a list, and dutifully looked at landmarks and museums and galleries so that she could say, at the end of each day, 'I saw the Statue of Liberty! I saw MoMA! I saw Central Park!' But as she trudged through the crowded streets, feeling the hardness of the pavements beneath her feet, she realised she'd got out of the habit of spending time alone. She was tired and fed up. She was bored.

Lee turned out to be a tall, athletic Californian who was something to do with brand management in Ursula's office. She said they were just flatmates, but her eyes followed him everywhere.

One afternoon Sara couldn't be bothered to trail round the latest tourist attraction, so came back to the apartment and wandered about looking for distraction. Lee's room seemed to be full of sporting equipment and motivational self-help books. Sara leafed through a pile of letters and invoices on his desk, but they were all to do with gym membership and air travel, so she couldn't be bothered to examine them closely. Ursula's room, on the other hand, was gloriously untidy, with clothes, scarves, make-up and jewellery spilling out of drawers and ending up, like driftwood at low tide, in a long line under the bed. Sara tried on some gold trousers, borrowed some lipstick, and sprayed herself with some of Ursula's scent. Then she pulled out one of the great big artwork folders that were lying under a pile of cushions on the bed.

It was entirely to Ursula's credit that her erotic story about a young woman's secret obsession with a tall, athletic Californian was so compelling – there was a lot of glistening and tumescence – that Sara didn't hear the front door. She didn't realise Ursula was home until she was standing in the room right in front of her.

Sara grovelled, apologised profusely, and promised never to snoop around Ursula's personal possessions ever again, but it was a long time before Ursula calmed down and stopped shouting.

Afterwards, thinking about the hurt and humiliation in Ursula's eyes, Sara realised there was probably a much deeper story running beneath the whole thing – a deeper story about unrequited love. She was surprised. Even mighty Ursula could be humbled by desire.

On the Friday night, they all went out to a Thai restaurant in the East Village. They had drunk quite a lot of beer by the time Lee arrived, late, with another young man called Simon. They were holding hands.

Sara didn't control her expression quickly enough. Lee caught her looking at Ursula with shocked sympathy, and realisation dawned. He hadn't known about her feelings for him. The air was thick with embarrassment. Ursula stood up, placed her napkin on the tablecloth, and walked out.

The next day, in a voice clipped with anger, she accused Sara of betraying her. She said Sara had deliberately let Lee know. This had ruined not only her personal but her professional relationship with him and would make working together impossible. Mike, who was some way behind, played peacemaker. Ursula turned on him with fury and said he had no idea what was going on. As he stared at her in some astonishment, she said she'd been trying really hard to put the past behind her. She'd decided it was wrong to bear a grudge against Sara for splitting up her friend and her brother – love is messy and unpredictable, and it wasn't fair to let her loyalty to Carys colour the way she thought about her sister-in-law. But she couldn't keep quiet any longer, because this latest incident with Lee proved what she'd known for some time, which was that Sara was the kind of cruel and vindictive person who deliberately set out to destroy people for her own amusement. She said that Sara had lied when she'd claimed to know nothing about Carys. She'd known about her right from the beginning, right from the first moment she'd laid eyes on Mike. The truth was that Sara had seen a stable, long-term relationship and had set herself the challenge of breaking it up. She hated other people being happy because it was something she didn't understand. She wanted everyone to be as lonely and miserable as she was.

Mike had been staring at his sister open-mouthed. When he shook his head and said she'd got it all wrong, Ursula screamed at him to shut up, to shut up and listen, because he didn't know anything, he was going round with his eyes shut, and it was all because of him that Carys had tried to kill herself.

There was a terrible silence. All the blood left Mike's face. He looked old and almost ugly.

In a much quieter voice, he asked her what she meant. At first, Ursula didn't want to say anything. But he wouldn't let it go. He kept on and on at her. Eventually she said that Carys had jumped in front of a car. She'd broken some ribs. She was out of hospital. She was OK.

Sara felt sick. She made an excuse to leave the room and stood in the bathroom with her head against the tiles, trying to make sense of what she'd heard.

Later that afternoon, Mike rang friends in London. They

told him Carys had got drunk at a party and walked out into the road. Not a suicide attempt. An accident.

Sara said to Mike, 'I want to go home.'

He was distraught. 'I don't know why she's being like this.'

'Why did she lie about Carys? It was horrible. She could see what it did to you.'

Mike said, 'She must have thought it was true.'

But Sara shook her head. 'Even if it was, she shouldn't have told you. She should have protected you. Not passed on some shitty piece of gossip.'

Mike put his face in his hands.

Sara said, 'And what she said about trying to break you up – that wasn't true either. I'd no idea you were with someone when we met.'

Mike looked up. 'I know you didn't.'

'I didn't find out about Carys for months.' Sara's eyes filled with tears. 'I'd never have started seeing you if I'd known.'

He leaned forward and took her hand. 'But that's why I didn't tell you.'

'I never wanted to hurt her.'

'Of course you didn't.'

'I don't know her. I've never met her. But you were together a long time. Of course she was going to be upset.'

He hung his head.

'You should have told me in the art gallery. Right at the very beginning. But you didn't even mention her.'

'I couldn't risk it. I thought if I told you, you wouldn't even let me buy you a cup of coffee.'

They sat in miserable silence.

Sara said, 'Why does Ursula think I broke you up?'

Mike shook his head. 'I've no idea. I've told her so many times.'

'Carys is her friend. I understand that. But she can't go round accusing me of things I haven't done.'

'I'll talk to her. I'll talk to her now.'

Sara sat in the bedroom, listening to their raised voices. The argument went on and on. After a while, Sara heard the front door slam. Mike came to find her. He looked exhausted. The story, when she finally got it out of him, was unbelievable.

Some months earlier, Ursula had shown Carys a picture of Sara on her phone. Carys, shocked, had recognised her straight away. She said they'd all lived in the same block when Mike and Carys were renting a flat in north London.

Sara frowned. 'When was this?'

'It was only a few months. The summer when Carys and I were looking for somewhere to buy.'

'But I've never lived in north London.' Sara was bewildered. 'She must be confusing me with someone else.'

Carys was adamant that she knew Sara well. Sara was house-sitting for a colleague at work who'd gone away for the summer and needed someone to feed his cats – she told Carys she'd never lived anywhere so luxurious and was loving every minute of it. They used to chat in the grand entrance lobby. Sara was really friendly and wanted to hear all about Carys's life, and what she liked doing, and her job at the children's charity, and conversation moved on to Mike, and his IT company, and how long they'd been together. Sara had wanted to know every detail of their relationship because she thought it was so romantic, first love, teenagers at the school gates, still together after all these years. Carys was surprised Mike didn't remember her too.

Mike remembered the block of flats – a 1930s art deco development that looked like an ocean liner from outside, with great sweeping white balconies – but he was sure he'd never met Sara.

'Because I never lived there,' said Sara.

Mike nodded. 'I told Ursula that Carys must have got it wrong.'

'But she won't listen?'

'No.'

Sara felt a little icy clutch of fear. 'So what did you say?'

'I said we were leaving.'

'Oh, Mike.'

'Ursula's stubborn. I've always known that. Decides something and sticks to it – she'll never admit she's wrong. But this is different. This really matters. I said to her, I don't know what Carys's problem is, but Sara doesn't lie. And if you're asking me to choose between them, you know what I'm going to do.' Mike looked desolate. 'Ursula said I just couldn't face the truth, so I said I was sorry, she was my sister and I'd always love her, but I thought we needed some distance between us.'

Sara couldn't bear to see the misery in his eyes. 'I'm sorry.'

'It's not your fault.' Mike tried to smile, but the muscles of his face weren't working properly. 'It's just a misunderstanding, that's all. We'll work it out. We'll look back on this in years to come and wonder what all the fuss was about.'

Ursula was very stupid. She didn't apologise – not then, not ever. Once or twice, when the boys were little, Mike suggested they should go and see her – she was in Australia by then – but Sara always found plenty of practical reasons why it wasn't a good idea. He stopped asking her in the end.

Sara knew that Mike and Ursula patched it up eventually. She knew they spoke on the phone and that Mike had even seen her a couple of times when he was away on business. But she suspected there was always a little crack in their relationship. Ursula could never quite forgive him for what he'd done to Carys.

Sometimes Sara wondered if Mike couldn't forgive himself either. Perhaps that's why he stayed with her, propping himself up with the odd affair, burying himself in his work. He'd already destroyed one woman's life. He couldn't face destroying Sara's too.

It was twenty years before Sara saw Ursula again.

By that time, Mike was dead.

It started innocuously enough. They had all filed back into the courtroom after lunch and were waiting for the coroner to reappear. The usher said, 'All rise,' as the coroner came into view, and everyone settled back down on the pale wooden benches.

Everyone, that is, apart from Ursula. She stayed on her feet, tall and straight, her whole body rigid.

People at the back of the court might not have heard her exact words because she started off in quite a quiet voice. 'I'd like to ask a question.'

The coroner had already shown himself to be a very polite man who recognised how stressful an inquest can be for the recently bereaved. 'Please go ahead.'

'Why is it a non-suspicious death?'

The coroner stared down at the stack of papers in front of him and said the information had been in the police reports, which he was happy to read out again if that would help. Ursula said she remembered the police statements, but that she didn't understand.

'What don't you understand?'

'Why the police made that decision.'

Sara started shivering as if a cold wind was blowing through the room.

The coroner frowned and said that he wasn't clear how he could help her, not because he didn't want to help her, but because the decision about whether or not to treat a death as suspicious is taken by the police officers who first attend the scene, in consultation with superior officers who review their conclusions.

Ursula said – and everyone in the court must have heard this, because her words rang out like a cry of pain – 'And that's it? We just take their word for it?'

Sara's hands were shaking so violently that she had to press down hard into her lap to make them still.

The coroner looked at Ursula over the top of his glasses as if they were the only two people in the room. He said that he'd explained at the beginning of the day's proceedings that the purpose of the inquest was to establish the facts about her brother's death – who he was, when and where he died, and the medical cause of his death. From this, he would decide by what means the death had occurred and record a conclusion. It wasn't a trial, and there could be no language of blame or accusation.

Then he paused for a moment, to be sure he had her full

attention, and said, 'We welcome any information you may have that might increase our knowledge and help us to understand the facts. Is that the case? Do you have further evidence to give us today about Mr Parsons's death that we have not already heard in court?'

Ursula sat down very suddenly as if her legs could no longer support her.

The coroner leaned forwards. 'Is there any further evidence that you would like to tell us about?'

There was a moment of tension, when it felt as if the whole courtroom was holding its breath.

Ursula shook her head.

And at that point, Sara knew it was over.

The ending came quickly after the long and tedious proceedings. It was all dressed up in fastidious legal language, but the decision was quite clear: accidental death.

The relief was so great that Sara couldn't see or hear for a while. It was only after she was outside in the reception area and she had been hugged so many times that she felt like a child's flannel, dirty and slightly damp, that it finally began to sink in. Joy spread through her, running like electricity through her veins.

Mike's death had been an accident. No blame. No horrible repercussions. The period of waiting was over. Life could begin again.

It was, of course, natural that there should be a bit of discussion about Ursula's embarrassing interjection as they all milled about in the lobby afterwards. There were odd mutterings and a few raised eyebrows. But luckily most people hadn't really heard what she'd said, and thought she'd just got in a muddle about one of the police statements. Someone said they'd always thought she seemed a bit flamboyant, and perhaps she'd just wanted a moment in the spotlight before the final decision.

Ursula herself was nowhere to be seen.

Eventually everyone started to leave. Mary Miller was picked up by her old friend Ailsa – the sexual health nurse – in a small red Audi, and all the others spread themselves out between various cars for the drive back to the village. By the time Sara had found Katie and they were ready to go, the sky was pale grey and there was a sharp wind picking up litter and sending it scurrying along the pavement.

As Sara and Katie left the courtroom, they saw Ursula standing on her own by the iron railings smoking a cigarette. The car park was almost empty – just a few lone cars.

Sara said, 'Do you want a lift?'

It seemed important to be magnanimous in victory.

Ursula turned to face them, her eyes black against the whiteness of her face.

Sara kept her voice neutral and friendly. 'I could drive you to your hotel if you like.'

Ursula stared across the shallow stone steps, her dark hair blown round her head like the brim of a wide hat.

Sara said, 'Or you could come back with us for something to eat.'

Ursula pulled her coat more tightly round her tall, thin body, dropped the cigarette butt, and ground it out with the toe of her shoe.

Sara hesitated, standing there with Katie, both of them buffeted by small gritty gusts of wind.

Ursula said, in a loud carrying voice, 'You killed him.'

She began to walk towards them, each long slow stride

reducing the space between them. Sara couldn't help herself. She looked over to the car, parked by the exit barrier, measuring the distance, wondering whether to run.

Ursula stopped right in front of her. 'I don't know how you did it. But you got him to take an overdose. You crushed up the pills and made him swallow them. And then you lay down next to him all night while the hours passed and his heart beat more and more slowly. And then it stopped. And in the morning he was dead.'

A blast of wind blew round their legs, flapping coats and scarves.

'I thought, if I came back today, someone might listen.' Ursula's eyes were glittering with tears. 'But they didn't. No one listened. They didn't want to know.'

Katie shot Sara a quick glance. But Sara wouldn't look at her. She kept staring at Ursula.

'My brother was a good man. He could have been happy.'

Sara felt very tired. 'You don't know what you're talking about.'

'But I do, Sara. That's the problem. I do know what I'm talking about.'

Katie found her voice. 'I don't think—'

'I know everything you did. All the punishments and humiliations you put him through day after day. For what? I don't know. For not being the man you thought you'd married. For not loving you enough. For not understanding your emptiness and loneliness and self-hatred. But it doesn't make any difference. Because there's nothing I can do. Nothing.' The weariness in her voice was bone cold. 'I can't fight you any more, Sara. I give up. I'm going home.'

Ursula turned and started walking away.

Katie said, 'She can't just—'

'Let her go.'

'But Sara—'

Sara said, her voice sharp, 'Let her go.'

They stood there, shivering, watching as the black line of her body became more and more distant before disappearing altogether round a street corner.

After that final confrontation Sara could hardly stay upright. She wanted to sink down on to the old gravelly tarmac, among all the windblown litter.

Katie insisted on driving. She said Ursula's mad accusation must have been a terrible shock. As she drove, she kept shooting Sara anxious glances, but Sara just sat there on the front seat, staring straight ahead. She knew that Katie wanted to talk – wanted to help neutralise Ursula's latest vile calumnies – but she couldn't face any kind of conversation. Even the thought of it made her feel sick. All she could focus on was getting home. When the silence in the car became oppressive, she turned on the radio. There was a drive-time chat show with a phone-in about the closure of the local psychiatric hospital. No one cares about mental health, said an angry voice, cracked with pain. My wife was so depressed she ended up killing herself.

There were roadworks on the bypass, and they got stuck at the red lights behind a long line of cars and a horse-box.

It was nearly five when they picked up Edward from school. She hadn't wanted him to come home on the bus to an empty house so had arranged for him to stay on. He seemed tired and disoriented, staring at Sara with a blank expression as if he wasn't really sure who she was. The journey home was interminable. By the time they crunched over the gravel past the stone urns, every part of Sara's body was prickling with misery. The last thing she needed was Bundle's enthusiastic welcome as he hurtled into the hall with a joyous volley of barks.

Katie took charge. 'I'll take him out.'

'You've done enough. You should go home.'

'Just a quick walk.' Katie was determined. 'Or he'll bark all night.'

The silence, once Edward and Sara were alone, was like a cool bandage on a swollen wound.

She took a deep breath. 'It's all over now.'

He said, 'Over now.'

Which, as she thought later, just goes to show how wrong you can be.

Sara and Katie should have talked. That's what should have happened. When Katie got back from walking Bundle, they should have gone to the kitchen and made supper and opened a bottle of red wine. Later it was obvious how much they needed to confide in each other. Sara was at breaking point. If they'd talked, Ursula's accusations outside the court would have been taken apart and seen for what they were – grief that had become ugly and evil and intent on destruction. How could Sara have crushed up painkillers and made Mike swallow them? Was he the kind of man who would meekly do what his wife said? Why would she want to make him take an overdose anyway? The whole thing was ridiculous.

That vicious remark about Sara having no friends was equally stupid. Sara had lots of friends. They'd been there in the courtroom, supporting her.

She and Katie should have pulled apart everything Ursula had said and dismissed it all as a package of lies.

But that night, coming back from the inquest, Sara was terrified. There was too much emotion. Her head was filled with noise, like the sound of crashing waves, and it was only by ignoring it that she had any control at all. If she turned to face it, if she allowed herself to see the force of all that energy, she would have been overwhelmed. She would have drowned.

When Katie returned with Bundle, Sara said she felt unwell and had to go to bed. Katie looked concerned, and sad, but what could she do? She said she'd be back in the morning.

After Katie left, Sara settled Edward in front of the TV and rang James. They'd already had a brief exchange of texts outside the courtroom, but she wanted to tell him exactly what the coroner had said.

He listened in silence. When she told him again about the conclusion of accidental death, he said, 'We always knew it was. But I'm glad everyone else knows too.'

Sara said, 'I can't believe it's all over.'

'But it is. That's it. No more mysteries.'

Sara didn't mention Ursula, or what she'd shouted out at the inquest, or what she'd said afterwards in the empty car park. James didn't need to know about any of that.

When the call was over, Sara went upstairs and ran a bath, and lay there in the deep water for a long time. She knew she should feel relieved. She knew she should feel the tension floating away. But this was the moment, out of all the weeks and months of pain and anxiety, when she finally hit rock bottom. She felt completely alone. As usual, Mike's voice was around somewhere (*Didn't quite work out the way you planned, did it, Sara?*), but only as background noise, like the radio turned down low. And although Edward was in the house, he'd never been much of a comforting presence. Companionship wasn't something he was able to do. You could be in the same room as Edward, even exchanging the odd word, but he would be in his head, and you would be in yours, and the only communal activity would be breathing the same air.

Sara started weeping into the bathwater. She shouldn't have turned Katie away. She missed her. It's easy to pick up on conversations you've had to abandon halfway through if you live in the same house. But now Katie was in her own house – probably, by now, in her own bed, wrapped round her beloved Danny – and Sara was the other side of the fence, and Katie had no idea how much she needed her.

Sara had always known that it would be hard when Katie left. But she still felt her absence acutely. Her heart hurt. Lying there in the tepid bath, she closed her eyes and imagined what it would be like if Danny went away again, and Katie gave up her damp and mouldy house and came back to live in the Old Rectory. Now that the inquest was over, there would be no anxiety, no financial worries. They would put the past behind them. The house was big enough for each of them to have their own space. They would live together in perfect harmony.

But that's not going to happen, is it, Sara?

An hour or so later, Sara cooked some pasta and she and Edward had a silent supper. Shortly after that, Edward went to bed.

Sara stayed at the table, looking out through the glass of the extension, the black night all around her. Her mind was fizzing with slivers of memory. Ursula was wrong. There was no emptiness, at least not in the early days. It was her confidence that had attracted him. When he finally told her about Carys, she could see why the relationship had been such a mistake. From the sound of it, Carys was clingy and insecure, leaning on him for emotional support. He didn't want someone weak and insipid. He didn't want someone who took up all his time. Sara's cool detachment must have come as a welcome relief.

She had looked at herself in the mirror of his adoration and liked what she saw. And he had gazed back at his calm, composed, self-sufficient wife and had congratulated himself on making such a clever choice.

Soon after they first got together, he said, with the big smile that broke up his rather pushed-together and dough-like face into something startlingly good-looking, 'You really don't need me, do you?'

'What do you mean?'

'I could disappear tomorrow, and you'd be fine.'

She didn't have a clue how to respond. He seemed to want her to agree. But how would that make sense? There has to be a certain amount of wanting the other's presence for a relationship to work at all.

She said, 'Are you planning to disappear?'

He laughed. It was hard to remember where they were when they had this conversation, but she could see the sun shining on the side of his face, lighting up the reddish stubble on his skin. He said, 'I'm going to be around for a long time, Sara.'

Which turned out to be true.

He loved her independence. It meant he never had to worry about her. If you set up your own company, you work long hours. You're hardly ever home.

She said, soon after they married, 'You're just trying to avoid me.'

'You don't believe that.' He looked anxious.

'Don't I?'

He took her face in his hands. 'It's all for you. I'm doing this all for you.'

Was that true? It's a convenient excuse when you're buried in a job you love. Work is selfish. You need enough money to live, to eat, to pay the rent. But after that, it's just extra.

He said, 'I'd give it all up in an instant if I believed that's what you wanted.'

But she'd never asked him to, so she didn't know if that was true either.

Sara stared into the darkness. Towards the end, when she'd got used to living without him, he said his only function was to bring in money and her life would be a lot easier if he wasn't there. It was one of his jokes, of course – his trademark dark humour, flung out on cold winter mornings as he crashed out of the house in a bad mood. She was never quite sure what to say. Disagreeing with him would have been dishonest because, by that stage in their relationship, his analysis was largely correct. She would have preferred a different kind of marriage, but that's what they'd ended up with, seemingly by mutual consent. So she couldn't disagree with him, but she couldn't pretend it was funny either, because it would have been too strange to stand in the hall laughing as her husband told her that he was unnecessary to her happiness. So instead she just looked at him, and he stared back, and after a while the silence became ominous and unpleasant and he said something angry like, 'For fuck's sake, Sara, I've got to go,' and slammed out of the house.

You would think they would have got the hang of conversational exchanges after twenty years. But it seemed to get harder, not easier.

She didn't want to remember any of it. She wanted to sit at the table and have nothing in her head at all, nothing but cool, empty darkness.

Once, out of the blue, he said, 'You make me feel like nothing.'

She didn't know what to say.

He said, 'Not wanting me. You make me feel like nothing.'

It always came back to sex in the end.

Sara thought, but sex is only a transaction. A contract agreed by both parties. You have to keep it in perspective.

He stayed because he couldn't walk out on his autistic son. That would have felt like failure. He needed his internal image of himself to be squeaky clean. He needed to admire himself.

If he'd been more of a bastard, they would both have been free.

A bastard. A bully and a bastard.

When she finally went to bed, she was sure it would be another night of insomnia. But she must have fallen asleep immediately, because she opened her eyes and there he was, the bulk of him just standing there, silent and accusing. She sat bolt upright in bed and stared straight at him as the outline of his body became less and less distinct, finally swallowed up by the darkness. She lay down again, shivering.

The dreams that followed were vivid and frightening. Part

of her knew they weren't real – just sickening delusions, a kind of waking nightmare. But they seemed so real, more like memory than fantasy. At one point, she was sitting in the grand, polished, black-and-white entrance hall of a block of flats – which she knew, as you do in dreams, was art deco, and that from the outside its sweeping white balconies made it look like an ocean liner – and watched as Mike and Carys came down the stairs. She could see her so clearly – blonde hair, a floppy faded dress in some kind of floral print with tangled tendrils of tiny leaves. Mike always said she was a bit of a hippy. More interested in incense and spiritualism than building up a business from scratch.

Sara marvelled at the detail of Carys's appearance, the way her mind had conjured up something so complete from remembered clothes in a wardrobe.

Mike and Carys reached the bottom step. There must have been something they had to decide about their plans for the day, because they stopped and looked at each other, standing there just in front of her, and their closeness was such that one glance was enough, one brief exchange that summed up all the possibilities, everything they'd discussed, and they laughed and made little clowning gestures as if to say, *Who cares? It doesn't matter*, and the decision was made and they could move on.

But that couldn't be right, could it? When he eventually admitted to Carys's existence, Mike said the relationship was over, that he and Carys had nothing in common, that they were only staying together out of habit and convenience. So how could they be so intimate? How could they talk with their eyes?

As Mike opened the heavy wooden door and stepped out

into the sunlight, his hand was beneath her elbow, guiding her through.

Sara's dream then cut to the same polished entrance hall, but this time she and Carys were sitting together on the curved wooden bench. Was this their first conversation? Their second? Sara was asking her how long she'd known Mike, and Carys smiled with the kind of bashful diffidence that seemed to be her trademark and said, 'Forever. Since we were thirteen. I can't imagine life without him.'

And Sara felt a cut to her heart – loneliness, perhaps, or grief, or a sense that something terrible had happened that could never be repaired and was somehow all her fault.

Just before dawn, she woke, covered in sweat. She could hear someone crying. After some time, she realised that the sound came from her own mouth and that her face was wet with tears. She sat up. The feeling of loss was a physical pain in her stomach, cutting her in two. Rocking backwards and forwards, soothing herself like a small child waking from a nightmare, she found herself shouting to the empty room, 'I never wanted to hurt her!'

Of course you didn't.

She looked round wildly, but he wasn't there – nothing but a grey and uncertain light as the darkness receded.

'She was kind to me.'

She was kind to everyone.

'She was my friend.'

You wanted to step inside her. You wanted to live inside her skin.

Sara shrank back, horrified.

You didn't really want me. I wasn't important – just an accessory, a way of feeling what it was like to be loved.

'That's not true.'

All that planning. All that effort.

She shook her head, trying to get rid of his voice.

Just so that I would look at you the way I'd looked at her.

She said, in a whisper, 'And then you stopped.'

There was no answer.

'Mike?' It was a plaintive cry, an exhalation of grief. 'Why did you stop? Why did you stop?'

But the room was silent.

The next morning, when Katie arrived to walk Bundle, the atmosphere in the house was tense and fractious. Sara's head was thick from dreams that clung to her like wet silk. Edward had only just left for school and Bundle was in particularly high spirits, jumping out at himself from behind hidden corners and knocking over the kitchen chairs.

Katie said, 'Are you feeling better?'

Sara nodded, unwilling to go into detail. 'Just tired.'

'I know what you mean.' Katie looked washed-out, as if she hadn't slept much either.

'Is everything all right?'

Katie hesitated.

'What is it? What's happened?'

Katie said, in a great gabble of words, 'I just wanted to say that I won't tell anyone what Ursula said. None of it, I promise. All that stuff about crushing up painkillers and making Mike take an overdose.'

There was a small awkward pause. Sara said, 'I didn't think you would.'

Katie swallowed. 'I thought you might be worried. Because of what happened at the funeral.' Her voice dropped to a whisper. 'Telling everyone about Mike.'

Sara said, in a cold voice, 'As I've said a number of times, that's all forgotten. We've drawn a line under it.'

Bundle barked, a short imperious yap to remind them that he was waiting.

Katie said, 'You can trust me. I want you to know that. I promise, on my life, I would never do anything to hurt you.'

Sara forced a smile. 'Of course you wouldn't.'

'I hated all the things she said. I kept thinking about them all night. They kept going round and round in my head.' Katie looked desperate. 'It's so frightening. You don't know what she's going to do next.'

'She can't do anything.'

'What if she comes back? What if she comes back and tries to stir things up again?'

Bundle let out a drum roll of barks.

Sara said, 'It wouldn't matter if she did.'

'What do you mean?'

Sara took a deep breath. It was important to reassure Katie that everything was going to be fine. 'We've had the inquest. The coroner heard all the evidence and recorded his conclusion. So we don't need to worry about Ursula's madness and anything she might say in the future. She can rant on all she likes. No one would believe her.'

'You're sure?'

Sara said, her voice calm, 'I think we should forget all about her.'

There was a moment while Katie thought about this. Then the cloud of anxiety lifted from her face and she smiled.

After Katie had left, Sara sat quite still, staring into space.

She hadn't anticipated Katie's reaction. This frightened her. She didn't like feeling out of control.

An hour after this exchange, the doorbell rang. Sara dragged herself to her feet and went to answer it.

There on the stone steps, against the background of red and golden leaves, stood not only a windblown Katie and an over-excited Bundle but a short balding man in a grey coat and wire-rimmed glasses, gazing at Sara with friendly recognition.

'Sara,' said Katie, 'it's Mr Roslyn.'

Sara recoiled. The last time he'd been in her kitchen, he'd gone on and on at her with such ferocity that she'd dissolved into tears.

Mr Roslyn said, 'Would it be convenient to have a word?'

'Not really,' Sara said. 'It was my husband's inquest yesterday and we're all exhausted.'

But somehow after that small explosion of defiance, all the fight went out of her, and she stepped back and let him in.

It was lucky that Katie had come back with Bundle just as Mr Roslyn was leaning on the doorbell. His interrogation would have been much worse if Katie hadn't been there to defend her.

As Sara led Mr Roslyn across the stone floor of the hall, Bundle raced ahead, all the way through to the kitchen extension, and started yapping at the garden. Sara put the kettle on while Katie slid back the great glass doors, and they watched as the dog shot over the lawn and disappeared into the shrubbery out of view. Soon afterwards, they heard his usual manic barking.

'It's the compost heap,' said Katie.

Such was the bewildering surrealism of the morning – a private investigator arriving hours after an inquest – that this remark passed without comment.

It was a relief to sit down with a full pot of coffee. Sara thought she might fade away altogether without an injection of caffeine. After only a small hesitation, because she didn't want to encourage him, she offered Mr Roslyn the biscuit tin. 'So how can we help you?'

Mr Roslyn must have thought they looked tired and distracted, because he went right back to the beginning. He had been hired to find Sara's old au pair Hilda, who had managed to go travelling without telling anyone where she was going. Although she'd tried to impress Sara in her original job interview with stories of a big family and a huge number of brothers and sisters – perhaps to make herself seem like the kind of easy-going person who would be good with small children – she was, in fact, an only child with very few relatives. As a result, the emails, texts and phone calls that normally fly around a close family were non-existent. No one had been in contact with her for some time. Mr Roslyn, because he had very little else to go on, had decided to go all the way back through her life in order to track down where she might have ended up, which was why he'd paid that very fraught visit to the Old Rectory some weeks before.

Although on previous showing a rather pushy interrogator, Mr Roslyn took some time to warm up on this occasion and didn't immediately answer Sara's question as to how they could help him. Instead he began a rather lengthy explanation of standard procedures in the search for a missing person. Because of all the stress and exhaustion of the past few days, Sara found it impossible to concentrate. At some point, she drifted off, only coming to when she realised that both Mr Roslyn and Katie were looking at her expectantly. It was clearly some time since Mr Roslyn had stopped speaking, and she couldn't recall a single word he'd said. She had no choice but to play the sympathy card. 'I'm sorry. I'm so tired from yesterday that I wasn't really listening. What did you say?'

Mr Roslyn frowned. 'That I haven't been able to find any evidence of her whereabouts since the time she lived here with you.'

Sara was surprised. Most people don't admit so readily to failure. 'So what will you do?'

He fixed her with a serious stare. 'I wondered if we could talk again about what happened on the day she left.'

'Sara is really very tired, Mr Roslyn.' Katie's expression was stern. 'If there's any chance that we could do this another time—'

He cut her off. 'I'm asking a lot. I do understand that. But without more information I'm at a dead end.'

Katie opened her mouth to speak, but this time it was Sara who interrupted. Her voice was high and strained. 'A bargain, Mr Roslyn. I'll tell you what I know. But then you must go. Do you understand? After that, no more questions.'

After a brief hesitation, he nodded.

In fact, there were no great revelations. It all boiled down to such a small story. Sara told Mr Roslyn that she'd known about Hilda's affair with Mike, but had hoped, if she ignored it, that the whole thing would just peter out. She explained that she had been utterly dependent on Hilda, because Hilda had been so good with her autistic son – she was one of the very few people he tolerated when he was small – so Sara had been wary of doing anything to upset her. But then came the day when she came home from shopping, laden down with plastic carrier bags, to find four-year-old Edward lying on the floor with a livid bruise on his forehead. Sara said that it was hard to explain quite how much that had affected her, except to say that the bond with her son was such that, on seeing the contusion, she felt as if she, too, had been coshed. She felt the pain. She felt dizzy, as if she were losing consciousness. Hilda rushed to reassure her. She and Edward had been in the garden, and she'd been distracted for a moment, just a moment, had turned her back, and he'd fallen down the stone steps near the willow tree. He hadn't cried for very long. It looked worse than it was. He'd let her apply some arnica.

Sara's response had been totally irrational. The whole thing was clearly nothing more than an accident. But she shouted at Hilda. She told her she was stupid and incompetent. She accused her of not caring. She said she couldn't trust her.

Hilda became tearful, and then angry, and at some point in the row that followed, with Edward screaming on the floor with his hands over his ears, she said that Mike was right, and Sara was totally insane. When Sara asked her what she meant, Hilda said, 'You know what I mean.'

They stood there, staring at each other, and Sara said, 'Don't. Please don't.'

And Hilda said, 'What do you care? You don't want him.'

It was hard to explain the significance of that exchange, but both Hilda and Sara knew exactly what it meant. Hilda was challenging Sara to face up to her affair with Mike. Obviously, she had thrown out the words in the heat of the moment. They weren't meant to have any lasting impact. But for Sara it brought everything to a head. As she explained to Mr Roslyn – Katie watching, her eyes huge with sympathy – she realised with sudden clarity that the situation couldn't continue. She took a deep breath, and asked Hilda to leave. Hilda tried to apologise, but Sara wouldn't listen. She just kept saying that she had to go. Eventually Hilda saw that she wouldn't be able to change Sara's mind, so she went upstairs, packed her stuff together, and left.

'What time was this?' Mr Roslyn was busy scribbling in his notebook.

'I'm not sure. Around lunchtime.'

'Do you remember what she was wearing?'

'No.'

'And where did she go?'

Sara shook her head. 'I don't know. I didn't talk to her again. I was in the kitchen with Edward and heard the front door slam.'

Mr Roslyn looked up. 'She didn't drive, and she didn't have a car, so she must have got a lift? Or a taxi?'

'Or walked,' said Sara.

'With a heavy suitcase?'

Sara felt hopeless. 'I don't know. I don't know what she did.'

'You didn't worry about her? Want to check to see she was safe?'

Quite suddenly Sara couldn't stand it any more. The strain of the day before collided with the stress of remembering an incident she thought she'd buried a long time ago, and she wanted him out of the house. Her voice was shaking. 'We had a bargain, Mr Roslyn. I said I would tell you what I knew. And then, once I'd finished, you'd go. No more questions.'

The light from the window flashed on his glasses. 'Yes, of course. I'm sorry. You've been very kind to give me so much of your time.'

As he fussed about, gathering together his belongings, Sara wondered if she should get up and see him out, but exhaustion seemed to have crept into her bones and immobilised her.

Katie went with him to the door. On the threshold of the kitchen, he turned and faced her. 'Just one more thing, Mrs Parsons. Did anything get left behind?'

'Like what?'

'I don't know. Anything that belonged to her. It can happen when people leave in a hurry.'

'No.'

'Nothing?'

'No.'

As his footsteps echoed in the hall, she felt a clamp around her forehead, and a weight on her chest, making it hard to breathe.

On Saturday morning, coming out of the village shop, Sara found herself face to face with Rachel. Her heart sank.

'I'm sorry I couldn't come to the inquest last week. I couldn't get time off. But I heard it went well.'

Sara nodded.

Rachel said, 'You must be so relieved.'

Sara always found it irritating to be told what she must be feeling. She would much rather come to her own conclusions. What was the point of a conversation if everything was decided before you'd even started? 'I am, yes. I'm really glad it's all over.'

Rachel settled the hessian bag on her arm. 'I saw him in the village.'

Sara was lost. 'Who?'

'That young man of hers. The one in the black coat.'

Sara wondered why this was supposed to be interesting.

'Loitering by the post box talking on his phone.'

'Customers, I expect,' said Sara. 'Talking to customers about windows.'

'You'd think he might want to sit in his car to carry out business negotiations. The Ford Mondeo. With the alloy wheels.'

On the way home, Sara found herself gritting her teeth with irritation. Rachel wanted to make her feel uncomfortable. Why? By the time she'd put away the shopping, Sara had decided that she'd had enough of people altogether. They were too complicated. Much too hard to understand. She was exhausted.

Unfortunately, there was more to come.

When Katie finally turned up, an hour late, to take Bundle for his afternoon walk, Sara was so shocked by her appearance that she insisted she sat down and had a cup of tea. It transpired that Katie had been so busy dog walking that she'd somehow managed to skip both breakfast and lunch.

'Bundle can wait,' said Sara. 'You've got to eat.'

When she next turned round, Katie's face was awash with tears.

It didn't take long to get the story out of her. Katie hadn't wanted to bring it up before the inquest because it seemed so trivial compared with what Sara and the boys were going through, but the worry had been eating away at her. The night before the inquest, she'd met up with Anna in the Goat and

Anna had asked if Danny was looking for a job. Katie had been confused, and said that Danny already had a job, selling windows. Anna had shaken her head, and said, 'Not any more.'

According to Anna – who had heard this from Baz – Danny had come back to the area because he'd been sacked.

Sara was surprised. 'Sacked?'

Katie nodded.

'Why? What happened?'

Katie didn't know. But Baz said that Danny was working out his notice. In a month's time he'd have to give back the Ford Mondeo.

Katie was at a loss to know what was going on. It was true that Danny hadn't exactly lied. Technically speaking, he was still a window salesman with a company car. But shortly he wouldn't be. So he hadn't exactly told the truth, either. On one level, his equivocation was understandable. It's humiliating, losing a job. It's not something that's easy to talk about. But Katie was still upset. She'd thought the reconciliation between them was so complete that they could tell each other everything. Why had Danny wanted to keep this from her? Did he think she'd love him less if she knew?

'I wish he'd told me, Sara. I wish I'd known.'

'He probably didn't want to worry you.'

Katie looked dejected. 'I just don't want us to have any secrets from each other. Not after all we've been through.'

Sara didn't want to trash her romantic illusions, tempting though this was. 'He probably wanted to wait until he had some good news. I bet you he's out looking for a job at this very moment.'

Katie looked up, her face full of hope. 'Do you think so?'

'Definitely.'

After she'd finished her sandwich, Katie took Bundle off to Smith's Field and Sara was left alone to mull over their conversation. She thought about Katie's determined attempts to understand her worthless boyfriend and felt very sad. From what she'd seen so far, the only person who mattered in Danny's life was Danny. He was selfish and calculating, and never stopped to consider Katie's feelings.

With sudden blinding clarity, she knew that he was going to break her heart all over again.

Sara had neglected the garden. She could see that the next day, when she went outside the minute Edward had left for school. The chaos was no longer lovely but threatening and slightly needy, as if the plants were trying to leave the ground and march towards the house. Sara set to, pruning and cutting, taming the penstemons and anemones, the salvia and phlox. The day was brisk and businesslike, with clear skies and a gentle breeze, and she congratulated herself on the wisdom of getting out of the house and doing something she loved. You can analyse too much. You can end up thinking so hard that you miss the big picture altogether. Katie should be her focus. Katie had given her so much love and support, and now it was Sara's turn to repay the favour.

Quite soon, pulling and digging, clearing and weeding, Sara was covered in sweat. She thought about Katie's faith in Danny, her perpetual optimism. Katie was a romantic. She was the kind of person who liked pretty flowers but didn't want to think of their roots in mould and bacteria. But I know what sins people are capable of, thought Sara, straightening up. I know they're cruel and manipulative and driven by self-interest. Katie is innocent. She sees only the best in people. It's my job to protect her.

She had a sudden sharp memory of an argument with Mike years before. She couldn't remember what it had been about, but he'd been irritated, scornful.

He said, 'Why don't you just try getting on with people for once?'

She had looked at him in astonishment. 'What do you mean?'

'You always act as if someone's out to get you. What's the point? Live and let live.'

But compromise, thought Sara, lifting up an armful of leaves and stems and dank-smelling weeds to put them on the compost heap, has never been in my nature.

On the Monday afternoon after the inquest, Katie crunched back over the gravel, Bundle straining at the lead, to find a police car in front of the house. When she passed the open door of the living room and glanced in to see a uniformed police officer and his crackling radio on one of the big white sofas, her face was the picture of shock.

'Katie!' Sara said. 'Come in! Do you remember PC Bush?'

Katie said something about letting Bundle out into the garden, and while she raced after him towards the kitchen, Sara reminded PC Bush that he'd met Katie before – she was their dog walker and had been in the house the night Mike died.

Katie came back, looking anxious, and Sara took a deep breath and said, 'We've been burgled.'

'No!' Katie's cry was heartfelt. 'What's been taken?'

'All my jewellery.'

'Oh, Sara.' Katie sat down. 'That's terrible. When did it happen?'

Sara was embarrassed that she didn't really know. 'I found one of my rings on the windowsill in the bathroom, opened the drawer in my dressing table to put it away, and it was empty. Cleaned out. Everything gone.'

'Everything?' Katie's eyes were big with concern.

Sara nodded.

'Someone broke in?'

'Not that we can see,' said PC Bush. He turned back to Sara. 'Is there an alarm?'

She nodded. 'But I don't usually turn it on. Because of the dog.'

What she meant was that she couldn't risk it because Bundle was so unpredictable, leaping up walls and crashing into windows, that he might set it off. But she realised that she'd given the misleading impression that his barking was enough of a deterrent for them not to bother, which sounded so much more mature and grown-up that she let it stand.

PC Bush said, 'Is it possible that you left a window open or a door unlocked?'

Sara felt tears pricking her eyes. 'Very possible. I'm not really thinking straight at the moment.'

'You know about the inquest,' said Katie to PC Bush by way of explanation, and he nodded.

'I feel so stupid not even noticing.' Sara swallowed. 'I can't even remember when I last opened the drawer.'

PC Bush looked grave, as if he completely understood the strain she must be under. 'I'll have another scout round and see what I can find. And we'll send someone over to dust for prints, just in case. Although they usually wear gloves, I'm afraid, so we may not be lucky.'

Boots creaking, he went out to the hall.

Katie said, 'I'm so sorry, Sara.'

Sara could feel her mouth trembling. 'Even my engagement ring's gone.'

Katie reached out her hand.

'I've described everything as well as I can. And given him some pictures I took the last time we had the valuable items insured.' Sara shook her head. 'I just wish I could remember when I last saw it all.'

'With all you've been through,' said Katie with great firmness, 'it's not the least bit surprising.'

After PC Bush had gone, Katie stayed on for a cup of tea. Sara was pleased. Their chats were so infrequent these days. But it turned out that Katie was just killing time. Danny was going to be late home. 'He's gone to London to see a friend.'

'London?'

'I know. I thought it was a long way, too.' She looked anxious. 'But I thought maybe it might be about a job. He's probably pursuing all sorts of leads.'

Over the next few days they kept missing each other, so Sara didn't find out for some time that Danny's London visit had turned into a bit of a holiday. He didn't return for three days. As Katie rather reluctantly admitted to Sara later, this wasn't the first time it had happened – his movements were fairly unpredictable, and he quite often disappeared for long periods of time. But he got irritated if Katie started making a fuss about where he was going or what he was doing, so she tried not to ask too many questions.

Sara's heart sank. All the old habits were reasserting themselves – and Katie was colluding in it every step of the way. Sara had to keep reminding herself that Katie was very young, and it was natural for her to make mistakes. But it was still hard to see a friend heading off down the wrong path.

Poor Katie. Worse was to come. The next morning, as she followed Bundle through the graveyard on the way to Smith's Field, her mobile rang.

As she told Sara later, it had all begun when she turned on the shower one morning and got nothing but a freezing drizzle. The boiler in her dilapidated house had finally given up the ghost. She left a message with her landlord, asking if he knew anyone who could fix it. She wasn't expecting him to pay to have it mended – that would have been unreasonable, given that she was living there rent-free – but was just hoping for a recommendation or a steer in the right direction. Now, standing in a windswept corner of the field, Katie listened, her mobile clamped to her ear, as he told her that he'd been round to have a look, and the boiler was beyond repair – it just wasn't worth the risk. All the mould was a bit of a shock, too. He'd no idea it had got so bad and was worried it was breaching health and safety – he didn't want her getting sick and ending up in hospital with pneumonia. So basically he thought it was probably time for some major renovation.

'Oh,' said Katie, as she and the phone were buffeted by a sudden gust of air. 'What kind of renovation?'

This was the point in the conversation when the signal dipped, so she kept missing parts of what he was saying, but he seemed to be talking about not getting permission from the council, which didn't make a lot of sense. Then, as the wind howled about her, whipping her hair around her face, Katie suddenly heard his voice clear in her ear. '. . . so I've had a word with a mate, and he's going to go through and do all the basics – damp-proofing, rewiring, re-plastering, the whole works.'

'OK,' said Katie. 'That's fine.'

He sounded relieved. 'I know it's not easy finding some-where to live. But I'll keep my ears open.'

As Katie rather urgently made it clear that she wasn't sure she'd quite understood, he explained that he needed her out within the month so that the house could be gutted and renovated. For a moment, she felt intense relief. She and Danny would end up with a nice new house. But the reprieve was short-lived. Her landlord was going to do up the house as cheaply as possible because he was putting it on the market. The council wouldn't give him permission to concrete over the garden, and he wasn't allowed to knock it down and build something bigger, so he was just going to sell it. The minute the paint dried, he was getting rid of it.

Katie made a small, brave attempt to suggest that it might be better to have a tenant while he was renovating and selling, but he was quite adamant.

'End of the road, Katie.' He cleared his throat. 'You've got four weeks. End of November.'

When Katie had brought this rather brutal story to a close, she looked utterly defeated. She said, not meeting Sara's eyes, that she had no idea how she and Danny were going to be able to find a place they could afford and was really scared they were going to be homeless.

There was a small, awkward silence.

Sara said she'd love to help – of course she would – but there was a bit of a problem, which of course Katie knew about already. Edward was fine with Katie, and Katie was welcome any time, but he'd go into meltdown if a strange man came to live in the house. Sara couldn't do it to him – not now, when he was already so fragile because of the recent disappearance of both Mike and James. So she couldn't offer them a room. She was really sorry, but she just couldn't.

After a small pause, Katie nodded.

They sat there as the day gradually died, the silence stretching out in the empty space around them.

The next day, thinking that Mary with all her contacts might have some ideas about how Katie could solve her housing crisis, Sara paid a visit to her cottage on the main road.

As Daisy dozed at her feet, Mary listened to the whole story. She was sorry to hear that Danny had lost his job and wanted to know what he was doing to find another. Sara told her about the trip to London.

'I'm not sure that's going to help.'

She nodded. 'But Katie's hopeful. She has great faith in him.'

Mary sighed. 'I just don't see how they can afford to pay rent if their only income is a bit of part-time dog walking.'

The next morning, Katie arrived at the Old Rectory just before eight o'clock all lit up with happiness. Danny had come back from London with pockets stuffed full of cash.

Sara was astonished. 'How come?'

A little shamefaced, Katie said he'd put money on a horse. 'But it means we can afford a deposit now.'

Just after lunch, Sara fed this back to Mary over a cup of tea. As she chatted on about flat-hunting and how excited they'd be when they finally found a new place and were handed their very own set of keys, Mary seemed distracted.

Setting her cup in the saucer, she looked up. 'Keys?'

'To the front door,' Sara said, wondering what she was missing.

Mary looked worried. 'He's an honest young man, is he?'

'I've never met him.'

Mary was surprised.

Sara smiled. 'I just hear all about him from Katie.'

'When did he come back to the village?'

Sara thought hard. 'About a month ago, I think.'

'Moved straight in with Katie?'

Sara nodded.

'And when did Grace lose her grandmother's bracelet?'

They stared at each other across the table.

As soon as Sara understood the implications of what Mary was saying, she shook her head and said it was impossible. It just couldn't have happened. Mary, pink and flustered, agreed. But they carried on looking at each other with a kind of silent horror. The dates fitted. The facts fitted. It all seemed clear cut.

Sara said, in a hoarse voice, 'My engagement ring.'

'Of course, it might be a complete coincidence.'

Sara nodded.

After a pause, Mary said, 'Where does she keep the keys?'

Sara could hardly bear to answer. 'On little brass hooks in

the kitchen. But he wouldn't do that to her. It's the worst kind of betrayal.'

Mary's face was very sad.

Then Sara remembered what Rachel had said about seeing Danny in the village on the day of the inquest. She told Mary he'd been seen loitering by the post box, just five minutes from the Old Rectory.

'Oh no,' said Mary.

Somehow, at the exact same moment, everyone in the village started to make the same connections between people and events, and the vast beam of their suspicions swung round on to Danny. He had access to all the keys. He could easily have let himself into Grace's house in Meadow Rise – there had been no sign of forced entry – and stolen her grandmother's gold bracelet. On the day of the inquest, when the whole village was sitting in the courtroom listening to the sad story of Mike's accidental death, he could have strolled up the gravelled drive of the Old Rectory, unlocked the front door, and searched the house until he found Sara's jewellery. The trip to London was to get rid of it all. Shortly afterwards, his pockets were full of cash.

It was despicable. It was disgusting. How could he have taken advantage of Katie's neighbours like this?

By the time Katie, blissfully ignorant of all the gossip, had taken Dexter up to the top of Ogden Hill, the rumours had rushed round the village like a small fire.

Poor Katie, looking out over the bypass, knew nothing of this. Her mind was on Danny, and the puzzle of why he was so unenthusiastic about the viewing she'd arranged for a run-down short-let studio flat above the discount carpet warehouse on the industrial estate. She had spent the whole of the bracing walk wondering how she could persuade him that it was probably the best place they could afford.

When she finally delivered Dexter back home, Rachel sat her down and told her with characteristic bluntness that people were worried that Danny was responsible for all the recent break-ins. The rumour was that he'd gone to London to sell the stuff and was now flush with cash on the proceeds.

Katie came round to the Old Rectory, her eyes red from crying. 'How can people be so horrible?'

She'd had a shock. Sara put sugar in her tea. 'Don't worry. They've just got nothing better to do. It'll all die down very soon.'

But it didn't. Someone tipped off the police. Unbeknownst to Katie, Danny had been in trouble many times before. He had form. Officers went round to his last known address – his nan's house in the terrace by the railway line – and found in her spare room, in old shoe boxes piled high to the ceiling, stolen goods from local burglaries dating back over the past two years.

As Mary said, he'd be lucky to stay out of prison this time. You can try people's patience only so far.

Grace said he must have been kicked out of his job for thieving. It made sense. You only need a few rumours going round about a light-fingered salesman for a company to lose its reputation completely.

Sadly, Danny's arrest didn't help Grace or Sara recover their possessions. Grace's grandmother's rose gold bracelet was never found. None of Sara's jewellery turned up either. Danny must have already sold it. It had all completely disappeared.

★

Katie was heartbroken. She had only just got Danny back. And now, because of his criminal record, he could end up with a custodial sentence.

In the days following his arrest, this was all she could think about. She was desperate to help him. She sat with Sara for hours over cooling cups of tea, talking about books she'd read and films she'd seen, and how a good barrister could argue your case and get you off on a technicality. She was going to stand by him. She would wait for him. He could rely on her.

Sadly, she wasn't able to prove any of this. Danny cut off all contact. It turned out that he'd decided to blame her for the tip-off to the police. Once out on bail, he went back to the hovel when she wasn't there, let himself in, and picked up all his stuff. The only difference was that this time he left the spare key on the draining board by the sink so that she knew his departure was final.

It was torture. There were a couple of days after he dumped her for the second time that Katie didn't even make it in to walk Bundle. Sara went round to the house, but the curtains were drawn and no one answered the door.

In the village, the recent shocking events were endlessly discussed. A sudden death, a scandal about sex workers, a spate of burglaries – daily life seemed to have turned into some kind of soap opera.

Many of the conversations that Sara overheard were deeply unsettling. She once called into the shop to pick up some overpriced white wine and found Mary in full flow, Daisy like a large fur cushion at her feet. When Sarinda looked up and saw Sara standing there, she opened her eyes really wide to warn Mary to stop, but Mary didn't cotton on fast enough and said, 'You can't live with someone without picking up the odd clue. She must have known what was going on.'

Worse was to come. When Sara heard whispers that Katie had not only known about Danny's burglaries but was also his accomplice, she grabbed her coat, and rushed straight round to the portacabin. She had only been there a few minutes when she heard Sally Cook say that Katie was having a terrible time, what with being evicted from her house, and Mary said that it seemed Katie's parents had just abandoned her and were giving her no support at all.

Sara couldn't hold back any longer. 'That doesn't mean she stole anything.'

A small circle of faces turned towards her.

'There is no way that Katie knew what Danny was doing.' Her voice rang out. 'She wasn't involved at all.'

'Of course she wasn't,' said Mary.

Sarinda looked confused. 'Do the police think she was?'

Later Sara wondered if she'd made the whole thing worse.

It wasn't long before the slanderous rumours reached Katie's ears. Gossip as vicious as that whipped round the village like a virus. Katie wept, sitting at the table in the glass extension, wondering how her friends could think her capable of stealing from them.

'It's all a mistake,' said Sara. 'We'll sort it out.'

Katie looked up, her face stricken with fear. 'What if they decide they don't want me to walk the dogs any more? No one wants to employ someone they can't trust.'

'Don't worry, Katie. It'll all die down.'

'They might ask for their keys back. I would, if I thought someone was stealing from me.'

For her own part, Sara knew that Katie was guilty of only

one thing. She had loved Danny with all her heart. Her infatuation had blinded her to his true nature. It would never have occurred to her, as she hooked the keys on to the little rack in her kitchen, that he would use them to burgle her neighbours' houses.

As the days passed, Sara worried more and more about the febrile atmosphere in the village. Katie tried to ignore it but was constantly aware of people staring at her. She began to look drawn and ill. Sara was concerned that she was turning in on herself, becoming isolated and detached.

One afternoon she asked if Katie had made any progress in finding somewhere new to live.

She hung her head. 'I haven't been looking.'

This was quite a shock. 'But when do you have to be out?'

'About a week.'

'Where will you go?'

Katie swallowed. 'I thought I'd be able to stay with Anna. But it turns out her aunt and the twins are there until Christmas. So they haven't got any space. Not even on the living room floor.'

'So what will you do?'

Katie's eyes filled with tears, as if Sara had pushed her into a bed of nettles.

It was worse than Sara had feared. Depression had settled on Katie like a blanket, depriving her of the ability to act. Sara took a deep breath. 'Come back here. Just till you've sorted yourself out.'

Katie looked despairing. 'You shouldn't have to—'

Sara cut her off. 'Edward and I would love to have you. It's decided. You're coming.'

So Katie moved in, back into her old room, and Sara

heaved a sigh of relief. Now she could make sure that Katie was eating properly and went to bed on time and didn't spend hours staring at her phone, waiting for the text from Danny that never came. Sometimes she drove her all the way into lectures and picked her up again afterwards. She helped her with her coursework and her reading and bought her little treats whenever she went out shopping – dark chocolate truffles, peppermint tea.

Katie said, 'You shouldn't be doing all this.'

Sara smiled. 'Why not? We're friends.'

James sounded cool on the phone when she told him that Katie was living at the Old Rectory again. 'Hasn't she got a life?'

Sara said, 'It's just to tide her over.'

'She's like one of those ear mites that live on dogs. Or a bed bug. Or a tick. Something you can't get rid of.'

'James, stop it.'

'Hasn't she realised there's a world out there?'

'She's like me. She likes a quiet life. She likes living in the country.'

He laughed.

She said, hurt, 'I don't criticise your friends.'

'That's because I don't tell you about them.'

It was meant to be a joke, but it wasn't funny.

Sara ended the call soon after that, feeling unaccountably upset.

With Katie back in the house, the residual tension left over from the inquest – particularly the memory of Ursula's astonishing outburst – began to fade away. But Sara still felt unsettled. She slept badly. Time passed with great speed, even though she didn't seem to be doing anything useful – indeed sometimes, at the end of the day, she was hard-pressed to remember anything she'd done at all. To begin with, frightened by this blurring of hours, she was tensed for some of Mike's more cutting remarks, certain that he wouldn't miss this golden opportunity to point out how much her standards had slipped. But he seemed to have become much less critical in recent weeks. There was a warmth and friendliness about him that made his company enjoyable. Sometimes she could almost feel him smiling.

This was especially true when she was dealing with Edward. Mike was right in her ear then, showering her with praise. She'd always been the one to look after Edward because Mike had been away so much. Most of the time, she rose to the challenge. Edward was her son. It didn't matter whether he was four or fourteen – it was her job to take care of him. But there were days when she was tired and overwhelmed – when he went on and on and on about something new or uncomfortable or surprising or noisy that she just couldn't change, that she just couldn't make go away, so that she could almost see another version of herself, angry and irrational, turning on him, shouting at him, reducing him to tears – and then she could hear Mike saying, *It's all right, Sara. It's OK. You're doing your best* just like he did all the time Edward was small, her lifeline of reassurance when she needed more patience to cope than she could possibly drum up from the bottom of her exhausted soul, when the only thing that kept her going was his unerring belief that they'd get through it together somehow.

Mike wasn't a saint. He loved business, opportunities, making money. Sometimes he forgot to put his family first. But he had always tried, in his own way, to make things better, to make sure they had enough, that Edward's future was secure. It was true, what Mary had said. He made regular donations to three autistic charities. He said that he and Sara couldn't change the past, but they could try to make sure that other parents had a better experience of diagnosis and support, and weren't left on their own for years struggling to cope. He said, you have to hope for a better future. You have to look after those who need help.

Sometimes, digging outside with a trowel in the garden, Sara would sit back on her heels and think of the early days when the boys were small. They got lost somewhere, she and Mike. It was hard to pinpoint how and where it happened, but there came a time when everyday life was overlaid with a kind of mist. At the beginning, they could talk. He didn't always agree with the way she focused so completely on her younger son, but he understood that she had no choice. Later, as time passed, he was less sympathetic. He couldn't see why everything had to be so rigid, why she couldn't move beyond the designated pathways she insisted upon.

It became hard to remember a time when he looked at her with affection or spoke to her with anything other than irritation in his voice.

Then there was the affair with Hilda. Even now, Sara could close her eyes and see her standing there, blonde hair awry, her sweet expression screwed into pugnacious contempt. She was in the wrong, and she knew it. The weakness of her position made her spit like a cornered cat.

'Why do you care? You don't want him.'

After that, she had to go.

Sara was the loser in the end. The atmosphere in the house had been quite happy while Hilda and Mike were having it off. Once she'd gone, it became tight and mean. The sunshine had gone out of his life. He became angry and irritable, a default position that became so entrenched that the lines of his face were redrawn.

He had other affairs over the years. She was sure of that. Some months there was a lightness about him again – he would sing in the shower, and take James out to the park to play football, and buy her bunches of flowers. But he was careful never to grind her face in it again. He had learned that much.

His sustenance came from work. He was proud of what he'd achieved. Sara thought that most of his emotional life came from his colleagues and employees – a committed group of people with the same joint goals.

One afternoon, she was dusting the desk in his study – she liked to keep everything clean and tidy in there, just as she had when he was alive – when she came across the phone, the one she'd found in the glove compartment of his BMW. It lay there in her hand, a stubby little silver thing, and she couldn't believe that something so small had started a scandal with such huge repercussions.

He said, *Why did you do it, Sara?*

She didn't jump out of her skin. She had got used to him being inside her head, and nowadays this was a kinder incarnation, a man who sounded as if he genuinely wanted to know what she thought.

She said, 'I had to stop her. For the boys' sake. I had to stop people listening to her.'

But that story – that long story about the texts and the porn and the prostitutes. You made it up. The whole thing.

'It could have happened.'

But Sara, you didn't tell everyone it was a possibility. You said it was true.

She said, a little uncertain of her facts, 'Wasn't it?'

There were no texts. There were no prostitutes. There were no secret bank accounts.

'What about the phone?'

It was Edward's phone. Don't you remember? The first one he ever had. I bought it for him when he started school so he could ring you if he was afraid.

There were faint stirrings of memory. But she couldn't be sure. He might be bluffing, trying to put her off the scent. 'You were away so much. All those conferences. All those hotels. You had to be getting it from somewhere. If you weren't having affairs, you must have been paying for it.'

You blackened my name.

Sara took a deep breath. There was a limit to her patience. 'You deserved it.'

Why?

Her head was hurting, that sensation of something tight round her skull. 'Because you made me feel like nothing.'

She didn't want to hear his reply to this, so she put her hands over her ears, like a child.

That night, when she went to sleep, she curled herself into a ball, as far away from Mike's side of the bed as possible.

★

Because Katie had moved back in, Sara was able to help her through Danny's first appearance at the magistrates' court at the beginning of December. Even on the morning itself, she tried to stop Katie going. She knew that turning up at the hearing would set her back and churn up all the old unhappiness. But Katie was adamant. She said someone had to be there to support him.

As usual, she put other people before herself.

It was a miserable experience. Sara had been keen to see the legendary Danny in the flesh and had to concede, when she finally set eyes on him, that he had a certain louche charm. But she was shocked by the way he stood there smirking, as if the whole thing was a joke. All he had to do was confirm his name and address and put in a plea – he said he was not guilty, which was ridiculous – but he turned the whole thing into an excruciating pantomime, an elaborate charade, raising his eyebrows and pulling stupid faces. Where was his dignity and restraint? Sara was so embarrassed she could hardly bear to watch.

Outside, in the icy cold, Katie's normally dewy complexion had flattened into something papery and grey.

'Why don't we go and find a cup of tea?' said Sara, thinking that Katie looked as if she might collapse at any minute.

Katie shook her head. 'I just want to go home.'

After the hearing, the atmosphere in the house was bleak. It would be at least another month before Danny's trial, so they were stuck yet again in a period of waiting. Sara tried to be sympathetic. She didn't want to appear selfish and uncaring. But there was a tiny part of her that was getting slightly bored with all Katie's moping around. The outcome of the trial was a foregone conclusion. Danny would go to prison. Because the only possible variable was the length of the sentence, it was time for Katie to accept the inevitable.

More importantly, Sara felt that Katie was missing the crucial point. Danny had never been right for her. He had made it clear he didn't want her and had recently cut off all contact. Surely the time had come to move on. Katie, after all, was living with her best friend in a beautiful house in the middle of glorious English countryside – rent free, all bills paid – and had her whole life ahead of her. Wasn't it time to put the past behind her?

Of course, the intense local interest in Danny's arrest and court appearance didn't help Katie to master her feelings. Her sad coterie of friends in the Goat, excited by the scandal and the drama, gathered round to offer support. But their interest just stoked Katie's despair. She became the centre of attention at a time when she really wanted to hide away and grieve. As she said to Sara with some sadness, it wasn't even any fun going out for a drink any more – every session in the pub turned into an endless discussion of Danny's chances.

Further misery awaited her in the charity shop, where Katie had gone to seek solace from Anna. One Saturday afternoon, Katie looked up from a rail of frayed cardigans to find herself facing Maxine. This was horribly embarrassing. The last time they'd spoken on the phone, Katie had been brimming with confidence. Danny had just returned to her welcoming arms, and she'd told Maxine that everything was going so well she didn't need therapy any more.

When Katie relayed this later, Sara was slightly alarmed. 'But you're not thinking of going back to her, are you?'

Katie looked desolate. 'I don't think she'd want me.'

Maxine had apparently been in a bit of a hurry – some

kind of counselling emergency – so couldn't hang around chatting. But she had given Katie one of her withering glances and said she'd heard all about the arrest. She hoped Katie now realised that she had idealised Danny and projected all her fantasies of true love on to someone totally inappropriate.

As Maxine's gleaming black boots marched out of the shop, Katie had hidden herself in the stockroom and wept.

Somewhat to her surprise, Sara found herself thinking that Maxine was completely right.

Over the next few days, Sara decided that what they all needed to cheer them up was the prospect of a happy Christmas. She felt a little thrill of joy at the thought of James coming home. Katie hadn't mentioned anything about going to Spain to see her parents. Was it possible that she too might be persuaded to spend Christmas at the Old Rectory? Sara could see it now – turkey and Brussels sprouts, silly jokes and paper hats. She imagined them all in the great glass room at the back of the house, sitting round the table laughing.

One afternoon Katie took the Polo to pick up two heavy bags of Bundle's special diet dog food from the vet. Because she disliked him so much, Sara often overcompensated where Bundle was concerned. Even his Welsh wool dog blanket was handmade.

On her return, Katie dragged the bags to the utility room and sat down with Sara at the table, looking thoughtful.

'Tea?'

'Yes please.' Katie hesitated. 'You know that time you saw Grace's Ryan down the alleyway?'

'When he was with that girl?'

'Yes.' Katie screwed up her face, puzzled and confused. 'I was thinking about it when I was driving back from the vet's, and feeling really sad, because Grace and Ryan are so unhappy without each other. And I was driving past Sainsbury's Local and the Goat, just like you did, and the lights went red, and I stopped. And I looked out of the window and I couldn't see down the alleyway at all. You can't even see the start of it. You have to be a lot further on down the high street.'

'How funny,' said Sara.

'It's strange, isn't it?'

'I definitely saw him. You couldn't mistake Ryan.'

After a pause, Katie said, 'Maybe it was after the lights. Maybe you were stuck in traffic.'

But Sara had got up to open the great glass doors for Bundle who was hurtling towards the house from the end of the garden, hoping it was time for his walk.

Grace found her bracelet. It had fallen down behind the curtains and settled itself into the tiny gap between the carpet and the skirting board. She was lying in bed reading, with just the lamp on by her side, and she'd seen something glinting at the far side of the room. At first she thought it was a trick of the light. But she was curious enough to get up and investigate, and when she realised what it was she was so overcome with joy and relief she burst into tears. She couldn't think how it had got there. She must have taken it off, and put it down on the windowsill, and been distracted perhaps by something going on in the street outside, and drawn the curtains forgetting what she'd done. And then, somehow, it had slithered off the windowsill, fallen to the floor, and hidden itself from view.

She was mortified. As Katie told Sara later, she took time off from the salon specially so that she was at home in Meadow Rise when Katie came round to walk Lulu. She made Katie a cup of tea, and sat her down at the kitchen table, and said she was really, really sorry. The bracelet had been in the house the whole time. No one had stolen it. Her Danny was completely innocent.

'Oh, Katie,' said Sara, who had been listening attentively.

'He never broke in. It had nothing to do with him.' Katie looked grief-stricken. 'But it's not just that he didn't steal anything from Grace. It's that people jumped to conclusions because of Grace's bracelet and your jewellery, and all sorts of horrible rumours started flying round, and because of that someone told the police, and they went to his nan's house and found all the shoe boxes. If they hadn't gone round there, he'd still be free.'

Clearly the police would have caught up with Danny eventually. But Sara felt this wasn't the moment to point this out. 'It's so sad.'

'Grace was really upset about Danny's arrest. She said she knew what it was like to lose the love of your life.' Katie paused. 'And I said to her that if she still felt that about Ryan, she should go straight round and make it up with him.'

Sara was surprised. There was a different tone to Katie's voice. 'What did she say to that?'

'She cried quite a lot. She said it had hurt so much when she thought he was cheating on her. And I said, well, that was only a rumour, too. A bit of gossip flying round the village. So maybe that wasn't true either.'

Sara bridled. 'I saw him.'

'I know.' Katie kept her eyes on Sara's face. 'I know you saw him. But it doesn't matter, does it? What's important now is that they get back together.'

It was such an unusual experience having Katie stand up to her that Sara was unable to think of a suitable reply.

Sara had the uncomfortable feeling that things were sliding out of control. It didn't help that she was finding it harder and harder to sleep. She tried everything – warm baths, milky drinks, lavender oil on her pillow – but felt so wide awake when she got undressed at night that she found herself gazing at the big, wide bed with despair.

She gave Mike short shrift if he tried to start a conversation in her head. To be fair, he was still being kind rather than critical. But he kept asking questions she couldn't answer, like why she'd tried to make Katie believe that he was up to no good whenever he shut the study door. He said he knew that Sara had a very low opinion of men in general, and that there might be husbands and partners who spent hours every evening watching porn on their laptops, but it wasn't true in his case, and he'd only ever been trying to catch up on work. Sara found this rather whiny self-justification very irritating because it was all water under the bridge and there was really nothing she could do about it after all this time.

Sometimes she was tempted to be quite rude and tell

him he had no right to demand explanations. But then she remembered he was dead, and felt sorry, because he was probably feeling at a bit of a loose end.

There were times when she got tired of lying there hour after hour staring into the dark and decided it would be better to get up and occupy herself with useful tasks. She couldn't keep her mind on reading or listening to podcasts or watching films, but practical jobs like cleaning shoes or clearing out drawers were somehow both soothing and absorbing. The difficulty at night was making sure she was quiet and didn't disturb Katie or Edward. She didn't always manage this. Once, in the early hours, she was rearranging the occasional tables in the living room when Katie appeared in the doorway, anxious and sleepy, wondering what she was doing. Sara had to pretend she'd been tossing and turning worrying about a lost earring and had decided in the end that she might as well just get up and look for it.

Her great joy, of course, was using these periods of wakefulness to prepare for Christmas. Katie said she thought her parents were spending Christmas Day with another ex-pat couple they'd met on the golf course, so she probably wouldn't be going to Spain at all. She was very touched to be invited to the Old Rectory, but a bit worried about barging in on a family celebration. She thought that James might like to have his mother and brother to himself. But Sara was adamant that they'd love to have her and, in the end, Katie tentatively agreed.

In celebration, Sara bought an enormous tree – the ceiling height could take it – and abandoned her usual minimalism in favour of sparkle and bling. Every single branch bristled with decorations, many of them home-made. Sara surprised herself with creative wellsprings she hadn't even known existed. Many of her more exciting nocturnal adventures involved paper and glue, and she had even experimented with stringing up dried pasta bows that she'd painted red and sprinkled with glitter.

During the day, Sara cleaned the house. She quite enjoyed polishing and dusting. For a while, when she was working in the wills and probate department, they'd employed a cleaner, but Sara had always hated the idea of a stranger snooping through her personal possessions. Quite apart from this, she loved the Old Rectory with such a passion – she had always been terrified that if she and Mike split up she might lose it altogether – that it felt only right she should be the one to buff it to a shine.

Sometimes, standing in the double-height hall as the cold December light gleamed on glass, marble and stone, Sara shivered with delight at the thought that the house, the whole house, now belonged entirely to her. Its lines calmed her. Its spaciousness enchanted her. It was her sanctuary, her refuge, her home.

One evening her phone rang, and James's voice filled her ear.

'Oh,' she said, suffused with delight, 'it's you! When are you coming back?'

'Tomorrow, if that's OK.'

Sara did a quick mental tour of the house. It was ready. Everything was prepared. 'Yes, of course. What time?'

'I was wondering if I could bring a friend.'

'A friend?'

'Yes.'

Sara felt suddenly cold. 'Of course.'

'You don't sound very sure.'

Sara swallowed. 'What kind of friend?'

'What do you mean?'

'Well,' said Sara, in a brisk kind of voice, 'will you be sleeping together?'

There was silence at the other end of the phone.

'I need to know.' Even to her own ears, she sounded much too loud. 'I might need to make up another bed.'

He sounded weary. 'It doesn't matter.'

'Of course it matters. They can't sleep on the floor.'

'Would you rather they didn't come?'

Sara felt a rush of embarrassment, or possibly horror, that made it impossible to speak.

James said, 'Just forget it.'

'No,' Sara was panicking now, 'no, you don't understand.'

'It was a bad idea. I see that now.'

'What do you mean?' Her voice came out as a wail.

'I thought it was Dad. But it wasn't, was it?'

'Please, James, please. Please come.'

He said, 'I don't want an argument. I really don't. I'll ring in a couple of days.'

'James—'

'Say hello to Edward for me.'

After he'd rung off, she stood there, quite still, a statue of ice.

It didn't seem possible that she and James had fallen out.

One afternoon, the doorbell rang. Sara wasn't expecting anyone. Edward was at school and Katie was out somewhere, probably walking one of the dogs.

When she opened the front door and found Rachel standing there, Sara couldn't believe her eyes. They weren't close friends. Sara was pretty sure that Rachel didn't even like her. But, more importantly, it was a weekday morning, and Rachel should have been at school, teaching algebra and percentages and haranguing teenagers about not doing their homework.

She said, 'Can I come in?'

Still dazed, and slightly apprehensive, Sara stood back and let her pass.

Rachel stopped in the hallway, as if struck by something strange. Sara was waiting for the usual comment about the hugeness of the space – the double-height hall, the chandelier, the sweeping stone staircase with the iron balustrade – but all she said was, 'Are you moving?'

'No. Why?'

'All the boxes.'

Sara hadn't really thought until that moment what the results of her recent nocturnal activity would look like to outside eyes. 'Just clearing out a few things.'

Rachel seemed surprised. 'But there's so much of it.'

Sara said, 'I don't like clutter.'

She led the way to the living room and Rachel sank down on to one of the big white sofas. For the first time, Sara was uncomfortably aware that the room looked rather strange. There was almost nothing in it apart from an enormous fir tree covered in rubbish. Had she gone too far? She was just wondering why she'd taken down the mirror above the fireplace, and what she'd done with the little grey button-back chair, when Mike wandered in and went to sit on the sofa next to Rachel.

Sara stared. Mike looked fit and relaxed, and was smiling the way he used to when they first met. The whole thing was extremely unsettling – it was awkward enough having Rachel in the house – but Sara resolved to carry on as if everything was perfectly normal until the situation became a little clearer.

She said, 'So what brings you here?'

Mike smiled. *Do I need a reason?*

Rachel said, 'I was just passing.'

The last two remarks had come out in stereo so it took Sara a while to work out who'd said what.

'Coffee?'

Rachel said, 'I can't stay long.'

That's a relief.

Rachel said, 'I'll come straight to the point. Katie's a bit worried.'

Sara was taken aback. She didn't think Katie ever confided in Rachel. 'Danny's arrest has been a nightmare for her.'

Rachel leaned forwards. 'She's worried about you.'

Why?

Sara's hands were trembling so much she had to lace her fingers together to keep them still. 'Why?'

Rachel said, 'She thinks you've been under a lot of strain.'

'Well, obviously,' said Sara.

It's only a few months since your husband died.

Sara glared at Mike to shut him up.

Rachel said, 'You're acting out of character.'

Mike laughed.

Sara said, 'It's not funny.'

Rachel looked taken aback. 'I didn't say it was.'

This isn't going very well, is it, Sara?

Sara was finding it hard to keep her temper. 'Keep out of it.'

Rachel looked shocked. 'Of course, if you'd rather I did. I just wanted to know if you needed help.'

Mike was grinning from ear to ear.

'Rachel,' said Sara, with some desperation, 'I don't mean to be rude. I'm sorry. I think it's grief. It makes me very abrupt.'

You were always abrupt.

'I don't want Katie to worry,' she said loudly, trying to drown out anything Mike might begin to say. 'She's probably right, and I'm not myself at the moment. But there's been so much going on.'

She thought, with sudden clarity, that it was very important not to mention James. She didn't want Rachel asking any questions about Christmas.

Rachel took a deep breath. 'She says you don't go to bed at night.'

Sara wanted to disagree but was suddenly unsure. She looked at Mike, who gave her rather a pitying look and shook his head in sorrow, as if this was something she should have worked out for herself. This was quite worrying. Sara knew she had periods of wakefulness but didn't realise she never went to bed at all.

'How does she know?'

Rachel's expression was very gentle. 'She can hear you pacing from room to room. Sometimes you even talk to yourself. When she asked you about it, you said you couldn't go to bed because there was too much to do.'

'I've got a lot on my mind.'

'Of course you have,' said Rachel. 'You've had a very stressful time over the past few months. But if you're having trouble sleeping, why don't you go and see the GP? Just to get yourself checked out?'

'I don't like doctors,' said Sara.

They didn't help me much, did they?

Sara found her eyes filling with tears. 'You know, I still can't believe Mike's dead.'

'That's perfectly natural.' Rachel fixed her with her usual steady gaze. 'But you don't have to cope alone. We're all on your side, Sara.'

Don't believe a word of it.

'I'm not on my own,' she said. 'I've got Edward. And Katie.'

And me.

Rachel hesitated. 'Katie's got her own problems, though, hasn't she?'

That made Sara very cross. Katie hadn't got any problems at all now that Danny had gone. It was just taking her a long time to realise it. She said, in a tart voice, 'It might have helped if people hadn't spread such horrible rumours about her.'

Rachel gave her a very strange look. For a moment, Sara thought she was going to come out with one of her more abrasive remarks. But instead she took a deep breath. 'You're absolutely right. Malicious gossip doesn't help anyone.'

Eventually, after a little more conversation about stress and looking after herself and promising not to empty the house of all its furniture, Rachel said she wouldn't keep her, because she was sure Sara was very busy, but she must promise to call if she needed any help.

After she'd gone, Sara stood in the hall, thinking about what Rachel had said. She couldn't be entirely sure when her habit of staying up at night had started, but she had an uncomfortable feeling that she hadn't slept properly for several days.

I must ring James, she thought. I'm still not clear when he's coming home for Christmas.

She went into the kitchen to make a cup of tea. Mike had got there first and was sprawled at the table, comfortable and relaxed. When he saw her, he looked up, his expression slightly sheepish.

She said, 'I do wish you wouldn't interfere.'

You've never liked her.

'That's not the point. It was kind of her to visit.'

Was it?

'You shouldn't even be here.'

But I can stay, can't I?

'For the moment,' she said, in what she hoped was a firm voice. 'Just until I've worked out what to do.'

Mike's face stretched into one of his more attractive smiles.

Katie was out when PC Bush turned up.

Sara smiled. He had such lovely blue eyes.

'May I come in for a moment?'

Sara led the way to the huge empty living room.

He said, 'Getting ready to decorate?'

Sara didn't answer.

'My wife's the same. Always wants the house spick and span for Christmas.'

Sara gave a tight little smile. She wasn't sure she liked being compared with his wife, who might be a very nice person, but might equally be someone of limited intellectual abilities.

He hesitated. Sara sat down and he followed suit.

She said, 'So how can I help you?'

PC Bush had taken off his helmet and seemed to be studying it closely. 'We've had a visit. A Mr Roslyn.'

'Oh yes?'

'I believe he's spoken to you a couple of times?'

Sara looked vague but didn't disagree.

'He's making enquiries about a young woman who went missing twelve years ago.' The constable hesitated, choosing his words with care. 'There have been discussions at quite a high level . . .' He stopped, as if he needed to be sure that these were the right words '. . . and our Chief Constable has asked us to make further enquiries.'

Sara put on an expression that she hoped conveyed both surprise and co-operation.

'I do realise this is a busy time of year, and we all know how difficult it's been for you recently. But we wondered whether you might be able to come in to the station and give us some assistance?'

'In what way?'

'If you could answer some questions and make a statement, that would be very helpful.'

'But my son's due home at any moment. His first term at university.'

PC Bush nodded as if he completely understood. 'Maybe one day next week? I said I'd ask, as I was passing. I wanted to explain in person.'

'Next week? The week before Christmas?'

'It wouldn't take long.'

Sara sighed. 'Is it really necessary?'

He looked apologetic. 'I think it might help.'

He really did have such lovely blue eyes. 'I could probably find half an hour. Perhaps when I'm out shopping. Shall I give you a ring when I've had a chance to look in my diary?'

PC Bush smiled. 'That would be very kind, Mrs Parsons.'

In the hall, just as they reached the front door, he turned to face her. 'You can't think of anyone else, can you, who might be able to help with our enquiries?'

Sara shook her head. 'It was all so long ago.'

After he'd gone, Bundle started barking, so Sara opened the glass doors and watched as he raced up the garden. I don't really mind making a statement, she thought. It's only fair. The police were so kind when Mike died. And from a selfish point of view, it might put an end to Mr Roslyn's rather disturbing visits. He did seem very persistent given that there was so little to say.

The frozen garden stretched out in front of her, petrified in the cold sleep of winter. She thought she might just prune the dead wood from the acer, a particularly lovely tree with leaves that turned dark red in the autumn. You had to be very gentle, of course. You couldn't rush in and cut any old how. You had to know when to stop.

When she came in from outside, her face cold, Mike was in the kitchen. It was a slight shock to see him in person again, but at the same time immensely reassuring. He really did look well – so much younger than when he'd died. The lines of pain and anger had disappeared. He had his shirt-sleeves rolled up like he always used to in the old days, and he seemed relaxed and content, as if he'd just been sitting there at the kitchen table thinking about nothing very much while he waited for Sara to appear again.

She smiled at him, and he looked up and said, *Will you tell them?*

'Tell them what?'

Will you tell them what really happened with Hilda?

She pulled a face to show him what a silly idea that was.

What about me? Can you tell me?

Strangely, she didn't feel surprised or defensive. She didn't rush to change the subject or try to distract him. It seemed for the first time an entirely reasonable request. Why shouldn't Mike know what had happened? So Sara put down her secateurs with the sharp curved blades and bright red handles, and peeled off her thick protective gardening gloves with padding round the base of the thumb so that you don't get blisters when you've been digging in the earth all day, and she sat down opposite him, in the great glass extension at the back of the house, and told him the same story she'd told Mr Roslyn, the private investigator, some weeks before.

But this time she added in a lot more detail. She wanted to give the best account she could. Mike deserved that, after all this time.

She didn't shirk. She told him that she and Hilda had been arguing about their affair, and that her dear little face had been twisted with fury and contempt when she spat out, 'Why do you care? You don't want him.'

Poor Mike. That was hard for him to hear. Years ago, all she'd said was that Hilda had left suddenly, and he hadn't pressed her for details. How could he? He'd been sleeping with the au pair under their roof. He had to accept whatever she decided to tell him.

But now Sara said that after packing her stuff and coming downstairs, Hilda hadn't walked through the hall and slammed out of the house, as she'd told Mr Roslyn, but had come into the kitchen to say goodbye to Edward. This was a kind and sensible thing to do. It had the potential to upset him, of course, but Edward was going to be upset anyway once he realised she'd gone. Hilda was one of the very few people he could tolerate when he was young.

So Hilda put down her bag and her grey wool coat and squatted down next to his chair. Edward – who still had the livid bruise on his forehead, the original cause of their argument – gave her a quick blank look and turned back to his cars. He had five small metal cars that he carried around with him everywhere – green, red, blue, yellow, black.

She said, 'Goodbye, Edward. I'll miss you.'

He adjusted the fine positioning of the yellow car so that it was exactly in line with all the others.

Sara said, 'It's time to go.'

Hilda stood up, her usual sweet expression back in place – she really was extraordinarily pretty – and said, as if they were talking about something charming and inconsequential like Faroese puffins, 'You know, I wasn't the first, and I won't be the last.'

That hurt, but Sara didn't let it show on her face. She wanted the ending, at least, to be civilised.

Sara followed her back out to the hall. At the foot of the stairs, Hilda stopped to put her coat on, easing her arms into the sleeves. She said, in a speculative kind of way, 'I don't like going without saying goodbye to Mike.'

He was away on business in Berlin.

Sara pushed her. It might have been that she was frightened Hilda was going to change her mind and wanted her out of the house as quickly as possible. But she had forgotten how small and light she was. One shove sent her flying. Her bag at her feet tripped her up and her arms were straitjacketed in her coat, so she fell backwards, unable to save herself. Sara heard the crack as her head hit the black iron banister. She ended up half standing, half sitting, against the curve of the stairs, her blonde hair over her face, like a drunk propped up by a brick wall. Sara tried to pull her to her feet, but she said something angry and incomprehensible, so she backed off. It was humiliating and embarrassing for them both. In the end, because she couldn't get her balance without the use of her arms, Hilda let Sara help her take off her coat, but she was obviously still in shock. Sara said she should sit down for a while.

Edward swivelled round as they came back into the kitchen, Hilda leaning on Sara's arm.

Sara said, 'She fell down, Edward. Just like you did in the garden.'

Hilda looked pale as if she'd hurt herself more than she wanted to say.

Edward said, 'Bang.'

Sara smiled. 'Bang.'

After a while, to her relief, Edward turned back to his cars.

She tried to apologise but Hilda wasn't really listening. After a while she interrupted and asked if Sara could call her a cab to the station, which Sara felt was the least she could do in the circumstances. Because she was flustered, and couldn't find her phone with all the taxi numbers programmed in, she began one of those hopeless searches that get more and more impossible the longer they carry on. She was in the hall, hunting through a pile of flyers and junk mail, when she heard a noise behind her. Hilda had pitched forwards on to the stone floor and was lying full length on her side, her eyes wide open.

As Sara told Mike all those years later, sitting at the table, it was obvious she was dead. But at the same time it made no sense at all. Can people die like that? One blow to the head? Sara knelt down on the floor next to her, staring at her blank eyes, trying to work out what to do. There didn't seem to be any point in ringing for an ambulance, because no hospital could bring her back to life. She thought of the repercussions of reporting her death. Then she thought about not reporting it at all. James was at school, but due home in a few hours' time. Edward was still in the kitchen, playing with his cars. The boys were her priority.

Eventually, Sara grabbed hold of Hilda under the arms, lifted her shoulders from the floor, and dragged her through to the downstairs toilet. She wasn't heavy, just lumpen and unyielding, as if she was being deliberately unhelpful. Sara covered her face with the hand towel. Then she locked the door from the outside.

Later she said to James, 'Hilda's gone home. Back to the Faroe Islands.'

Edward said, 'Bang.'

She smiled at James. 'Your brother hurt his head. He fell.'

Edward's bruise had turned dark purple.

The next day, she and Edward came home after taking James to school and she spent all day digging a big hole in the garden, about halfway up by the vegetable patch. Edward was quite happy playing with the woodlice under the terracotta plant pots on the patio, and racing his cars down a wooden plank into a puddle, and they only had to stop a couple of times – once to make a sandwich, and once when the yellow car fell into the drain. James was going out to tea with a friend straight from school, and being brought back home later by the friend's nanny, so at the end of the afternoon, when Edward was inside watching TV and the whole garden was pitch black, Sara dragged Hilda out through the sliding doors.

The Old Rectory was surrounded by very high hedges. And these were pre-Bundle days, of course – there was no dog to get overexcited over a small rigid body.

The following day, Edward and Sara went to the garden centre and bought a very large wooden composter, which they had delivered, for an extra fee, a few hours later. It was quite expensive because it was made of sustainable wood and high-quality durable materials, but Sara thought it was probably a good investment. It looked good on top of the newly dug earth. The delivery men, after she'd tipped them, helped her hammer the posts into the ground so that it was completely secure, a permanent fixture.

Sara said to Mike, 'I had to think of winter weather. Storms and gales and high winds.'

Mike seemed to understand. His expression didn't change.

The next day, she burned most of Hilda's clothes on the bonfire, constantly stoking up the flames to be sure that everything was reduced to ash. Edward watched from a safe distance. He didn't like the sting of smoke in his eyes, or the crack and snap as the wood caught fire.

A few of the better items she took to the charity shop in the nearest town – the one that Anna ended up working in as a volunteer years later. It seemed wrong just to destroy things that could make money for a good cause.

Sara didn't tell this last part to Mike, because it didn't seem that relevant – all water under the bridge – but she did exactly the same with his antique Rolex after she'd stolen it from under his nose. It had been an impulse to hide his most treasured possessions and watch him lose his temper when he couldn't find them – a silly, childish, pathetic impulse, born out of a desire for revenge. But she had cause. All those weeks of autocratic bullying when he couldn't go in to work and had to run his business from the sofa. All those weeks he shouted at her so that she couldn't think straight and kept locking herself in the bathroom to cry. To make herself feel better during that period of incarceration when she was his secretary, his chauffeur and his personal servant, she carried out all sorts of petty acts of defiance, like pretending she'd misheard and bringing him extra strong mints when he was shouting for his painkillers, and making sure she was out of the house at the exact moment when an important delivery of company documents was scheduled to arrive. It was sad to look back on it. But she'd wanted to hurt him as much as he was hurting her.

Later she couldn't remember whether she'd even got any enjoyment from it in the end, stealing his valuable possessions and watching him stomp round the house in a rage looking for items that had mysteriously slid out of reach. She did wonder whether she should own up, or come up with some story about tidying them away in the wrong place, but she didn't have the courage once he'd reported everything to the police. It seemed easier to let sleeping dogs lie.

The keys and the laptop she took to the council refuse

centre wrapped in a black plastic sack, and hurled them into one of the bins.

But she couldn't bear to trash the watch. It was valuable, and a thing of beauty. She wrapped it in newspaper and posted it through the letter box of the charity shop.

It didn't seem too much of a risk. It really wasn't likely that anyone would suspect a loving wife of playing a horrible trick on her husband.

James wasn't answering his phone. This didn't worry her. He was probably very busy packing up all his stuff and getting ready to come home.

Outside in the cold December air, Sara walked through the garden, leaning down to pick up stray twigs and leaves. It was so peaceful. You couldn't hear any of the neighbours, of course, because the house was so isolated. But you couldn't hear any traffic either. The Old Rectory was much too far from the main road and hardly anyone came this far up the spindly lane. James would be so looking forward to recharging his batteries in the quiet and calm of the countryside. You could really relax when you were this far away from other people.

She wasn't concerned about their slight disagreement. It bore no resemblance to the explosive arguments she had with her own mother all those years ago – standing on the scuffed wooden boards of the hall floor, shouting up the stairs at top volume that she was going to London the minute she finished school because she was being suffocated, she couldn't breathe, she needed to get out while she could. Sara smiled. She had a very different relationship with James. Her own mother had been frightened and depressed, using every trick in the book to stop Sara leaving home because she didn't have the inner resources to cope alone. Sara, on the other hand, fully accepted James's need for independence. She had completely understood that he had to leave to continue his education – she had even persuaded him to change his mind when he'd been thinking of spending a year at home after Mike had so unexpectedly died.

Of course, when he'd finished his studies, he might come back to the Old Rectory. It was hard to find the money for rent when you were just starting out, and it made sense to take up offers of free accommodation from friends and family. Sara enjoyed picturing the four of them in the house together, pursuing busy independent lives – James and his brother, she and Katie.

Sara could feel Mike on the edge of her consciousness, desperate to know how he fitted in. She blocked the thought.

The secret, she thought, was all in the planning. So many people didn't bother to think ahead. Imagining all those wasted opportunities made Sara feel sad. You can't blunder through life, reeling from crisis to crisis. You need to be sharp. You need to be clever. You need to use your brains.

Sara remembered how Katie had once, with great earnestness, tried to persuade her that they should dig up the compost heap to see what Bundle was barking at. The postman had told her that non-stop noise wasn't normal animal behaviour. He could hear the poor dog all the way round the cul-de-sac.

Sara had said, as gently as possible, 'Do you have any idea what goes on in a compost heap?'

Katie bit her lip.

'All sorts of tiny animals and insects are busy breaking down decaying leaves and rotting vegetable peelings and old tea bags and shredded paper. And all these slugs and snails and beetles and earwigs are attracting birds and frogs and hedgehogs. So what you've got is a warm, smelly, rustling pile of movement and constant surprises. It would be extremely strange if Bundle didn't find this interesting. And unfortunately he's the kind of irritating dog who expresses his interest with continual loud barking.'

Katie looked embarrassed. 'So we don't need to dig it up?'

'No.'

'Because it's completely normal.'

'Sadly, yes.'

'The postman seemed so sure.'

Sara smiled. 'You shouldn't always believe what people say.'

The last thing Sara was expecting was a difficult conversation with Katie. She had genuinely thought that the turbulent events of the past year had been laid to rest, and that they could all look forward to the future with confidence.

A lovely Christmas, after all, was just on the horizon.

But it turned out that she was wrong.

It was a normal, mid-week morning. Edward was at school,

and Sara had just come back from one of the cheaper super-markets on the other side of town where she still went sometimes to stock up on bulk buys of essential food items like tinned plum tomatoes and basmati rice. Since the insurance policies had paid up, money was no longer a problem. She was very well off. But old habits die hard.

It was nearly eleven o'clock by the time she hauled her carrier bags through the front door, so Bundle had already been taken for a walk and was back outside in the garden barking at the compost heap.

As Sara unpacked the last of the shopping, Katie came in to the kitchen. They knew each other very well, so Sara could tell just by looking at Katie's face that something was wrong. But because of Katie's fragile state – she was still so upset about Danny – Sara didn't press her straight away but asked if she'd like a cup of coffee.

Katie nodded in a distracted kind of way.

They sat down at the table underneath the great expanse of wintry grey sky, and Sara asked her what she'd been up to that morning, expecting nothing more than an update on her core module of contemporary business management for hospitality organisations.

Katie said, 'I was looking for some Sellotape in Mike's study and I found all your jewellery.'

Sara stared. It was, of course, a terrible shock. Various possible reactions to Katie's rather bald statement ran through her mind, from outrage that Katie had been snooping through Mike's desk to some kind of simulated astonishment at the miraculous reappearance of stolen goods. But for some reason her usual decisiveness deserted her.

'I don't understand.' Katie's voice was so quiet that Sara

could hardly hear what she was saying. 'It was all there. Everything you reported missing. Even your engagement ring.'

It was a very distinctive ring – Edwardian, Arts and Crafts, with emeralds and diamonds – so Sara wasn't surprised that Katie had recognised it straight away.

Katie's eyes were full of confusion.

Sara said, 'I won't pretend it was for the insurance money.'

It was a rather hopeless attempt to lighten the atmosphere. But Katie didn't smile. In fact, Sara could see from the look of entreaty in her eyes that she was still hoping there was some kind of rational explanation. Katie was, as usual, clinging to the possibility of a favourable outcome long after any sane person would have given up.

'Danny was hurting you.' Sara tried to sound calm. 'I had to do something.'

Katie was trembling. 'So your jewellery was never stolen.'

'No.'

'There was no burglary. It was just like Grace's bracelet. Danny had nothing to do with it.'

Sara leaned forward towards her. 'He didn't steal anything from me or from Grace. But there were lots of other burglaries all over the place. He's guilty, Katie. You told me yourself right at the beginning. And you heard all the charges in court. He's been thieving from old ladies for years.'

'Did you tell the police?'

'You know I did. You were here when PC Bush came round.'

Katie shook her head. 'Did you tell them you thought it was Danny?'

It was tempting to prevaricate. After all, Katie knew the way that gossip worked in the village – a little bit here, a little bit there. It could have been a collective effort. No one could ever have said, with any degree of certainty, who had finally tipped off the police.

But Sara decided, on the spur of the moment, to tell the truth. She met Katie's eyes with what she hoped was a steady gaze. 'I suggested to PC Bush that they might want to investigate him.'

Katie seemed to slump in the chair.

'For your own good, Katie. I couldn't bear to stand by and do nothing. Not after what he put you through last time.'

Katie just sat there, staring down at the table.

Sara leaned forward. 'I had to make you see what he was really like. You kept blaming yourself. But it wasn't you. It was him. I knew he was going to do it again. He was going to leave you and break your heart. And I couldn't let that happen.'

The silence felt ominous. Sara thought, with some sadness, that honesty came at a price. She'd had a sudden urge to tell the truth, and it had been the wrong call. She was normally so careful. She hardly ever gave in to impulse. It so often played out in her head – crashing the car into the back of someone who'd just taken her parking space, pushing over the cyclist who'd just ridden into her shin. But she had learned over the years that it's far better to think ahead – to work out every possible outcome and adjust your plans accordingly. It takes a little longer, but it leaves you with more control in the end. The last thing you want is a messy, unpredictable result.

Katie lifted her head and looked straight at her, and Sara realised with a pitch of dismay that she was going to pay heavily for her mistake.

Katie said, 'Have you lied about other things?'

It seemed better to be straightforward. 'Yes, sometimes.'

'I mean things that matter.'

'Like what?'

Katie looked serious. 'Everything to do with Mike.'

'Our relationship?'

Katie nodded.

'No, I didn't lie about that. We weren't happy. I wish we had been.' Sara looked down at her hands. Her head hurt, as if she'd drunk too much, or spent hours squinting at strange objects that were just out of focus. She wished she could lie down in a dark room with something cool and comforting pressed against her forehead.

'What about Ursula?'

Sara wasn't really sure how to answer that. 'You saw what she was like.'

'You said she wanted Mike all to herself.'

'Yes.'

'And that she was mad.'

Sara took a deep breath. 'I think she's emotionally unstable. I don't know if that amounts to the same thing.'

Katie was still staring at her across the table. Sara was beginning to worry that she wouldn't have clear enough answers to everything Katie might want to know, when Katie said, 'Was it an accident?'

Sometimes, when you hear something unexpected, you can't immediately work out what's being said. For some reason, Sara had been convinced that Katie was about to ask her about phone sex and fictional prostitutes, so this simple query, which got to the whole nub of the issue rather too quickly, completely threw her. 'What?'

'Mike's death. Was it an accident?'

There was a sudden collapse of time, a flashback so intense that Sara caught her breath. One minute she was sitting with Katie at the long wooden table on a weekday morning in the middle of December, and the next she was standing by the white sink, all alone, on a Friday evening at the end of June. When vivid memories flood back like this, you're almost convinced you can smell and touch, that you can experience all the sensory impressions that imprinted themselves on your mind when they first happened. The window was open, and the night was hot and still, full of the scent of star jasmine and honeysuckle. Sara could remember the heaviness of her eyes, the ache of her muscles, the thick sound of rural silence. Edward and Katie were both upstairs in their rooms – Katie was probably already asleep after her deep and soothing bath.

In his basket by the wall, Bundle was lying stretched out, dead to the world, his throat wheezing with faint, almost inaudible barks.

It had been a backbreaking day of cleaning, polishing, cooking and furniture-shifting in preparation for Mike's fiftieth birthday party. She had pushed herself beyond the point of tiredness. Standing there by the open window, Sara's mind drifted to James, lying somewhere in a grassy field under the serious moonlight, surrounded by friends, drinking beer, listening to music. Of course, she missed him. But just at that moment, she wasn't anxious or afraid. Her lovely house was shining. Everything the guests might need had been prepared. She hadn't wanted to organise a big, expensive celebration. She'd hated the idea of an invasion of strangers. But she'd agreed to do it – out of obligation, out of duty – and now that everything was ready she was proud of what she'd achieved. It was done. It was finished. She was offering her difficult, irascible, demanding husband the best party he'd ever had.

Sara's phone rang and Mike's name flashed up. 'I'm coming back now.'

She was surprised. He'd said he wouldn't be home till midnight. He was going to take the client out for dinner. 'Is everything OK?'

'I'm not staying. We're going to meet up again next week.'

Her heart sank. His voice was angry. She knew the signs by now. 'Did you forget your painkillers?'

'Don't start.'

Quickly, to distract him, she said, 'Did it go well? The meeting?'

There was the kind of pause that makes you wonder if the signal has gone. Then he said, 'You'll have to cancel it.'

'What?'

'The party.'

'But I—'

'Don't start, for God's sake.'

There was another strange, blank silence.

She said, 'Have you eaten?'

'I'll get something on the way back.'

'But all the—'

'It doesn't matter. It's not important. Sara? Are you listening? Just cancel the party.'

'It's—'

'Get hold of Gemma if you don't want to do it. We spoke earlier. I said it might not happen.'

Her voice came out all floaty and light. 'OK.'

'Sara?'

But now her throat was tight and she couldn't speak.

After she'd ended the call, she stood there at the sink, her hands on the cold white enamel. The night was black all around her, pressing down through the panels of the great glass extension. Various random phrases were floating through her head – *It's just the pain – He'll be all right in the morning – He didn't mean to sound ungrateful – It'll all be fine – Don't make any decisions now – It's late – You need to go to bed.*

He wouldn't find anywhere open at this time of night. Motorway services, maybe, but she couldn't see him dragging himself out of the car for old chips and watery coffee. And he couldn't take the pills on an empty stomach. He'd been told that so many times. She opened the massive great fridge, full from top to bottom with luxury food for the party, and closed it again. With jerky, mechanical movements, she began a fruitless search through both store cupboards for something that might do. She was beginning to move beyond pleasant weariness to a state of fractious exhaustion. She knew him. He was always saying he'd stop off for something on the way, but he never did. He was incapable of doing anything in the kitchen. He couldn't even boil an egg. He'd come back irritable and hungry, expecting a full meal, as usual, to be waiting for him.

For a moment, Sara fantasised about going upstairs and packing a suitcase. She could see herself placing neatly edged piles of ironed clothes against the soft grey quilting, tucking in underwear and socks, adding a silky dressing gown. She thought about leaving this beautiful, empty, shiny house – her creation, her sanctuary, her home – and walking down the lane past the high hedges smelling of laurel and yew. She saw herself disappearing into the darkness.

Bundle, in his basket, sighed.

Upstairs, Edward and Katie were asleep.

She found an onion, some celery, some garlic, half a bottle of white wine, a packet of Arborio rice. She unwrapped a block of Parmesan. She made up a jug of stock. She thought of Mike driving home through the night, his mind screaming with pain.

Around her, the house waited.

Just before she started to cook, she went upstairs and hunted around for his painkillers. He didn't like her doing this. He didn't want her anywhere near his medication – hated any kind of interference. But she couldn't risk the thunderous clash and clatter of furious searching in the early hours as Mike rampaged around, turning the house upside-down. She found a full pack of pills right at the front of his desk drawer. She stood there, staring at it in her hand. Perhaps leaving it behind had been intentional – the continual bravado of self-deception that he was perfectly able to do without painkillers.

Mike hated weakness of any kind.

Downstairs, alone in the kitchen, she chopped and crushed and stirred, and her back – as if in sympathy with his – sang with pain, because the day had been too long, far too long. As she worked, she found herself remembering something from years before, a kind of bright light, a kind of intensity, when he was her future, and she was his, and there was no sniping and misery and disappointment, only his smile and his warmth and the creases round his eyes.

And she knew, at that moment, how tired they were, and how hard they had tried, and how it was time now to let it stop.

Sara stirred in the last ladle of stock.

And when it was done, because he needed to be rid of the agony of the pain as quickly as possible, she pushed the pills out of the little blisters of their flat plastic trays, crushed them in the base of the big stone pestle and mortar, and stirred them into the warm, thick, unctuous risotto. And then she sprinkled it with Parmesan and parsley, and covered the bowl with clingfilm and stood it next to the microwave, just as she always did, so that he'd know it was the same routine, and all he had to do was reheat on full power for two minutes.

She left the empty packet of pills next to the bowl so that he could see what she'd done.

And then she went to bed.

Katie seemed to be waiting for something. Sara said, 'I'm sorry – what did you say?'

'Mike's death. Was it an accident?'

They stared at each other across the table.

Sara felt the past stretching out behind her, blurred and muddled. She felt an overwhelming sense of tiredness.

Katie said, 'I just keep feeling there's something I don't understand.'

'Like what?'

'I don't know. Something that isn't right. It's been going round and round in my head for days.'

Sara said, 'I wish you'd let it go, Katie. It's all over now.'

Katie looked uncertain.

Sara kept her voice calm. 'There was an inquest. Witness

statements, medical reports. The coroner took it all into account and came to a conclusion of accidental death.'

Katie said, 'Why didn't Ursula believe him?'

'Because she wanted it to be my fault.' Sara leaned forwards. 'Don't you remember? She said I drove Mike to suicide. And after that didn't work, she came up with the idea that I'd killed him.'

'She said such horrible things in the car park.'

Sara's voice was cold. 'Which you promised you'd never repeat.'

'I won't.'

'On your life, you said. You promised on your life.'

Katie nodded, eyes wide with sincerity.

Sara looked out through the big glass doors. She wondered if she should go out into the garden after lunch and cut back the ivy on the fence. But she wasn't sure she had the energy.

Katie said, 'It's just that everything feels different now.'

With difficulty, Sara dragged her mind back to the present. 'What do you mean?'

Katie said, her voice indistinct, 'Because of what happened with Danny. It's all changed.'

They could hear Bundle barking.

With great weariness, Sara said, 'You're angry with me.'

Katie looked up.

'But you must understand I was trying to protect you. He was going to hurt you and I couldn't let that happen again. All those weeks, Katie, all those weeks we sat here talking about him because you couldn't accept what he'd done. I couldn't bear to see you go through that a second time.'

It was, of course, tedious to have to run over all the arguments when the whole thing was so glaringly obvious, but

271

Sara tried once more to explain, as gently as possible, why Danny was so wrong for her. Poor Katie. Even after all this time, the hold that Danny had on her was so strong that she couldn't be rational and objective. Sara touched on his grandiose delusions, his unpredictability, his criminal tendencies. She said that it was all to Katie's credit that she had been so loyal and stood by him, but there was a danger that her open and trusting nature was blinding her to all his faults. Danny had preyed on Katie's gullibility and abused her trust. It was time to face up to the truth.

Katie was silent.

Sara said that Katie was kind and good-hearted and determined to see the best in everyone. But she had to understand that there were people in the world who would happily take advantage of that and manipulate her to their own ends. She had to see through lies and exploitation and learn to stand up for herself.

This finally prodded her into speech. Katie said, her mouth trembling, 'You sound like Maxine.'

'I'm saying it for your own good.'

'But don't you see?' Katie's eyes were huge. 'None of this is important.'

Sara was lost.

'You took Danny away. I thought you understood. I thought you understood how much I loved him. But you took him away from me.'

Sara felt a small flash of irritation. 'I didn't take him away. I suggested that the police might want to investigate him.'

'And they arrested him.'

'Katie, I don't know how to get through to you. Danny wasn't right for you. He didn't deserve you.'

'But wasn't that up to me? Wasn't that my choice?'

Sara looked at her with exasperation.

Katie said, 'You've been so kind, and I don't want to sound ungrateful. I know you were trying to do the right thing when you told the police about Danny. But I wish you hadn't. I wish you'd kept quiet.'

Sara glared at her. 'It didn't make any difference. The police would have caught up with him sooner or later.'

Katie wouldn't back down. 'You don't know that.'

Sara was having to work very hard to keep her temper. Bubbles of rage kept blistering through her mind, shouting words that she could only just keep silent. Katie was being obtuse. There was no logic to anything she was saying. Clearly Sara had saved her from an abusive relationship that would have destroyed her. It was stupid to pretend anything different. For a moment, she stopped listening, lost in a grey mist of irritation, and only came to when Katie said, '. . . and they think I shouldn't be spending so much time with you.'

'Who?'

'Anna and Baz.'

Sara looked at her with astonishment. 'Why?'

Katie was clearly finding this difficult. 'They say it's been a bit intense.'

'Intense?'

'With the funeral and the inquest, and now all this with Danny.'

Sara said, 'It's been a very difficult time for both of us.'

But she could see from Katie's expression that this wasn't enough. With a great effort of will, Sara pulled herself back under control. It seemed these vacuous friends from the foul-smelling Goat had said something that Katie had decided was important. 'Why shouldn't we spend so much time together?'

Katie was hunched over. 'Because you're so much older than I am.'

Sara stared.

'They say you're old enough to be my mother.'

Sara felt a cold shiver run down her spine.

'And in the pub,' said Katie, wretched with embarrassment, 'people are saying it's more than that. More than just being friends.'

There was an awkward silence.

Sara said, 'It's just gossip. You should never listen to gossip.'

They could still hear the distant sound of Bundle barking. No one, it seemed, was taking any notice of what he was trying to tell them.

With a stab of sadness, Sara realised that everything was about to change. She could feel it in the air. It had crept up when she'd been looking the other way, when her attention had been distracted by trying to explain. For the first time, Katie was making her feelings plain. She was daring to criticise, to risk offence, to say the unsayable. It seemed – incredibly – that her love for the ridiculous, pathetic, insignificant Danny had suddenly made her brave. She was finally speaking up for herself.

Perhaps if you have your back to the wall, the only choice is to turn and fight.

Katie looked up. 'I was talking to Rachel the other day. She said that people are always changing their minds about where they're living, even halfway through the year, and it's worth asking around to see if there are any spare rooms in any of the student flats. Or even a shared house somewhere in town.'

Sara could hardly bear to listen.

'She said you get more of the student experience that way.'

Sara felt a band of tightness in her throat. Why was Rachel interfering?

'I may not be able to find anywhere.' Katie was having trouble meeting Sara's eyes. 'But I thought I could have a look and see what's out there.'

Sara said, keeping her voice neutral, 'Can you afford it?'

'I can get a loan. Lots of students get loans to cover their rent.'

'It seems a shame,' said Sara carefully, 'when there's so much space here.'

There was a kind of pleading in Katie's face, a longing to be understood. 'It just seems a good idea.'

Sara couldn't speak.

'I'll carry on with the dog walking. Maybe not twice a day. But as often as I can. I love Bundle. I don't want to let him down.'

Bundle? Bundle? With difficulty, Sara said, 'So you're looking now?'

Katie was clearly finding this hard. 'I've talked it over with Anna, and she says I can stay with her. So I can grab things when they come up. View straight away and put down a deposit.'

'I thought there was no room at Anna's.'

Katie swallowed. 'Her mum said there's always room.'

'So when will you go?'

'I'm not sure.'

Sara said, forcing herself to sound calm and sensible,

'It's entirely up to you, of course. You must go whenever you like.'

Katie bit her lip. 'Maybe I should go now.'

'Now?' There was a kind of pressure in Sara's ears as if she was being held underwater. It made it hard to speak. 'What about Christmas?'

Katie still couldn't look at Sara directly. 'I think I should probably go and see my parents. Mum was really upset when I said I wasn't coming. She said they'd been really looking forward to it.'

Sara said, 'So you're going to Spain.'

Katie nodded. 'Anna's for a few days. Then Spain.'

'This is all happening so fast.' Sara smiled. 'I didn't know you were making so many plans.'

'I wasn't, really. They've sort of made themselves.'

Sara tried to look as if she knew exactly what Katie meant. 'So you're going to leave now?'

'I think so.'

'Won't it take you a long time to pack?'

'Not really. It's just clothes and a laptop.'

'And they're all expecting you?'

Katie shifted in her chair. 'Not exactly. But Anna said I could stay whenever I wanted. And Mum said, just turn up when you can. It'll be a Christmas surprise.'

Sara thought it all sounded rather vague and slapdash. The last thing anyone wants is uncertainty about dates in the middle of the festive season – Katie was being extremely inconsiderate. But it seemed the decision had been made. She cast around for something to say, feeling that the only important thing was to save face and maintain a façade of normality. 'We'll miss you. Especially on Christmas Day.'

'Is Polly coming?'

This was almost her undoing. 'Polly?'

'I thought James might bring her home for Christmas.'

'Oh,' said Sara, her heart plunging in shock, 'I don't think they've decided yet.'

'Maybe they'll do Christmas Day here and Boxing Day in Wales.'

Sara nodded as if she had even the slightest clue what Katie was talking about. The thought that James might be seeing someone – someone with whom he was so intimately involved that her family played a significant part in Christmas festivities – made her feel sick.

The conversation had brought itself to a close. Katie remembered, with sudden panic, that she'd half arranged to meet Anna in the charity shop, which would work out really well because then they could go back to Anna's house together when she finished work. Katie stood up so quickly that her chair fell backwards and clattered to the floor. Everyday life flooded back into the room and the tension – the awkward, tortuous silences, the pauses filled with hidden meaning – vanished without trace.

It was astonishing, really, quite how much had been communicated in such a short time.

'Sara?' Katie – rushed, dishevelled – stopped on the threshold.

'What?'

She hesitated. 'You're not upset?'

'Of course not. I completely understand.' Sara glanced up at the kitchen clock. 'If you're sure about going straight away, I can give you a lift into town if you like. As long as we leave in the next half hour, I can still be back in time for Edward.'

'Really?' Katie's face lit up. 'Yes, please.'

Sara tried to find just the right level of warmth and indifference. 'Of course, I'm still hoping I can change your mind.'

Katie shook her head. She seemed so grown-up suddenly, so certain of her decisions. 'I think it's time to go.'

'You're sure?'

'Yes.'

'Quite sure?'

Katie nodded.

Sara smiled. 'Promise me one thing.'

Katie waited, her face full of the old eagerness to please.

'I know you want to look around and see what's out there. But remember that the Old Rectory is your home. Forever. There's always room for you here.'

Katie's eyes were solemn. 'Thank you.'

After Katie had gone upstairs, Sara stayed at the table, looking out into the garden. She sensed Mike was around somewhere, wanting to speak, but she wouldn't let him get a word in. He had no place in this moment. It would just make everything more complicated, because it really had nothing to do with him. It never had.

Sara felt very calm. It was a relief to have some clarity of thinking at last. Of course it had all come as a bit of a shock, because she hadn't expected Katie to surprise her with a radical change of plans, but there was no point in getting emotional. The important thing now was to act in Katie's best interests, whatever the personal cost. She felt a rush of anticipation, a fluttering of her heart. It was time to face up to what had to be done.

Sometimes it takes a good friend to push you in the right direction.

Overhead, she heard drawers opening, cupboard doors shutting, the thud and crash of haphazard packing. She imagined Katie throwing her clothes into a bag – in an untidy, messy way, because she was hopeless at anything practical – and gathering up the chaos of bottles and make-up from the bedside table. Sara wondered how long it would take for her to clean Katie's room once she'd gone – to wipe away the finger marks and coffee mug rings, the blobs of foundation, the ash from her incense sticks. She thought about the splodges of nail varnish on the duvet cover and the smears of mascara on her pillow. It all seemed so sad. For a moment Sara was filled with a sense of weariness, as if she were doomed like some kind of fairy tale character to repeat the same tasks again and again, the work never-ending, the job never done.

She heard footsteps walking over the floor above, the creak of a floorboard, and then silence as Katie made her way across the landing and down the stairs. The house was so big, you couldn't ever really hear progress from one room to another. Sometimes you just had to imagine it.

She thought about Katie walking down, step by step, her hand on the black iron balustrade. She thought of her putting her heavy bag on the floor and lifting her coat to push her arms into the sleeves.

Sara took a deep breath. This was so hard. But it was time to go out into the hall to say goodbye.

Acknowledgements

Thanks to Nicholas Rheinberg, PC Stephen Bush from the Metropolitan Police, Professor Annie Bartlett and Dr Gwen Adshead for their professional advice – all errors that have crept in despite their best efforts are entirely my own. Thanks to friends and family for their love, support and editorial suggestions – Alexandra Fabian, Yvonne Wilcox, Sally Eden, Gabriel Firth, Luke John Oxlade, Tamsin Kelly (who read every draft), Joe Kavanagh, Ben Kavanagh, Alice Kavanagh, and my husband Matt Kavanagh. Finally, thanks to my agent Veronique Baxter and all at David Higham Associates, and to everyone at Hodder & Stoughton – particularly my kind and brilliant editor Ruth Tross.